Love Finds You™

IN

TOMBSTONE

ARIZONA

Love Finds You™

IN

TOMBSTONE

ARIZONA

BY MIRALEE FERRELL

summerside
PRESS™

Summerside Press, Inc.
Minneapolis 55438
www.summersidepress.com

Love Finds You in Tombstone, Arizona
© 2011 by Miralee Ferrell

ISBN 978-1-60936-104-4

Scripture references are from The Holy Bible, King James Version (KJV).

The town depicted in this book is a real place, but all characters, other than known historical figures addressed in the Author's Note, are fictional. Any resemblances to actual people or events are purely coincidental.

Cover design by Lookout Design | www.lookoutdesign.com

Interior design by Müllerhaus Publishing Group | www.mullerhaus.net

Photos of Tombstone provided by Miralee Ferrell.

Summerside Press™ is an inspirational publisher offering fresh, irresistible books to uplift the heart and engage the mind.

Printed in USA.

Dedication

....

My mother's loving influence and support have helped shape me into the woman I am today. She remains one of my closest friends and is among the first people I turn to when I have a problem or want to celebrate an answer to prayer. Thanks, Mom, for always being there for me, and for the many times you've gone beyond what I could hope or expect.

Acknowledgments

....

Special thanks to my readers who wrote e-mails wanting to know more about Christy Grey. We first met her in the book *Love Finds You in Last Chance, California*, and she gripped readers' hearts. I'm happy to present Christy's story, as well as return briefly to the town of Last Chance and the friends made there.

If you haven't read *Love Finds You in Last Chance, California*, don't worry; it won't spoil the story to read this one first. But you'll definitely want to go back and pick up a copy of the book to learn where Christy's journey began.

My desire in writing *Love Finds You in Tombstone, Arizona*, is to show the redemptive power of God's love. I hope you'll find little nuggets of truth scattered throughout that will encourage you along the way.

So many people have contributed to making this story what it is today. Family, friends, editors, agent, critique partners, and prayer partners who offer an ongoing covering have all been such a help and blessing during the writing and editing process.

Special thanks go to my critique group. Kimberly Johnson, Sherry Kyle, and Karen O'Connor made suggestions that helped strengthen my book from start to finish. Each one is a talented writer, and I'm blessed to be on the same team. And to Kristy Gamet and Tammy Marks, who have both read my books in advance. I so appreciate your input on my stories and characters. Also, my heartfelt gratitude goes to Debbie, Barb, and Kay for their prayer covering. You are each such a blessing to me.

I can't forget to mention Rachel Meisel, senior editor at Summerside Press—thank you many times over. Your brainstorming sessions and willingness to allow me to use a character from another book as my heroine were such an encouragement—as well as permitting Ramona Tucker (I love that woman—she's a joy to work with!) to do the edits.

Susan Lorher did a preread and targeted areas needing to be expanded. Susan, you're an amazing editor and friend, and I thank you from the bottom of my heart. You took an interest in my work early on and have been my champion ever since.

Tamela Hancock Murray, I'm so grateful to have you as my agent. You've believed in me from the beginning and stood behind me on every project. Bless you.

Marnee, my daughter, and Steven, my son, along with their spouses, Brian and Hannah: you've all been encouragers—cheering me on, asking questions about my work, and truly caring. And to my husband, Allen, who without fail asks how many words I've written each day, lets me ramble on about my characters, plot, and writing, even when he doesn't always have a clue what I'm talking about. Thank you; I'm honored to be your wife.

More than anything I give all the glory to God. I pray each of my books will in some way impact lives for the Lord and draw readers to Him. I wouldn't be writing if it hadn't been for His hand on my life, and direction to do so. I'll write for as long as He asks me to and give Him the honor for any success I might have.

And to my readers, whom I choose to think of as my friends, thank you. If it weren't for you, there would be no more books. I love hearing from you and enjoy knowing what you think, feel, and experience as you read my stories. Bless each and every one of you as you follow my career and the stories God lays on my heart. Drop me a note, or visit my website (www.miraleeferrell.com) or my Facebook page. I'd love to meet you there!

Tombstone, Arizona

IN THE 1870S ED SCHIEFFELIN SPENT A GOOD DEAL OF TIME PICKING up rocks in Arizona Territory while serving as part of a scouting expedition aimed against the Chiricahua Apaches. On a number of occasions the soldiers told him that if he stayed after they departed, the only stone he'd find would be his own tombstone. When Schieffelin finally discovered silver in 1879, he remembered those words and named his first mine The Tombstone.

Within two years the small mining town of Tombstone, Arizona, exploded into a booming city of more than twenty thousand souls, bringing with it a wide variety of characters, including Bat Masterson, Doc Holliday, Big Nose Kate, Curly Bill, and the Earp clan. The gunfight at the OK Corral is only one of the wild episodes that make up the history of this colorful town. Saloons and gambling halls outnumbered every other business, and it was almost two years after the city's birth before the first church building, St. Paul's Episcopal Church, was completed. Eventually families arrived, bringing schools and respectability, but the early years were rife with outlaws, shootings, and violent deaths.

When the miners tunneled six hundred feet and deeper, water began flooding the depths of the mines, and eventually they were forced to close. Tombstone, often called "the town too tough to die," dwindled to about 150 people. In the 1900s a surge of fascination with the Old West brought new life to the area, and it now boasts approximately fifteen hundred people. Four blocks of the old downtown section were preserved, containing some of the original buildings dating back to the early 1880s. The residents pride themselves in keeping alive the history and heritage of their ancestors and bringing the Old West to life for the thousands of visitors who flock there each year.

Miralee Ferrell

Chapter One

....

Late March 1881
Last Chance, California

Ma needed her. Christy Grey mouthed the words, just to see how they tasted. She stood on the boardwalk in front of the telegraph office in Last Chance, California, staring at the slip of paper clutched in her trembling fingers. Once again she read the words from her younger brother, Joshua.

> *Ma sick. Stop. Can't care for her alone. Stop. Come soon.*
> *Stop. Joshua*

Hope sprouted a tender shoot and quickly withered as the bright heat of reality settled around her. Christy almost laughed. She'd allowed herself to be fooled. Joshua, not Ma, needed her. Ivy Malone's life revolved around her husband at the time—number three being the most recent. Thankfully, Christy had had a stable stepfather while she grew up, following her own father's death. But after burying two husbands, Ma had foolishly married a man named Logan Malone, and Christy had little use for him.

She sighed and drew her double-breasted wool cloak tighter around her. It was past time to head to Miss Alice's. The older woman would be disappointed at her impending departure, but it couldn't be helped. Joshua wouldn't have written if their mother wasn't in danger. Ma wouldn't allow it.

A blast of cold air blew snow under the overhanging roof and lifted the hem of her skirt. That was one thing she'd never gotten used to—the deep snow and cold winters of the Sierra Nevada Mountains. When her fiancé, Ralph, was alive, she'd figured she'd live here forever, but after he died three years ago, her life had floundered more than once. If it weren't for the fact her seven-year-old nephew Toby lived here, she might have moved on long ago. Of course, her friendship with his stepmother, Alexia—or Alex, as she liked to be called—and his father, Justin, had been a factor in her decision, as well.

This might be the change she'd been seeking, though. She loved the small hamlet of Last Chance, but maybe it was time for a new place and a more promising future. She appreciated all her close friends had done when they'd drawn her in and accepted her in spite of her past as a saloon girl. But so often she felt like someone on the outside looking in. While many of the townspeople were kind, her past always hovered in the background. Some had never forgiven the poor choices she'd made.

The last three years had seen her float about with no purpose or sense of direction. Nothing in her life had turned out as she'd dreamed when only a young girl. So many *if onlys* followed by one disappointment and wrong choice after another. She'd hoped to start her own business here in Last Chance but had drifted down the easier path of working for Miss Alice at her boardinghouse. She desperately needed to figure out where she belonged—where she could make a difference.

A sense of excitement combined with dread warred inside her. She'd miss her young nephew terribly, and dealing with Ma's querulous attitude would be difficult, but the thought of starting over where no one but family knew her brought a definite exhilaration.

* * * * *

The two days since the telegram arrived had been a whirlwind of activity, saying good-bye to friends and packing for the trip. Christy stood in front of the general store choking back the emotion threatening to swamp her. She hadn't realized how hard it would be to leave these people she'd grown to love.

Alex leaned against her husband, Justin, who held their two-year-old daughter, Grace, in his arms while seven-year-old Toby clung to her skirts. So many bittersweet memories centered on this family. Like the time she'd ridden down the hill and gotten her first glimpse of Justin and Alexia's ranch. The two had been outside giving three-year-old Toby a riding lesson. The child's shriek of joy carried across the meadow, and his delight in "widing the horsey" had almost turned her from her less-than-honorable pursuit of snatching the boy from his father. Thankfully, all had ended well and she'd grown closer to these three people than she'd ever hoped or imagined.

Christy reached for Alex and gave her a hug. "You've been like a sister to me." She choked out the words. "I wish I could take you all with me."

Alex squeezed her back and took a half step away. "Me too. Are you sure you need to go? You can't bring your mother here to live?"

"No." Christy shook her head as a deep certainty swelled in her heart. "My younger brother needs someone in his life, as well. I want to make a difference, Alex. I haven't been able to do that here."

"But you have! Toby adores you and so do we."

"I know, and I love you all. But that's not what I mean. I want my life to matter in some deeper way. I feel like I've wasted so much of it in the past. Maybe caring for my mother will fill the longing in my heart. I'm hoping things will have changed between her and me, now that she's ill. And Joshua's not had the best of influences with Logan, Ma's recent husband. Joshua is only nineteen, and I'm afraid he's making poor choices. My presence might help turn him around."

"I understand." Alex glanced at Justin and smiled. "I know my life changed after meeting Justin and Toby. I hope and pray something equally wonderful will happen for you."

Christy turned to Justin and raised her face to his. "I need to talk to you about something personal. I hope you'll hear me out."

He shifted his daughter to his other arm. Alex reached out and Grace went willingly to her mother, wrapping her small arms around her neck. "What is it, Christy?"

Alex grasped Toby's hand and drew him aside while cradling the little girl on her hip. "Let's go look in the shop. Maybe we'll find something you can take home after Aunt Christy leaves."

Toby gave a shout of glee and rushed to the door. "Thank you, Mama. I'd like some lollipops."

"All right, but we'll hurry so we can come back and say good-bye to your aunt." The bell on the door tinkled as they made their way inside.

Christy smiled as the boy disappeared from sight.

She sucked in a sharp breath and blew it out through her nostrils, trying to form the words that needed to be said. Why did it feel like she was about to betray her sister? That didn't make sense, since Molly had been dead almost five years. "I want to thank you." Her voice choked.

Justin patted her shoulder. "Nothing to thank me for."

She gripped his hand and held on tight. "Yes, there is. Molly..." She forced herself to continue. "Molly didn't deserve you." She suddenly felt the need to release the pent-up dam that had been growing higher the past few months and now must come toppling down. So much had accumulated over the past five years. The loss of her sister, the discovery of her nephew, Toby, Ralph's untimely death, and her need to discover where she belonged. The words came in a rush. "She had everything. A husband who cared enough to stay with her, even when he knew her child wasn't his. A son should have been enough reason for her to get up every morning with joy, instead of drinking herself deeper into sorrow over a no-good man who didn't deserve her love."

Justin shook his head. "No, Christy. You don't have to do this. She was your sister."

"Yes, and I loved her in spite of all the wrong choices she made, but that doesn't excuse what she did. I want you to know I honor and respect you for loving Toby and being such a wonderful father. What Molly did was wrong, but she taught me so much about what's really important. Because of her, I decided to leave the life I'd been living.

Because of her, I knew I'd never again allow a man to trample on my freedom or take advantage of me. Because of her, I know how valuable family really is." A sob cut her off, and Justin wrapped his long arms around her and drew her close. She hadn't cried when she'd heard Molly had walked in front of a fast-moving team and died under the wheels of the wagon—she'd been too numb.

Justin hugged and released her, then withdrew a handkerchief from his pocket and pressed it into her hand. "But he's my son, no matter who fathered him. Nothing will ever change that. At one time I loved his mother, even if she never loved me, and Toby contains all the good things in Molly."

"I know." She whispered the words.

"Remember her when she was young, Christy. Think about the good times, not who she became. That's what I do."

"Thank you." She gave him one last hug and swiped the tears from her cheeks.

Justin stepped to the door of the store and called inside, "Hey, you three, hurry on out here. Christy needs to leave soon."

Toby raced out the door waving a fistful of lollipops, and Alex followed with Grace sucking on one.

Toby's face blazed with delight; he pressed all of the candy into her hand. "I got some for you, Aunt Christy."

"No, honey. I can't take all of it. Just one, okay?" She handed him back the rest, then leaned down for one last hug, wrapping her arms around the brown-haired boy. "Make sure your Papa and Mama bring you to visit me."

"Why do you have to go, Aunt Christy?" The little boy's lament nearly tore her heart in two.

"My mama is sick and needs me. If your mama were sick, you'd want to take care of her, wouldn't you?"

Toby turned a watery smile on Alex. "But Mama is fine. I want you to stay here with us."

"I know, sweetheart, but I have to go. We'll see each other again, I promise." She placed a firm kiss on his cheek and straightened.

"Alex." Christy had promised herself she wouldn't cry, but as the other woman's slender arms wrapped around her, the renegade tears rolled. "I'll miss you so much." She whispered the words, not wanting to upset Toby further.

Alex nodded against her hair. "Me too. You've become one of my closest friends, and I hate to see you go." She pulled back but retained her grip on Christy's upper arms. "Do you think you'll come back here to live?"

"I can't say. Joshua didn't give me any details about Ma's condition, so I won't know more until I arrive in Tombstone."

"I understand. We'll come visit when we can. Maybe after roundup is done, and the horses are shipped to market." She gave Christy one last hug. "Remember, God is in control. Trust Him with your future, and you'll come out all right."

Christy smiled but didn't reply. She'd never quite accepted the religion that brought such comfort to so many in this small town but didn't want to hurt her friend by saying so. Besides, she didn't need God to be in control. The past four years she'd made good decisions for her life and turned things around pretty much on her own. She doubted moving to Tombstone to tend to Ma would require God's involvement.

A burly man with long whiskers, rough clothing, and leading a string of pack mules motioned at Christy. "Miss, it's time to go."

Alex grimaced. "I wish you didn't have to take the mule train to Foresthill."

Christy forced a smile. "I'll be able to ride the stage from Foresthill to Auburn, and get on the train there until well past Tucson, so this will be the worst part."

The mule driver stepped closer. "We got to leave, Miss. Don't want to be caught in a canyon after dark. We'll make it to Michigan Bluff tonight." He took Christy's arm and guided her to a mule standing head to the ground. "You mind sittin' astride?"

"I'm quite capable." She set a foot in the stirrup, holding her skirt out of the way as she swung into the saddle. "I made this trip a few years ago and did fine."

Justin raised a hand in farewell. "You're always welcome in our home, Christy. If things don't work out in Tombstone, we want you to come back here."

"Thank you." Christy swallowed a lump in her throat. "I love you all."

She picked up her reins and nudged her mule forward as the teamster led the string down the main street of Last Chance.

Good things would happen in her future; she was sure of it.

Chapter Two
....

Albuquerque, New Mexico

Nevada King's hand hovered above the butt of his six-shooter. His eyes bored into the man standing thirty feet away. "Give it up, Malone. Walk away while you can. I don't want to kill you."

The man he'd only recently come to know as Logan Malone raised the corner of his top lip, but nothing else on his body moved. "Not gonna happen, King. I'm sick of hearing how fast you are with a gun, and I aim to prove I'm better."

"It's not worth dying over. You don't know what you're getting into."

"Ha. I know plenty. I seen you shoot that feller in San Antone, and you weren't so slick then. He got his gun out faster than you." Malone ran his tongue over his lips, and the hand hovering above his gun twitched.

"Yes, but he's dead." Nevada's gut clenched, and an icy calm washed over his body. A gust of wind blew a dry tumbleweed across his path, but only muted sounds from the typically busy Albuquerque street reached his ears as he focused all of his attention on this man. There was no hope for it. He'd have to shoot and ride away. Again. Right when he'd finally found a boss he trusted and a ranch he wanted to work for, not to mention hoping to have his own spread one day.

He kept his gaze trained on Malone's eyes. No need watching his hand. A man's eyes always revealed when he planned to draw. Logan's eyelid jerked, and his fingers gripped the butt of his gun.

Nevada moved almost without thought. His pistol slid out of the holster and he fired two shots close together, hearing the echo of Malone's shot a second after. The bullet zipped past his shoulder, nicking his shirt.

Logan's eyes widened and his lips formed a circle, but no sound came out. He swayed on his feet, then slowly toppled over, landing on his side in the dirt.

Voices echoed around Nevada, and footsteps echoed on the hard ground behind him. He swung around, gun leveled.

A wizened man with a limp plowed to a stop and raised his hands. "I ain't armed, mister, and I don't want no fight with the likes of you." He waved at the still form on the street. "It were a fair fight. I seen it all. But if I was you, I'd hightail it out of Albuquerque fast as your horse will carry you. Logan Malone's got a mean cousin, and he'll be lookin' for you."

Nevada holstered his gun and gave a brief nod. "Obliged, but I've never met his cousin and don't have a beef with him."

The old man wiped grimy hands against still dirtier trousers. "Won't matter. He'll still want revenge. Him and Logan woulda for shore ambushed you if you hadn't shot him dead. They's done it to others." He jerked his chin toward the body lying nearby. "Don't worry. I'll tell the marshal Logan here drew first. Weren't nothin' else you could do. 'Sides, I heard you tell him not to draw."

"Thanks." Nevada stalked to his horse and untied the reins from the hitching rail in front of the saloon. Seemed like every drunken wrangler, gambler, and no-account that spotted him wanted a piece of his hide.

Nugget snorted and sidestepped as Nevada stepped into the saddle. The fist in his gut hadn't started to unwind, but it wouldn't be long before it did. He needed to be out of town and on the trail before the dam of emotions broke, or he'd be an easy target for anyone hoping to plug him. All he wanted right now was to crawl into a hole somewhere until the sickness passed. He'd vowed to never shoot another man, but once again he'd been drawn into a fight against his will. Why couldn't these men be satisfied with their lives instead of wanting to brag about how many notches they could file on their guns?

Too bad he couldn't head back to the ranch and tell the folks there good-bye. He'd hoped to eventually purchase a ranch and settle down outside of Albuquerque. All he'd ever wanted was a place of his own, a wife who loved him, and the memories of his past wiped away. But with Logan's cousin dogging his trail, he'd best light a shuck out of this country and not look back.

Good thing the man had never seen him, but he'd heard rumors about Logan Malone and his cousin before this. Putting a gun in a dead man's hand after he'd been ambushed would've been their style.

He'd have to find somewhere far away, where people didn't know his name. No more working on ranches for now or associating with cowboys who pushed cattle up the trail. Someone would spot him, and it would begin all over again. It was time to make a new start.

* * * * *

Nevada shifted in his saddle and his stomach growled. Dusk was drawing near, and he'd yet to find a good site to eat and bed down. He'd been riding aimlessly for two days and his supply of grub was almost gone. After he'd ridden out of Albuquerque last week he couldn't decide where to land. He'd heard the town of Tombstone had hit a big silver strike. Might be a good place to start, since it lay less than a six-hour ride from here.

He turned his horse, glad to have one thing settled. Too much of his adult life had been spent wandering, trying to find a place to belong. He'd been followed from one rough town to the next by men hoping to prove their mettle with a gun. Sometimes he'd avoided a fight, and at other times he'd had no choice. Whenever that happened, the same old sickness assailed him and often took days to shake.

After shooting Logan, he'd ridden twenty miles and holed up in the brush without moving. Half the time he'd been on the alert, expecting the cousin to arrive, and the rest of the time he flat hadn't cared. As much as he wanted to leave this old life behind and start over, he had little hope it could happen.

He longed to keep the promise he'd made his mother so many years ago. She'd begged him to stay out of trouble and make a good life for himself—one she could be proud of. But so far that hadn't happened. At times he felt God had forsaken him, but in the early, predawn hours, when sleep evaded him, he admitted the lie—if anything, he'd abandoned God. Why was it so hard to stay out of trouble and settle down with a wife on his own ranch? Other men achieved

it, but the hope of finding freedom from his past constantly dangled just a step ahead, always elusive.

Nugget's ears pricked forward, and the horse moved from a walk into a trot. The flickering light of a campfire shone off in the distance. Nevada reined in his horse. Running wasn't part of his nature, even though he'd prefer to avoid a fight. The men around the fire could be enemies, but they could as easily be travelers on their way to Tombstone. Right now the thought of a hot meal and coffee urged him on. He'd hail the camp and take his chances.

A coyote yipped off in the distance and another answered. Soon a rising crescendo of barks and howls lit up the early evening. His horse moved through the desert chaparral, wending its way toward the fire. Several minutes later Nevada drew rein, bringing his mount to a halt. "Ho, the camp."

The cocking of rifles reverberated in the night air. Two figures pulled away from the fire and stepped into the gloom.

"Who goes there?" a rough voice off to the right called out.

"A hungry traveler hoping for a bite of grub and a cup of coffee, if you have it to spare." Nevada rested his right hand on his thigh, inches from the butt of his gun.

"All right. Walk your horse nice and slow toward the fire so we can get a look at you."

Nevada did as he was told, his senses alert and his eyes scanning the encampment. "Not wantin' any trouble, boys. Only thing I got left to eat is hardtack. Sure would be grateful if you could offer something more."

"Swing yourself down off'n that horse." A tall, burly man dressed in dark clothing stepped to the fore, a rifle cradled across his arms.

"Guess we can spare a mite of grub. Coffee's on, and there's a mess of beans still in the pot." He spat, then wiped the back of his hand across his bearded face.

"Much obliged." Nevada eased Nugget off to the side, facing the men. "I'll not wear out my welcome. I'll eat and be on my way."

"Sorry, stranger. Didn't mean to be unsocial, did we, fellas?" He motioned to his two silent companions standing in the shadows. "Me and the boys are a mite touchy right now. We're huntin' a man and don't care to get bushwhacked."

Nevada grunted and tossed Nugget's reins over a branch. "No danger of that. I'm only a travelin' cowpoke, hopin' to find work in these parts. Know of any jobs to be had?"

"You needin' a grubstake?" The one who'd done all the talking took a step closer.

"Maybe."

"Throw your bedroll off your horse and strip your gear. Bunk here tonight and we'll toss some money your way in the mornin'." He gestured toward the three bedrolls to the left of the fire.

"Thanks, don't mind if I do." Nevada tethered his horse and stripped off his gear, slinging his bedroll and saddlebag over one shoulder and hoisting his saddle against his hip. He made his way back to the fire and set his belongings at the base of a scrub manzanita.

By the time he returned, two of the men had rolled in their blankets, resting their heads on their saddles. The leader gestured at a pot of coffee slid to the edge of the coals. "Help yourself. What'd you say your name is?"

"I didn't." The brusque words hit the still air and vibrated over the camp. Nevada waited to see what effect they might have. Most

men in this country didn't put much stock in a name, unless it was printed on a wanted poster. He'd rather not bandy his about at the moment.

"Fair enough, seein' as how we don't care to share ours, neither." The leader laughed. "Now eat and turn in. We're plannin' on bein' up at daylight tomorrow." He beckoned toward a cluster of pans. "Beans in the pot and bacon in the pan, so help yourself."

"Thanks." Nevada scooped up a helping of beans, took the tin cup of coffee offered, and sat on a boulder. The sun had sunk below the horizon some time ago. He kept his eyes trained away from the fire. No sense in getting night blinded by staring into the light. Something about this setup didn't feel right, even though the men had given no solid reason to put him on edge. He'd been the first to refuse his name, so he couldn't complain about not knowing theirs.

Silence blanketed the camp as Nevada finished the last of his meal and set his bowl aside.

Crickets whispered on the night breeze and an owl hooted off in the distance. A sudden weariness struck him. He plucked his bedroll and saddle off the ground and moved away from the fire and into the brush, a good distance from the other men. He sank onto the dirt, placing his head on his saddle and drawing the wool blanket up over his shoulders. Tonight he'd sleep with one eye open and an ear tuned for trouble.

* * * * *

Nevada woke as the first flush of dawn brightened the sky. He reached for his pistol lying close to his side and sat up, throwing back the blanket in one easy motion. He hadn't removed his boots, so he rose to his knees and quickly rolled his blanket, then walked over to his horse tethered to the picket line. Nugget nickered a greeting and Nevada loosened the rope, leading the animal to a scanty patch of grass. He'd pick up some grain when he hit Tombstone, but for now this would have to do.

Murmuring voices came from the clearing along with the crackling of branches being broken and tossed onto the smoldering coals. The rattle of a coffeepot and the scrape of a pan indicated breakfast would soon be ready. He drove a stake into the ground and looped the rope around it, then sauntered back toward camp.

The big man looked up when Nevada approached. A jagged scar showed on his cheek above his beard. He motioned toward the coffeepot. "Should be hot soon. Grab a cup."

"Thanks, don't mind if I do." Nevada squatted on his haunches near the fire and reached for the pot.

An occasional grunt and the scrape of a knife against the bottom of a tin pan were all that disturbed the morning. Nevada ate the scant fare offered and drank the strong brew, grateful for the meager meal. His thoughts wandered ahead to Tombstone. The first order of business would be to find work. Maybe he'd take a stab at staking a silver claim if nothing else panned out.

The leader tossed the remnants of his coffee onto the fire and pushed to his feet. "Want t'make a couple of gold pesos, stranger?"

"What's your plan?"

"Like I said last night, me and the boys are huntin' a man that killed a kin of ours. He's an outlaw that might be runnin' with a local gunman, Curly Bill. Got word him and his gang are holed up nearby. They should be ridin' down the trail toward Tombstone soon."

"What do you need from me?"

"We'll all ride up close to the trail, then hoof it the rest of the way. You'll wait with the horses while we scout ahead."

"No need for pay. I'll trail along since I'm headin' toward Tombstone myself."

"I don't care to be beholden to a stranger." He flipped a gold coin in the air, and Nevada caught it. "Stay with the horses until we get back, and there'll be another waitin' for you." He motioned to his men. "Saddle up, and let's head out."

Fifteen minutes later the men broke camp. They swung aboard their horses and hit the trail through the brush heading toward Tombstone. Nevada let his gaze roam the surrounding area. Rugged mountains crested against the distant sky must have beckoned many a wandering miner to explore their shadowy crags. Manzanita and cactus dotted the landscape, and a scorpion scurried across the trail.

Finally, the leader raised his hand and drew to a halt. They stopped on a relatively flat area with undulating hills not far ahead. "This is a good place to wait. The man we're huntin' should be comin' just beyond this rise. There's a narrow spot in the trail where we'll hold them up without any gunplay, then take him back to the marshal in Tombstone for trial."

Nevada stepped off his horse. "Sure you don't want me to come along?"

"Naw. But you might need this, if anything happens." The man yanked a grain sack out of his saddlebag and tossed it.

"What for?" Nevada caught it and held it up for inspection. The bag had two holes cut side by side with a string attached near the opening.

All three men withdrew similar sacks and slipped them over their heads, tying the cords around their necks. "We aim to have the element of surprise and don't care to have these gents see our faces, in case we don't capture them all."

One of the men gave a coarse laugh. "Which ain't likely. But Curly Bill's a mean one. We'd hate to have him come gunnin' for us if'n he gets away."

Nevada tossed the bag on his saddle and shook his head. "Not for me, fellas. I'll wait here like you asked, but that's all."

"Suit yourself." The leader's words were slightly muffled, but his eyes gleamed from the holes cut in the bag. He yanked his thumb toward his men. "Let's go."

They stalked past the horses and headed up a shallow wash toward a rock-strewn hill. Their boots weren't suited to walking and one of the men stumbled. His curse rolled across the clearing. Within minutes they disappeared over the top of the low rise.

Nevada gazed at the spot. This setup didn't smack of an honest group of cowboys trying to round up a killer. He'd ridden on more than one posse in his younger days and never once found the need for a mask. He waited another ten minutes, then grasped his horse's reins and tugged. Time to see what those hombres were up to.

Chapter Three
....

Christy stepped off the train in the new town of Benson, Arizona, grateful to be rid of the dirty, noisy car. This journey had taken longer than she'd anticipated, and worry over her mother mounted. Joshua hadn't said how bad Ma's condition might be, or even what was wrong. Right now all she cared about was reaching Tombstone and seeing to her mother's needs. She chafed at the constant delays and prayed Ma wouldn't worsen before she arrived.

While train travel was somewhat faster than a stagecoach, it didn't have much more to offer in the way of comfort. The cars had jarred, jerked, and rattled their slow way across the countryside, kicking up volumes of dust that drifted into the windows. Her sage-green traveling dress and matching hat were covered with the stuff. Good thing she'd thought to wear a hat with a heavy veil covering her face. More than likely she'd be even more grateful for it by the time the stagecoach rolled into Tombstone.

Tucson had been a disappointment, although the train departed before she had a chance to visit any shops. She'd expected a grand city and only found streets of low adobe houses on the outskirts of town where the train passed through. She scanned the small station at Benson, wondering how many of the people who'd disembarked with her would be going on to Tombstone. Most of the passengers on the train were men, and more than one had given her a look of deep interest, which she'd chosen to ignore. Women had accompanied two of the men, but the rest traveled alone and apparently weren't immune to a single woman.

The stagecoach driver approached the knot of people standing on the siding. "Folks, anyone going on through to Tombstone has thirty minutes to buy their ticket and get some grub. Hustle along."

Christy rolled her head back and stifled a groan. She'd parted with ninety-eight dollars in train fare since leaving Auburn, California. Hopefully her brother was gainfully employed and kept the pantry stocked. At this rate she'd soon be out of the money she'd carefully saved. She walked to the side of a group of three men as they headed toward the way station.

The crude adobe structure stood alone at the end of the street. Two dogs chased a small boy who ran in circles, laughing and screaming, in front of the building. A chicken screeched and flapped out of their way. A woman stood off to the side, hanging clothing on a line strung between two poles planted in the ground, ignoring the visitors trooping across the hard-packed ground toward her.

One of the men wearing a bowler hat, trousers, white shirt, and vest poked his comrade in the side and snickered. "Looks part Injun. Wonder if I need to worry about my scalp."

Christy swung around and glared. "I don't know where you're from, mister, but any decent man in these parts will horsewhip a man who talks ugly about a woman."

A red stain crept up the man's neck, but his eyes narrowed and his chin snapped up. "None of your never-mind, lady. I wasn't talking to you."

"No, but I heard you." She squared her shoulders and marched past him. Ever since she'd taken her first job in a saloon at the age of sixteen and felt the ugly stares and heard the whispers of the decent folks in town, she'd been a champion of the downtrodden and misunderstood. What did it matter the race of the woman hanging the clothes on the line? She was a person with feelings, needs, and desires, like any other. Christy smiled at the dusky-skinned woman as she moved past her. The woman looked startled but smiled tentatively back.

So much prejudice in the world and so little compassion, Christy thought. Hopefully she'd find something better in Tombstone.

The door of the squatty building opened, and a young girl motioned her inside. "There isn't much time before the next stage leaves. Pa has a pot of vittles on the stove."

Christy crossed the threshold into a dimly lit room. Only one small window helped to illuminate the squalid setting. It was barely big enough to contain two rough-hewn tables surrounded by four chairs each, and a rude wooden bar ran well over half the length of the room off to the left of the door.

A man stood behind the waist-high barrier, and the people from the coach lined up before him. "Two dollars each for the trip and a dollar for your meal. Make it quick, folks. There's barely time to get your ticket and eat before the stage leaves for Tombstone."

Christy gasped and covered her mouth with her gloved fingers. Another three dollars? Her stomach rumbled, reminding her she'd eaten a scanty breakfast. She drew in a lungful of the odor emanating from the pot on the potbellied stove behind the counter and wrinkled her nose in distaste. If she guessed correctly, that meal had been brewing for days. She cast around hoping for something else to assuage her hunger and her gaze fell on a loaf of bread. No signs of black spots on the surface, so it might be safe.

She edged up as the man in front of her walked away, clutching his bowl of whatever concoction the establishment saw fit to serve. "I need a ticket for one, please."

"That'll be two dollars, Miss. How about a bowl of my wife's fine stew?" He grinned, showing a blackened tooth.

"Uh, no. Thank you. Might I have a slice of bread instead?" She dug into her reticule hanging around her wrist and withdrew the required payment for the stage.

"That'll be two bits for a slab o' bread. Sure you don't want the stew? I kin throw in the bread for free if you take 'em both."

"Just the bread." Christy laid a coin on the counter. She took the slip of paper declaring she'd purchased one-way fare to Tombstone, and grasped the edge of a small plate with a jagged slab of bread sitting atop it. Praise be, it appeared fresh. A quick step took her to a table not yet occupied, and she sank down in relief. If Ma wasn't up to cooking when she arrived, she'd fix them all a nice supper.

What a relief. Only a couple more hours till Tombstone.

* * * * *

An hour later Christy grabbed at the window frame of the stagecoach, steadying herself from being thrown into the lap of the man beside her. The gentleman wearing the bowler hat sitting across the coach grunted and scowled. "Consarned uncomfortable contraption, if you ask me. Good thing some of the passengers wanted to ride up top, or we'd be jammed in here like sardines. The alkali dust is enough to kill a person."

A rotund man sitting next to the bowler-clad gentleman nodded and patted the arm of the woman beside him. "I agree. I'm thankful the driver allowed us to get out and walk on some of the roughest areas. Thought my teeth would rattle out of my head a couple of times."

Christy smiled but didn't comment.

His female companion had kept to herself most of the trip, clutching the man's arm whenever the coach lurched or jolted. She stared across at Christy's neckline and her eyes widened. "That's an exquisite cameo." She leaned forward and squinted. "Are those pearls around the edge?"

Christy touched the brooch. "Yes. It was a gift from my grandmother before she died."

The woman sat back, a genial expression lighting her face. "It looks valuable. I've heard Tombstone is quite a wild city. You might want to be careful where you wear it."

"Thank you. I hadn't thought of that."

The group inside the stage settled into silence, and Christy was left alone with her thoughts. This brooch contained so many loving memories from her childhood when her papa's mother still lived. She'd stayed with them from the time Christy was eight until she turned twelve and her grandmother had passed. Every year on Christy's birthday she'd been allowed to wear the piece for the entire day.

That last day, as the sweet older lady rested in her bed, she'd pressed her cameo into the young girl's hand, closing her fingers over the small treasure. "It's yours, my love. It's been in my family for three generations. Maybe someday you'll have a daughter you can give it to. Tell her about me, will you, child?"

Christy had treasured the cameo and kept it close from that day forward, always anticipating the time she'd have a family and be able to pass it along with the fond memories of her grandmother. Now she wondered if it was too late. She was twenty-five years old and the closest she'd ever come to marriage was Ralph, back in Last Chance. Some would say she was an old maid and beyond hope, but in her heart-of-hearts she still believed the right man would come.

A loud "whoa" emanated from the driver, and the team slowed its pace. "Hold on, folks. We're goin' down a pretty decent grade," his voice boomed from on top of the box. "When we reach the bottom it'll be some better. You can get out and stretch your legs a mite if you've a mind to, before we start up the other side."

The stage tilted and slowed its forward progress, as the driver continued to haul back on the reins and call to his horses. Once again Christy gripped the opening in the door as the wheels encountered ruts and rocks, jostling the passengers from side to side. Why hadn't the man allowed them to walk this stretch? It seemed the horses would have less work holding back the extra weight in the coach if it were empty. She was tired of being thrown into the man next to her, although from the smug expression she'd noticed a time or two, he didn't seem to mind.

A gunshot from somewhere ahead electrified the five travelers inside. The man she shared a seat with leaned toward his window and peered outside. "By Jove, it looks like a holdup! There's a man with a rifle standing in the middle of the road."

The stage didn't slow, and another gunshot cracked. "Stop your team, or we'll shoot one of the horses," a rough voice echoed against the hillside.

"I ain't stoppin' for nobody." The driver shouted the words, and a gun barked from on top of the stage.

Christy's heart jumped, and a knot formed in her stomach. They were so close to Tombstone, and now someone wanted to rob them? Half of what she had left was inside her small purse. She unpinned the cameo from her dress and held it in the palm of her hand. Bandits would surely notice a piece of jewelry this fine, and she couldn't allow it to be stolen. Slipping her reticule from her wrist, she placed the brooch inside, then searched the interior for a place to hide it. Nothing presented itself as an option.

The seat. Her bag was small and might fit. She turned and jammed the bit of cloth between the seat and its back, stuffing it hard into the crack. The two men continued to peer out the window, but the woman's gaze followed her movements. Christy raised her eyes and met the woman's, giving her a tight smile.

"Do you think they'll kill us?" She whispered the words and clenched her hands in her lap.

Christy shook her head. "Not if we do what they say. If they stop the stage, obey their orders and don't argue or complain. Most robbers won't harm a woman."

* * * * *

Nevada's chin jerked up at the gunshot. He'd almost crested the hill, and he dug in hard, scrambling through the brush and over the top, pulling his horse behind him. They hit a patch of loose rock and slid for several yards, his gelding scrambling to remain on his feet. He held fast to the reins and jumped to the side, getting out of the way as Nugget lunged over a boulder and skidded to a stop. "Whoa, boy. Easy now." Stroking his mount's neck he waited, surveying the area below. On the far side of the gulley, a brace of horses pulled a stage down the hill, the driver hauling back on the reins trying to slow the team. Three men wearing sackcloth masks waved their guns and shouted, but the driver didn't appear to notice.

What had he stumbled into? This wasn't a group of cowboys intent on arresting a killer and carting him to town. Nevada reached for his gun and peered more closely at the stage. Looked like three men riding on top with others inside, like they did when transporting a Wells Fargo payroll to the mines outside of Tombstone.

* * * * *

Another gun exploded nearby, and Christy felt a searing pain in her arm, just above the elbow. She gasped and cried out, staring at the blood now soaking her sleeve.

The woman across from her screamed and then started to shriek, her voice escalating in fear. "They're going to kill us all! Help! Somebody help us!" She buried her face against the chest of the man sitting next to her, but her now muffled screams continued.

The stage rattled and jumped over rocks in its hasty descent into the shallow valley below. Christy wrapped her gloved fingers around her arm, staring at the stream of blood gushing from the wound. She'd been injured more than once in her life, but nothing like this. Something akin to terror gripped her mind, and she struggled to push it aside, tightening her hold on her arm and praying it would slow the bleeding. She couldn't die out here in the wilderness, only a short distance from her family.

She hadn't had nearly enough time to experience life—at least not the kind she'd always hoped and planned for. Scenes from her past rushed at her faster than the jostling coach, reminding her of the years wasted in shameful living. She'd finally found her purpose in helping her mother recover her health, and hopefully gaining some kind of family relationship where none had existed before. Bleeding to death before she even arrived was not an option.

The stage finally drew to a halt, and loud, angry voices erupted outside. Christy sat up straight and gazed around. None of the passengers appeared to have much courage—even the men wilted into limp caricatures of the male race. If she had to demand that someone take care of this wound to ensure her safe arrival at her mother's bedside, so be it. If the outlaws didn't kill them all first.

* * * * *

Nevada scrambled the rest of the way down the hill, pulling his snorting horse with him. No way could he slip away now, not with women on board and someone possibly hurt. He eased his gun out of his holster. It was three against one, but he had the element of surprise.

He crept forward, dodging from bush to bush. The man he recognized as the leader had his gun aimed at the stage, as did the other masked man standing off to one side. The third had disappeared, and Nevada stopped to get his bearings.

A masked man stepped out from behind a boulder, gun drawn and trained on Nevada. "You got two choices. Help us, or get yourself shot."

Nevada hesitated, weighing his options. He could probably take this man without too much trouble, but the gunshot would alert the others. The stage had rolled to a stop, and a glance showed two men climbing down from the top and a male passenger stepping out the door. If he moved forward with his plan and took this man down as he wanted to, it was highly probable some of the passengers would be killed in the ensuing gun battle. His gut clenched, and he tightened his grip on the butt of his gun. Something told him he would do better falling in with these men than trying to stop them, and getting himself and others killed—even if it meant pretending to be a criminal. "I'll help you."

The man's eyes seemed to glow as he peered through the holes in the mask, but his gun didn't waver or drop. "You don't get nothin' but what Jake promised, and you'll get a dose of lead if you try anything funny."

Nevada holstered his gun and raised his hands, palms out. "Sure. Take it easy, friend. Just want to lend a hand, that's all." He sent a prayer heavenward, his first one in years, and hoped this time God would see fit to listen. Maybe once he got close to the stage he could still overpower the outlaws and keep this robbery from happening.

"All right." The gun dropped a couple of inches but stayed trained on his belly. "Ya still got the mask the boss gave you?"

"Yeah. In my saddlebag."

"Put it on. Unless you want your face plastered all over the county on wanted posters." He gave a sharp bark of a laugh. "That might be a good thing. They'd be chasin' you, 'stead of us."

Nevada stepped toward his horse. He withdrew the sackcloth mask from his saddlebag and drew it over his head, wrapping the string around his neck to keep it from slipping. The smell of mold almost gagged him. "What'd you have in here?"

"Some old grain that went bad. Now tie your horse and get a move on." He motioned with his gun and waited for Nevada to follow his orders, then walked behind him toward the other two outlaws.

Nevada peered through the eye holes at the motionless stage and stopped short, still a number of yards away from the coach. His heart rate accelerated. A man climbed out and an older woman followed, her wails splitting the air. Her companion patted her back and drew her close, trying to quiet her sobs.

The outlaw leader stepped forward and uttered a low growl, then raised his voice in warning. "Shut your trap, lady. You don't look hurt a'tall. Quit your caterwaulin', or I'll give you somethin' to complain about."

Her eyes grew round and she gasped, then her lips clamped shut. A slender woman wearing a green dress, a hat, and a veil stepped to the ground. The white glove gripping her arm was stained red and a distinct whimper came from under the veil.

The burly leader turned at Nevada's approach and stalked toward him, stopping a good distance from the stage. "Came to help us, did you? Good thing you covered your head. Wells Fargo don't look too kindly on havin' the payroll stole off their stage."

"You shot a woman?" A growl laced Nevada's words.

He placed his hand on the butt of his gun but kept his gaze trained on the man. Conflicting thoughts raced through his mind. No way could he get into a shooting scrape now. Avoiding more bloodshed must be his primary focus, even if it meant quelling his own desire to end this thing. He fought a hard battle inside—and all the years of violence and living by the gun almost won out. But a glance at the woman standing so silent, gripping her arm with only the one whimper, decided the question for him. He loosened his hold on his gun and relaxed his arm.

"Not a'purpose, we didn't. One of the men got nervous when the driver wouldn't stop and shot at the stage. Winged her. Come on, you kin help us relieve them of their valuables."

"I don't care about the money you offered." Nevada dug out the gold coin the man had paid him and tossed it toward him. "I agreed to stay with the horses, and that's all. I had no idea you planned on robbing a stage."

"Good." The leader snatched it and walked back to the scene playing out in front of the coach. He walked to the far side and stepped up onto the wheel, dragging down a case from on top of the stage.

The woman still gripped her arm and drops of blood dripped on the ground. The hat and veil covered her hair and most of her face, revealing only a nicely shaped chin and curved red lips drawn down in pain. "I say, you over there." She tilted her chin in his direction. "I don't care to bleed to death. Can't someone help me?"

"Yes, ma'am." Nevada stepped forward. He walked up to her, marveling at her near perfect form and slender waist. He reached for her arm, but she pulled back.

"Not here in front of everyone." Her hand clutching the wound trembled. "I'd appreciate some privacy, please." Nevada cast a look at the outlaws, but they didn't appear to notice, as two were busy relieving the driver and passengers of their belongings and the third unstrapped the small box taken from the top of the stage.

"All right. Let's step over here." He motioned to an outcropping of boulders and brush. He reached out, hoping to help her over the rough terrain, but she shrank away. Hot anger drenched his skin with perspiration. Why hadn't he paid attention to his gut back at the camp? Those three men were obviously up to no good, but he'd ignored the warning. The woman believed him to be part of the gang. He'd never be party to harming any lady, and this was most certainly a lady.

A sudden shout went up from the coach and a gleeful voice drifted toward them. "Hey, looky here. Someone hid this bag in the seat. It's got a real pretty doodad in it, and some gold coins. Whoo-whee!"

The woman walking beside him suddenly sagged, and he reached out to steady her. "What is it? Are you feeling faint?"

She placed her hand over her heart. "My grandmother's brooch. I can't lose it. Oh, please…" Her breath caught in a ragged sob, and she bowed her head.

"I'm sorry, Miss, but I'm more concerned with this gunshot wound and getting the bleeding stopped." He paused and studied her. "I'll not touch you unless I need to, but you'll have to let me look at that wound."

She stopped behind the dense brush, then removed her grip on her arm and hesitantly offered the injured member to him. "Can you stop the bleeding?"

"I think so." He peered at her sleeve. How to get to the wound without destroying the sleeve? Of course, it already contained a bullet hole that would need to be repaired. "Can you push your sleeve up above your elbow?"

"I'll try." She gritted her teeth and pushed at the material loosely draped between wrist and elbow. It slid partway up but didn't quite reveal the affected area. "You'll have to help." She raised her head, and he barely caught a flash of green behind the veil.

The sackcloth mask kept slipping, making it difficult to see clearly through the small eyeholes. He tugged it back in place and bent over her arm, only to have it move again. There was no hope for it. Either he took the thing off so he could see properly, or he wouldn't be much good to this woman. "Ma'am?"

"Yes?" Pain spilled from her voice, and she bit her bottom lip.

"I can't see much through this blasted mask."

"Remove it, then."

"I need to tell you something first, and you have to make me a promise." He could see she struggled to keep from crying, but he had to extract the promise first, as much as he hated seeing her suffer. "I'm not part of this holdup."

Her chin raised and she frowned. "You're wearing a mask and carrying a gun, and you're here, aren't you?"

"I know. I rode into these men's camp last night looking for a meal and they asked me to stay with the horses this morning." He shrugged. "I knew better, but I was in no hurry to go anywhere."

She sucked in a quick breath. "Right now I don't care. I'm going to bleed to death if you don't do something."

"I'll take my mask off and help, but you've got to promise you'll never tell anyone what I look like, or point me out if you see me in Tombstone."

Christy lifted a determined chin. "Fine. I won't tell anyone what you look like. But please hurry and bind this wound."

Nevada jerked off the mask, thankful for the fresh air and better vision with the musty piece of burlap removed. "I need to cut your sleeve."

* * * * *

Christy nodded but didn't speak, afraid to trust her voice now that the bandit had removed his mask. Deep brown eyes tried to probe the veil. Her heart jumped to her throat, and she struggled to breathe. The outlaw was undoubtedly one of the handsomest men she'd ever encountered. She'd always thought Alexia's husband Justin attractive, but this man with his broad shoulders, narrow hips, cleft in his chin and dark, wavy hair was downright rugged and masculine.

She stared up into his rich brown eyes, thankful he couldn't see hers, because she was embarrassed at the direction her thoughts had taken. He was an outlaw, for goodness' sake! There was no place in her life for interest in a man like this. No, five years ago she'd sworn she'd never again be duped by a handsome face, no matter the circumstances. Especially not someone who carried a gun and appeared to know how to use it.

A slight shudder shook her body, as she remembered the man who'd coerced her into traveling to Last Chance in the first place. He'd been no good, and she hadn't been strong enough to stand against him. *That* Christy no longer existed, and she'd found the strength to do the right thing in the end. She'd grown and changed in the intervening years, and nothing would make her waver from the path she'd chosen now—caring for her mother and younger brother, and hopefully making their lives better.

* * * * *

Nevada squinted at the veil, wishing he could see beneath it and into the face of the woman standing so calmly before him. He'd seen the color course up her neck and then noticed the slight shiver that shook her body. Was it shock from the bullet wound or fear of further injury at his hands that consumed her? Best finish this as soon as possible and hightail it out of here. He cursed himself for getting hooked up with this crew and drawn into this mess.

Then another notion penetrated the dark thoughts swirling in his mind and drew him up short. What would this woman's fate have been if he'd not come along when he had? Based on the greed and uncaring attitudes of the group robbing the stage, he doubted any of them would've seen to her wound.

He pulled a finely honed knife from a sheath on his belt and sliced the material, then spread it wide. A deep gash in the fleshy part of her arm continued to ooze blood, but the bullet didn't appear to have cut deep enough to hit a bone. He dug into his back pocket and withdrew a clean bandana. The one around his neck was covered with trail dust and wouldn't do to cover the wound but would tie off the blood flow. "Here, hold this for a moment." He shoved the bandana into her hand and yanked off the one around his neck, then tied it a couple inches above the bleeding.

She winced when he tightened the cloth and knotted it but didn't utter a word.

He cut a corner off the clean bandana and made a pad, placing it over the gash, and then tied the rest of it around the area where she'd been shot. "There. That should do it."

A tiny smile tipped up the corner of her mouth. "Thank you. I won't forget your kindness, even if you are a bandit."

Nevada started to reply, then tightened his jaw. He'd already explained, and she didn't believe him, so what was the point? He pivoted on his heel and tugged the mask back on. Hopefully this holdup would end soon, and the stage and its passengers could be on their way. The young woman had seemed sincere when she promised not to divulge his identity. He hoped no one in town would convince her otherwise. The last thing he needed was his mug hanging on a wanted poster for something he hadn't done.

Chapter Four

Nevada stood his ground in front of the outlaw leader. "I want the brooch your man found in the coach, nothing else."

The man rubbed his unshaven jaw and chortled. "Got to you, did she? Quite the looker, if you ask me." He leaned over and spat. "That stage ain't too far down the road yet. Maybe I should trot after it and see if the lady wants company from a real man." His cheeks stretched in a leering grin.

Nevada sprang forward, landing less than a foot from the bandit. He grabbed the rough cloth of his shirt and jerked the man's face within inches of his own. "Leave her alone or answer to me."

Out of the corner of his eye he saw one of the outlaws reach for his gun. Nevada shoved the leader away and swiveled toward the man, his hand hovering over the butt of his pistol. "Don't even think about it, unless you want your gizzard filled with lead."

Hesitation showed in the eyes staring into his own. Finally, the outlaw relaxed and took a step back. "Don't get all riled up now, pard. The boss was funnin', wasn't you, Jake?"

A low snarling curse rolled from the leader's throat. "Like thunder I was. Who are you anyway, mister?"

Nevada kept his hand poised above his gun and pinned both of the men with his gaze. "That doesn't matter. You promised me payment. I'll take the brooch."

The third robber who'd kept silent stepped forward. "You didn't do nothin' to earn it but tend to some woman's arm."

Nevada swung his attention around. "And you'd best be glad I did. If she'd bled to death, you'd be wanted for murder, as well as robbing the stage."

"Ha! Like you ain't gonna be wanted too." The leader dug into his pocket and withdrew the brooch. "Fine, take it. Looks like it's probably nothin' but junk anyway. Now get out of my sight." He tossed the bit of jewelry through the air and Nevada caught it with his left hand.

"Suits me." He backed away, keeping an eye on the men. Good thing he'd left his horse tethered close by in a stand of mesquite, and the rest of this crew had to walk over the hill to find their mounts. He wouldn't put it past any one of the three to plug him in the back if given half a chance.

✳ ✳ ✳ ✳ ✳

Christy's arm throbbed and her head hurt, but she thanked the Lord she'd been spared the indignity of having her person searched. Shortly after the handsome bandit had dressed her wound and ushered her back with the others, the outlaws had gathered up the guns from every member of the party and disappeared over the top of a nearby hill. The driver had checked on her with some degree of solicitude, asking after her arm, and then urged the passengers to enter the stage.

"Miss?" The woman sitting across from her leaned forward and touched her knee. "Are you all right?"

Christy lifted her veil. "Yes. I hope Tombstone has a doctor, but at least the bleeding has stopped."

The gentleman next to her nodded. "Yes, ma'am, Doctor Goodfellow will fix you right up. He arrived in town last fall and is an expert on gunshot wounds. Good thing. Lots of shooting used to go on betwixt the miners and such, but it's slowed down tolerable now we've got a county sheriff and town marshal."

"My name is Molly." The woman gave a shy smile and motioned toward the portly man sitting beside her. "This here is my intended, Rodney. We're going to marry as soon as we arrive. Rodney is from Tombstone, and he's built us a house."

Christy pasted on what she hoped was a pleasant look, but a shaft of pain shot through her heart. Molly. Her sister had borne that name and died a number of years back when Molly's young son, Toby, was only a toddler. So many bad memories from her past continued to haunt her, and her sister's wasn't the only one. "Congratulations. I hope you'll be very happy."

"Thank you." Molly's face turned somber. "It'll set us back a mite, though, what with those bandits taking the gold we saved." Eager curiosity illuminated her countenance. "What did he look like? The man who fixed up your arm."

How could she convey to these people that the fingers that touched her arm had been tender, yet firm? His deference and care toward her had hinted at a gentlemanly upbringing, but his clothing and occupation belied that suggestion. These travelers wouldn't believe her, no matter what she said. The man had been riding with the outlaws and must be part of their group, regardless of his claims. "I'm sorry, but I couldn't say."

"What do you mean? Rodney here got a glimpse of the two of you when the robbers moved us toward the front of the stage. The man had his back turned and his hat on, but he removed his mask, so you surely got a good look at him."

Rodney leaned forward. "You need to give a description so they can round up the gang."

Christy didn't reply but looked instead out the window of the bouncing stage. The veil resting on top of her hat offered privacy, and she dropped it back. Distant hills could be seen through the clouds of dust kicked up by the wheels. They'd arrive in town soon, and hopefully she could distance herself from these people who seemed so intent on getting answers.

The man in the bowler hat cleared his throat. "Miss?"

"Yes?"

"You'll need to talk to the marshal about what happened."

"I understand. I'll do so after I've had my arm looked at and I've seen to my sick mother."

Molly's brows drew together. "Why won't you tell us?"

"I'd rather not discuss it, if you don't mind. My arm is throbbing."

"Oh." The woman sat back. "I'm sorry. I wasn't thinking."

Christy turned her attention back out the window. They passed the first buildings on the outskirts of Tombstone. Soon she'd see Joshua and her mother and get this arm tended to. Her heart faltered at the thought of her mother. If only things would be different this time. Ma had the idea Christy had abandoned her when she'd chosen to stay in Last Chance, but she couldn't return to her old life. The last thing she wanted was for her mother to remain angry with her and prayed coming to care for Ma would set things to rights.

She didn't know what she'd say if the marshal questioned her about the man who'd unmasked himself in order to help her. One thing Christy knew. She'd given her word, and she'd not break it no matter what anyone said or threatened to do.

* * * * *

Nevada pushed his horse hard, cutting across country and avoiding the road the stage would take into town. He wanted to be on hand when the coach rolled in and see if he could catch a glimpse of the injured woman's face.

He rode down Allen Street in the midst of Tombstone. He'd heard about this small city that grew up almost overnight but hadn't known what to expect. He'd been in many a cattle town over the years, but this mining town beat all. As Nevada rode he noted numerous saloons, hotels, stores, barbershops, gambling halls, restaurants, and a jumble of humanity thronging every side. Most looked like prospectors, but gamblers, cowboys, and teamsters helped fill out the crowd, along with an occasional woman. Some of those were pleasant, homebody types, but he spotted more than one woman who would only fit in a bordello or dancehall. Boardwalks lined the dusty avenue, and buckboards, wagons, and buggies of every shape and size rolled along its length.

Hotels and several homelike edifices with a signboard advertising them as boardinghouses beckoned to weary travelers. Looked like plenty of places he could hang his hat. First stop would be the livery where he'd put up his horse. Nevada's thoughts slipped back to the woman he'd helped. He'd loved to have skinned those varmints who held up the stage, but the last thing he wanted was another shooting laid at his door.

His mind drifted to Albuquerque and the grisly scene that played out with Logan Malone lying dead in the street. How many times in the past had he wished things had turned out different? Right now all he wanted was a new occupation—one that didn't include gunplay. He'd stashed enough money to purchase a small ranch, if he found one that suited him. This might be a good area to start checking. Riding herd on cattle for other men had lost its fascination years ago. He was sick of traveling from town to town and never knowing where he'd sleep.

A shout up the street caused Nevada to turn in the saddle. He'd wondered how long the stage would take to arrive. No need to question any longer, as the driver smacked the lines against the horses' backs and cantered them up the road. A billow of powder rose from its wheels. People cleared a path when it slowed at the business district and finally halted less than half a block away. He leaned his hands on the pommel. Maybe he'd get a glimpse of the lady with the injured arm. His heart rate accelerated, remembering the perfectly shaped lips, lovely voice, and pleasing figure.

A crowd gathered around the coach, partially obscuring his view. He nudged his gelding with his heel, urging him forward. Nevada's elevated position allowed him to scrutinize the scene. A sudden thought checked his forward progress and he reined to a halt, his mouth going dry. The woman from the stage was the only one other than the robbers who'd seen him. She'd promised to guard his identity, but what did he know of her? Nothing. If she saw him sitting nearby she could easily point him out and call for the law. Nevada tugged his hat low over his eyes and dropped his head an inch or two. No sense in taking chances, but he'd be hanged if he'd walk away without getting a glimpse of her.

"We're in Tombstone, folks." The driver stood up and pointed his whip at a young man standing nearby. "Hey, you boy."

"Yes, sir?" The lad wore an expectant look.

"Run and get the marshal. We've been robbed again, and we've got an injured lady onboard this time."

The boy took off running. No one on the street seemed overly concerned with the announcement, but curious faces peered into the stage.

The driver laid aside his whip and wound the reins around the brake, then clambered from his seat to the ground. "Ma'am, I sent for the marshal, and we'll have the doc look at your arm if you'll sit tight for a few minutes."

Nevada's gut clenched and he reined his horse back, stopping in the shadow of a store. He didn't care to have anyone from the stage recognize his clothing.

The coach driver pointed a hand to a nearby building. "That there is the Grand Hotel, and the Golden Eagle Brewery is across yonder. You folks can sleep, eat, or drink, whatever your pleasure might be. Now get yer gear and hop on out."

Two other men shimmied over the side and the first one reached the door, swinging it open. The man and his woman companion disembarked, then the gent with the bowler hat, another portly gentleman, and lastly the woman with his bandana wrapped around her arm, the veil still covering her face.

A whoop went up from the crowd. A miner jumped forward and threw his arm wide. The bowler hat went flying into the dust, landing at the feet of a nearby laborer. He gave it a kick, sending it on to the next pair of boots, who sent it along to the next.

The stunned city slicker stared as his prized headpiece bounced down the Tombstone street. Catcalls and hoots of laughter filled the air. "Hey. Stop that, do you hear? I paid good money for that hat."

A man wearing a double-breasted vest with a watch chain dangling from the front pocket stepped up, his thumbs hooked in his belt. "Sorry, mister. We don't cotton to city folks. You need to get yourself a decent head covering. Doesn't appear that one's going to survive long in this town."

Grinning wide, a miner trooped up to the gawking stranger, dangling the now battered and dusty object from his finger. He turned to the rest of the laughing crowd and shoved the disreputable headpiece into the hands of the nearest man. "Pass this around, gents, and let's get this man a decent sombrero."

Cheers resounded and men tossed coins and bills into the offered basket. The miner turned with a smile. "Hold out your hands."

The stunned city slicker did as he was told and the miner pushed the hat into them. "Hop on over to the dry goods store and tell the clerk to fix you up proper." He gave the city slicker a shove in the direction he'd indicated. The crowd gave another cheer, then started to disperse. Apparently that hour's entertainment had ended, and it was time to find something else to amuse them.

Nevada rubbed his chin, surprised at what he'd seen. If this didn't beat all—that was a cowboy trick, for sure. He wondered what the motley assortment of men would have done had the stranger put up a serious fuss. Probably sent him rolling down the street after his hat, instead of taking a collection.

A jolt shot through him, and he swiveled around. Where had the woman with the veil gone? In the excitement he'd completely lost track of her before he'd gotten a look at her. He let loose a low groan and urged his horse forward. He didn't have a prayer of discovering her identity, but he could ride up the street a ways and see if he could spot her.

Another searching glance brought him up short. A man with a gold star on his vest strode toward the stage. Looked like the law had arrived. All he could do was hope the woman would keep her word. Time for him to slip into the background and disappear.

* * * * *

Christy eased farther away from the laughing group of men, only slightly disturbed by the scene that had played out before her. It had been a number of years, but the memories rushed back quite easily. Men having sport at another's expense—be it a city slicker, a drunk, or a tenderfoot. So many of the folks in Last Chance had been decent, law-abiding citizens that she'd almost forgotten how this part of the world lived. She shook her head. Time to get out of here and see if she could find her brother.

Too bad she'd been unable to let Joshua know what day she'd arrive, but hopefully it wouldn't be too hard to discover his and Ma's whereabouts. A dark-frocked man wearing a flat-brimmed hat and a gold star on his lapel pushed his way through the crowd. Christy shrank back, not caring to face his questions right now. All she wanted was for her arm to be treated and to find where her mother lived. The details of the stage holdup could come later.

She took a few more steps away from the laughing crowd and cast a look around for someone familiar. Fingers touched her arm, and she turned. A tall, slender man stood before her. He was dressed mostly in black, his broadcloth suit neatly pressed and a flat-crowned black hat snugged down on his dark hair. He wore a white shirt with the stiff collar turned up and a pair of dust-covered black boots. She'd wager he was a gambler. It may have been nearly five years since she'd escaped the dancehall life, but she could still spot a man of chance with her eyes half closed.

"May I direct you somewhere, dear lady?" Dark blue eyes peered from beneath slender, raised brows.

"No. Thank you." She turned to go, then realized she'd have to speak to someone. A glance revealed no other women in the area, and none of the men sauntering nearby looked much better. "Excuse my manners. I would appreciate being directed to the doctor's office."

He gave a half bow and extended his arm. "Allow me to escort you?"

Christy shook her head. "That won't be necessary. If you'd point it out, I'd be most appreciative."

His eyes narrowed, and he touched the end of his small mustache. "Most assuredly, but I must insist on at least accompanying you. My name is Gordon Townsley, and I'm one of the managers at the Oriental." He said the words as though they should have special meaning.

"The Oriental?" She didn't smile. Men who were this forward didn't need encouragement.

"One of the premiere establishments in our fair city." He cleared his throat and offered his arm again. "Please, I insist. A lady like yourself could easily be accosted on this rowdy street. I'd hate to have anything untoward happen as you make your way there."

Christy hesitated. She had no idea where the doctor's office was located, or how to find her brother or mother. So far this man offered the only help in sight, and he'd given her no reason to spurn his assistance. She bobbed her head but didn't touch the extended arm. "All right. I'd be grateful if you'd show me the way, Mr. Townsley."

The corner of his chiseled lips quirked up, but no sense of warmth was conveyed. He lowered his arm and touched her shoulder, turning her slightly toward him. "Right this way." He led her to the boardwalk running in front of a mercantile and assisted her as she stepped up. "What did you say your name is?"

"Miss Grey."

He gave a slight start. "Grey. Any relation to Joshua Grey?"

Christy's heart leapt. "Yes. You know my brother?"

"I do. He frequents my establishment on a regular basis. Likeable fellow, if a little prone to provoke a fight at times. Does he know you're in town?"

"No. He sent for me, but I wasn't sure when I'd arrive." Her spirits sank at the realization this man's business must be a gambling hall. "I'd be pleased if you could direct me to him."

"I can't say if he's there now, mind you. But I'll certainly be happy to show you the way to the Oriental after you finish at the doctor's office." He steered her around a throng of miners surging out the batwing doors of a saloon. Their loud laughter and coarse voices drifted back, along with the distinct odor of alcohol. "If I may be so bold as to ask?"

He tipped his head toward the bandana knotted around her arm. "I see blood on that rag. What happened?"

"Our stage was attacked, and a stray bullet caught me in my arm. It's no longer bleeding and no bones were broken, although I must admit there's a bit of pain yet."

His eyes widened. "I should think so. I'm amazed you haven't swooned right at my feet. Why, you never even mentioned your discomfort."

A flick of his wrist directed her attention to a sign up ahead. Doctor Goodfellow was emblazoned in deep-blue letters on a sanded slab of wood hanging above a window on the second floor of the Golden Eagle Brewery. "His office is upstairs."

He directed her through a door and across to a staircase. "Most women I know would be screeching with pain or lamenting their experience."

Christy shrugged. "Not much to be gained by that. It burns like fire, and I'll be happy to have it cared for, but there's no need to fuss over it." No sense in letting this man see her anxiety. It would probably only encourage him. All she wanted was to get this arm tended to and find her family.

Admiration and something she couldn't quite decipher lit his eyes. She turned her gaze away, suddenly uncomfortable with this neatly dressed, dapper man. He pushed open the door, and a bell jingled above it. "Let me see if the doctor is here."

"That won't be necessary. I'm able to take care of myself." But her words fell on empty space as Townsley's frock-coated form disappeared through another doorway leading toward the back of the building.

Solid footsteps echoed on the plank floor, and a man who looked to be in his early thirties appeared at the door, Townsley right on his heels. "Sorry to keep you waiting. I just finished with a surgery. Bullet wound. Had to dig so deep I felt like I was performing assessment work." He grinned and cocked his head. "Rich in lead but too punctured to hold whiskey. Poor chap pulled through. Hopefully he'll not get liquored up next time when he decides to accost someone with a gun. Now, how can I help you?"

Christy held out her arm. "I'm afraid liquor had little to do with this bullet wound, Doctor, but there was certainly a gun involved."

Doctor Goodfellow had the grace to duck his chin. "Pardon my poor manners, ma'am. It seems I've been in the wilderness too long and no longer know how to address a lady. I graduated with honors from Cleveland Medical College, but you'd certainly not know it from my behavior today." He beckoned her toward the door. "Come. I'll take you back to an exam room and fix you right up."

Gordon Townsley stepped forward. "I'll wait for you, Miss Grey."

"No need. I'm sure Doctor Goodfellow can direct me once we finish. There's no telling how long this will take."

"Nonsense. I have no pressing business to attend to, at any rate." He settled onto a wooden chair in the waiting area.

"All right. Thank you."

She followed the doctor beyond the open doorway and into a dark hallway. They walked three steps, then turned right into a cubbyhole lined with shelves on one side and holding nothing else but a cot with a small table alongside.

"You said your name is Miss Grey?" The doctor motioned to the cot. "Sorry I don't have anything better to offer. If you wouldn't mind taking a seat on the edge?" He reached for a clean cloth, a towel, and a pot of water while she perched on the canvas surface. "I'm going to soak this bandana before I try to remove it. You might want to spread this towel over your skirt so it doesn't get wet."

She did as he suggested, and the next few minutes passed in silence as the doctor carefully removed the cloth tied around her arm. He swabbed the blood-encrusted area and probed at the wound with skilled fingers but made no comment. Christy bit her lip to keep from crying out. The hole in her flesh started bleeding again, and a burning heat shot from her elbow up to her shoulder.

"I'm sorry. I know it hurts. Would you like some laudanum for the pain?"

"No. I won't touch it." She didn't care to tell him her sister, Molly, had used it more than once, and she'd always believed her dependence on alcohol started with the nasty drug.

"Up to you. I'll be finished shortly, in any case."

He reached over to the nearby shelf and removed a can, prying open the lid. A foul odor drifted from the canister and Christy wrinkled her nose.

"It smells bad," he said apologetically, "but it'll help seal the wound. It has turpentine in it, so it might sting , but that will pass quickly." He dipped his fingers in the concoction and smeared a liberal amount on a piece of gauze, then placed it over the gaping hole.

Christy gasped and gritted her teeth.

"Sorry." The doctor unwound a long strip of clean white cloth and wrapped it around her arm from her elbow almost to her shoulder, covering the entire affected area, and drew her sleeve back down. "There we go. I'll want to see you tomorrow."

"How much do I owe you?" She reached for her reticule and groaned. She'd tucked it into the seat of the stagecoach and the outlaws had found it. Thankfully the rest of her money still rested in her trunk.

"You can settle up after I see you again." Doctor Goodfellow pulled open the door of the small exam room and ushered her back up the hall to the waiting area. "Care to take any laudanum with you, Miss?"

"No, but thank you for seeing me, and I'll come back tomorrow." Christy extended her hand, and he took it, bowing over it for a moment.

Townsley rose from his chair and removed his hat, nodding first at the doctor, then Christy. "You ready to go, ma'am?"

Christy shot him a glance, torn between trying to get rid of the man and allowing him to help her. But right now family was uppermost in her mind, so she pushed her concerns about Townsley's character aside. "Yes. I'm anxious to find my brother."

He escorted her out the door and down the boardwalk. "It's across the street on the corner. Can't guarantee Josh will be at a table right now, but someone might know of his whereabouts."

They crossed the dusty side street and stopped at a two-story building flanked across the front with large windows. Several decorative pillars propped up the overhanging roof, and a number of rough-clad men stood under the shade of the porch. Loud music blasted out the open door along with brash laughter and the tinkling of glasses.

Townsley touched her arm and halted her. "Why don't you wait here, Miss Grey?"

Christy scooted sideways and peered around him. At that instant, the door swung open, emitting a miner who appeared to have imbibed liquor beyond his capacity.

The man swerved to pass her and paused, clumsily lifting his hat. "Good day, Miss. If you're comin' to work here, I'll be back. Don't see women like you around here very often."

Townsley stepped in front of Christy and placed a hand on the man's chest, shoving him backwards off the boardwalk. He hit the ground with a loud grunt.

Townsley towered over the prostrate man. "We don't want you coming back here, mister. Go down the street and try Campbell and Hatch's Saloon; they cater more to your kind." He turned around and eyed Christy. "I don't want to leave you outside. Most men in this town would never touch a lady, but there are those who might say something they shouldn't. Would you be willing to step inside while I look for your brother?"

Revulsion surged inside Christy, and her stomach knotted. She'd seen far too many of these places and had never planned on setting foot in one again. "I'm not sure…."

"I have a man inside who'll watch out for you. No one will get near you while you're here. I can't say the same if you stand outside."

"All right. It seems I must."

Christy lifted her chin and followed him through the doorway leading into the noisy Oriental Saloon. Her eyes darted around the room, barely grasping the opulence spread before her. A piano and a violin both played a brisk tune not far from the end of the highly polished bar running the width of the room. Lush carpet covered much of the floor rather than the typical rough-cut lumber she'd been accustomed to in businesses like this. The mirror behind the bar reflected the gaming tables scattered around the room, as well as the women drifting from one to another serving drinks. Christy wrinkled her nose as cigar smoke hit her. She'd always hated the smell, and now she remembered why.

Townsley beckoned to a tall, slender man in a dark suit who stood back from a faro table. "Doc, I need you."

The man called Doc moved forward, his gaze trained on Townsley. "How may I help?"

"This is Miss Grey, Joshua Grey's sister."

Christy noted a flash of surprise as the cold eyes met hers.

"I see." Some other expression crossed his face too. Speculation or anticipation…she couldn't be sure.

"This is Doc Holliday," Townsley explained. "He's usually at the faro table or sitting in a game of poker, but there's not a man in the place who will trifle with him. You'll be safe in his care."

Doc brought his arm across his waist and bowed low. "Pleased, ma'am."

Townsley dropped his voice, leaning closer to Holliday. "You see Grey today?"

"He was here earlier. Not sure if he's still around. I'll stay with the lady while you look."

"Thanks." Townsley pushed through the milling crowd.

Christy lost sight of him as he bent low over a table of men playing cards. She allowed her gaze to roam over the room once again, then slowly returned her attention to the man beside her, trying not to stare. Doc Holliday was a legend. His fame had even reached into the small mining community of Last Chance. He had a Colt

.45 strapped to his hip, and the handle of a knife protruded from a sheath to the left of his belt buckle. She'd heard of his prowess with both weapons. More than one man turned his attention away from her now when they noted the man standing close by. Somehow his nearness did little to assuage her anxiety, however. She didn't belong in this place, and neither did Joshua. When she got her hands on her little brother, she'd convince him to change his ways.

Loud voices lifted above the hum. Christy turned her attention toward the commotion. A man pushed back from a table halfway across the crowded gambling floor and threw his cards on the table. "You're a low-down cheat, Coulter."

A chill raced up Christy's spine. Her brother stood with his hand hovering over the lapel of his coat where she knew he favored hiding a gun.

A raw-boned man wearing a bow tie and a white shirt shoved his chair back and glared. "Watch what you call me, son. I'm a dead shot, and you'll be buried before sundown if you're not careful."

Joshua snarled a curse and his hand stiffened.

Christy sprang forward, pushing past Doc Holliday's out-stretched arm. "Joshua, wait!"

Her high-pitched cry froze the room. The piano and violin hushed, and the slowing roulette wheel clicked loudly in the silence. Joshua kept his gaze on the waiting Coulter.

Christy pushed through the men separating her from her brother. "Joshua, it's me, Christy. Please don't fight that man."

His hand wavered and then dropped to his side. He drew in a sharp, hard breath and broke his gaze free, sweeping his hand over the small stack of coins on the table and dumping them into his coat pocket. "You're gettin' off easy this time, Coulter. Next time you cheat, my sister won't be around to save your hide."

The buzz in the room resumed, and the men at the table picked up their cards and commenced playing as though nothing unpleasant had happened.

Christy rushed to her brother's side, barely sensing Doc Holliday's presence behind her. "What do you think you're doing?"

Joshua swiveled toward her and scowled. "You don't belong in here. Get out and go see Ma."

She jerked back, feeling as though she'd been struck. The brother she remembered would never have spoken to her this way. "Joshua, I don't know where Ma lives."

Gordon Townsley stepped over and touched her arm. "Miss Grey, allow me?"

Christy wasn't sure what the man planned, but right now she felt at a complete loss and could only nod.

He threw a hard look at Joshua. "Why don't you walk your sister home, Grey? She's had a long stage ride, and I'm sure she'd like to rest and see her ma. You can come back later when you've cooled off."

Joshua's jaw clenched. "Fine. Let's go." He stalked past Christy and headed for the door.

Chapter Five

. . . .

Nevada exited the livery stable where he'd put up his horse and strolled onto the bustling main street. He hadn't been able to get the picture of the injured woman out of his mind. If only he'd paid more attention when she'd stepped off the stage and not let her out of his sight. It occurred to him that she might need to purchase some things after arriving in town or even be staying at a local boarding-house. Spending time walking the streets wouldn't be a bad idea.

This place certainly lived up to its reputation as a booming min-ing town. Freight wagons rolled past, loaded with ore drawn by mule teams boasting ten and twelve strong. Men loitered on street corners, and a shopkeeper swept the boardwalk in front of his establishment while keeping an eye open for prospective customers. A cat raced between two buildings with a burly man not far behind. Nevada scratched his head and grinned at the comical sight. Must be a toler-able mouse or rat problem if men chased cats up the alleyways.

The door of a saloon a block away slammed open, and a young man stalked out. He didn't bother to check for passersby but bar-reled onto the boardwalk, pushing through anyone who got in his way. More than one man tossed an oath at his back as he headed up the street away from Nevada. Must have lost at the gaming tables. Nevada suppressed a chuckle. Hopefully the young fellow would learn early that a man and his money are easily parted in places like this one.

Seconds later a young lady dashed out, waving her hand. He couldn't understand the words she called over the noise in the street, but she looked fit to be tied. Poor woman. Must be hard up if she had to work in a saloon and chase down customers when they wanted to leave. Nevada made it a half block in the opposite direction when realization hit him hard. That green dress and hat...he'd seen it before—a few hours ago, to be exact. Why hadn't he paid closer attention? He whirled around and started forward, looking up the street on both sides. Straining to see through the crowd, he tried to get a glimpse of the green dress, but both the man and woman had disappeared as though they hadn't existed.

He slowed his pace, disappointment slapping at him. When had he started fantasizing the girl needed rescuing and he could be the one to do so? Obviously she could take care of herself if she'd already made her way to a gambling hall. Had she come to Tombstone for that reason and gone straight to the business wanting to hire her? He shook his head in disgust. Never had he understood women who lured men to drink themselves into a stupor for a living—or worse.

Yet, somehow, he still wished he'd gotten a glimpse of her face.

* * * * *

Christy's ire rose with each step and she clenched her fingers into fists as she hurried along behind her brother. Joshua strode ahead without looking back. When she caught up, she'd love to box his ears like she'd done when he was a little scrap. What had changed the young man she remembered into someone ready to pick a fight? Even two years ago, when she'd last seen him, he hadn't evidenced this degree of anger. She realized men in this country must stand up for what they believed, and if a card shark was cheating, it might be appropriate to call him on it. But drawing your gun and killing the man? No. That was too much.

They left the business district behind and entered a row of houses. Shacks, more like it. She shuddered as she looked around. Ma would never agree to live like this. At least she didn't have to worry about Joshua stopping at one of these hovels.

"Joshua." Christy raised her voice, making sure he could hear her, but he didn't slow his pace.

And men thought women were cantankerous creatures. She grasped her skirt with one hand and lifted her hem. Time to catch that young scamp before he arrived wherever he might be headed.

"I say, Joshua. Wait for me!" The increased pace jarred her arm and she gasped. She gritted her teeth and kept going. A few more trotting strides and she almost drew even with her brother. "Joshua, stop walking this minute."

He seemed to wake from an angry stupor and came to an abrupt halt, letting her plunge on past him two full steps before catching herself and stopping. "What? Can't you see I'm heading home?"

Panting for breath, she placed her hand over her heart to still its racing. "I had no notion where you might be headed, but I'll admit I'd hoped it wasn't home, considering our surroundings." She glanced around her at the low adobe buildings and the shanties built out of scraps of lumber—some covered with only a canvas roof that a strong puff of wind could easily remove.

Joshua rounded on her and crossed his arms on his chest. "You too good for the likes of this family now, that it? You been gone so long you forgot what it's like to be poor?"

Christy felt the blood drain from her face. "Poor? Like that?" She flicked her fingers toward the closest hut, where a woman stepped out of the door and onto the dirt road. From her scanty attire, barely covered by a shawl, her occupation was apparent. Was she going to work at one of the saloons, or did she bring her business home with her? The door opened again, and a grizzled, balding man emerged, snapping his suspenders and grinning.

Christy stared in horror as Joshua sped up again, then a block later slowed in front of a fence badly in need of paint. "Do you mean to tell me you actually live in one of these...houses?" Christy's heart lurched into her throat. She couldn't get out of this neighborhood soon enough to suit her.

"Yeah. What of it?"

"Joshua." She touched his arm, but he drew back. "What's happened to you since I last saw you? Why are you so...angry?"

"Ha. Angry, is it? Good question, big sister." The last two words came out with a sneer. "You're off livin' the high life with your fancy ranch friends while Ma and I are strugglin' to survive here in this hole."

"But I thought Logan left money for you before he headed to his mining claim. If you were careful, it should've lasted a long time. Ma could've had a nice little house in a good part of town. What happened?"

"Nothing. Everything." He dragged his fingers through his dark red hair, the only thing they shared in common besides their mother.

Her pa had died when she was young, and Ma didn't waste any

time marrying again. Christy had loved her stepfather, Michael Grey—also Joshua's pa—and taken his name. When Michael died, though, Ma took up with a no-account miner turned gambler named Logan Malone. Joshua idolized the man...even more so when he'd left them a sack full of gold before hitting the trail a year or so ago. Ma sent her a telegram at the time, asking if she wanted to come live with her and help celebrate her good fortune. Christy had gently declined.

"What do you mean, everything?" She placed her hand on her hip. "Where's the rest of the money?"

"We don't have much of it left."

Christy narrowed her eyes. Suspicion mounted as she pushed aside the throbbing in her arm. Dropping her voice to a whisper, she took a step closer. "What happened, little brother?"

"Never you mind. It's gone, and we can't get it back."

"Gone?" Christy grabbed his hand and drew him toward her. "Did you gamble it all?"

He jerked away as though her fingers were iron bands ready to clamp around his wrists. "Let's go home. Ma's gonna worry."

"Huh. Funny you'd think of that now." She knew when to back off, but one way or another, she'd get to the truth. A thought drifted through her consciousness—something she'd heard Alexia say more than once. *When all looks lost, don't believe what your eyes tell you. Pray instead.*

Christy hadn't put too much stock in prayer over the years. But peace appeared to be coming to an end, and prayer might be something she'd need to consider.

Joshua stomped away and rapidly covered another half block to an area parallel and behind the main business district. He then swerved and entered a weed-strewn yard through a gate hanging by one hinge. He beckoned her forward. "Forgot to ask. Where's your bags? Didn't you bring nothin' with you to wear?"

"Yes. I couldn't carry my trunk. The stage driver told us to pick up our belongings at the livery stable anytime today or tomorrow. Maybe we could rent a wagon and you can help me? I can't use this arm to lift much." She waved her bandaged limb away from her body.

"I don't have money for a wagon. What happened to your arm?" He walked the last short distance to the squat adobe house that didn't look big enough to house one person, much less three.

"The stage got held up, and a stray bullet took a chunk out of it."

He swung toward her, genuine concern clouding his eyes. "You need to see the doc?"

Tears sprang to her eyes at the caring reflected in Joshua's voice. "I already did, and I'll be fine." She reached out her good arm and drew him into a hug. "I've missed you, little brother."

His words were muffled, but his voice sounded softer and more like the brother she'd remembered from years ago. "You too, sis. I'm sorry for...everything."

The front door opened, and a young man bolted down the path toward them, skidding to a halt before he ran into Christy. "Sorry, Miss. Didn't see you." He glanced at Joshua and back at her, then sidled a little closer. "You belong to this house?"

"I beg your pardon?" Christy took a step back, unsure what the boy intended.

He held out his hand, palm up. "I need to get paid."

Joshua pushed forward. "For what?"

"I brung that woman in there a telegram. I was told by the man at the office she'd pay me. But all she did was snatch it outta my hand. I want my money."

Joshua shoved the young man backwards and skirted around him. "You're not gettin' nothin' from me. Now get along with you, and tell your boss to pay you next time."

Suddenly a loud keening broke the stillness of the early afternoon, sending a shiver up Christy's spine. It reverberated like a lost soul who'd discovered they can never return to where they belonged.

She bolted up the path on Joshua's heels. *Ma.* Christy had never heard the woman cry before, much less scream the way she carried on now. Another wail met her as she forced her way through the partly closed front door, right before the stench hit her. She wasn't sure which made her knees the weakest—the unearthly moans coming from a back room, or the horrible smell assaulting her senses.

Chapter Six

....

Nevada made his way to the Grand Hotel. He didn't like spending much money for a room, but he had to admit the idea of a soft bed, clean sheets, and no varmints skittering across the floor appealed to him. Besides, it was close and highly recommended. Once he got the lay of the land tomorrow and found a decent boardinghouse he'd find a different spot to live. One night wouldn't break him.

He'd bankrolled a sizeable amount over the years from working cattle. Other cowboys blew their pay on women and whiskey, but not him. The memory of the gold coin flipping through the air and landing in his palm made him groan. Maybe his desire to buy his own ranch had pushed him too hard to take whatever cash he could get, even when it meant riding on the ragged edge of shady.

From now on he'd go straight. No more taking mavericks off the range and herding them over the line to Mexico for a fast dollar. Sure, most ranchers agreed an unbranded calf running wild in the breaks was fair game. But he knew in his heart he didn't have a right to those calves.

Nevada pushed through the doors of the two-story edifice and stopped. He'd been in a lot of cattle and mining towns, but this hotel beat all. Maybe he couldn't afford this place for even one night. A wide staircase covered in carpet lay ahead, sporting a black walnut banister running all the way to the top. An open space to the right boasted a small sign introducing the traveler to the office, and beckoned to a sitting area for weary guests. Lavish furnishings with velvet drapes and walnut tables graced the room, and a bespectacled man sat busily writing at a desk that looked too large for his small size.

Nevada took cautious steps up to the desk, his hat clutched in his hands. His gaze dropped to his boots, and he winced. Street dust had left a trail behind him on the luxurious carpet. A desire to rush back outside and clean his feet or, better yet, find somewhere else to stay assailed him. A quick look to the side revealed another large, elegant room, and almost convinced him the impulse to leave was sound. It was too early in the day for supper, and no patrons sat at the tables in the dining area. Three ornate chandeliers hung from the ceiling, and walnut dining tables were covered with fancy cloths and topped with cut glass, china, and silver.

He could stare down the barrel of a cocked gun without flinching, but the sight of china and glass unnerved him. His early days growing up flashed before his memory. Mama with all her genteel ways, insisting he use the proper fork and fold his napkin when he finished his meal. Daddy smoking his cigar in their parlor after supper and Mama sitting with her embroidery. He hadn't cared for all the finery then, nor the airs the adults who came to visit assumed, and nothing had changed. He'd find another place to take his evening meal.

Someone nearby cleared his throat, and Nevada jumped. He gazed at the middle-aged man who rose from behind the desk. Nevada had totally forgotten the clerk while taking in the sights of the hotel.

"May I help you, sir?"

Nothing about the clerk's expression convinced Nevada he thought poorly of the cowboy standing before him. No doubt the man had been instructed to take money from anyone who could afford this opulent place. Many a dirty miner could be packing thousands of dollars in silver or gold, and most businesses in frontier towns didn't judge men by their attire.

"Are you waiting for the dining room to open? Or might you be looking for the saloon? Big Nose Kate's bar is in the basement and open all hours."

Nevada stepped forward. "No, sir. But I'd surely enjoy one of your rooms for the night, if you happen to have one open." He carefully enunciated his words and watched with amusement as the clerk's eyebrows rose.

"Glad to have your business." The clerk picked up a pencil and moved a large, open book toward the edge of his desk. "If you'd care to sign in, I'll give you a room on the second floor. We have sixteen in all, including one suite called the bridal chamber." He peered out the door behind Nevada. "I don't suppose you're in need of that one, sir?"

Nevada grinned in response. "Nope. I'm not hitched and have no plans to be, so one of your smaller, simpler rooms would suit me fine." He picked up the pen and hesitated, then wrote with a flourish *James N. King, II.* How many years had it been since he'd used his real name? More than he cared to remember, but somehow it seemed suitable here.

The clerk stepped from behind his desk and beckoned Nevada to follow. They walked up the wide stairs, their feet muffled by the deep carpet. At the top they entered an elegant parlor. Oil paintings lined the walls, the furniture was covered in silk, and a piano stood in grandeur in the far corner. They passed through a set of double doors and into a hallway where a myriad of rooms opened up along the way. Most were closed, but he got glimpses of empty rooms, each beautifully appointed with walnut furniture and carpet, and every one with its own window.

Finally they came to the end of the hall. The clerk pushed open a door and stood aside. "Will this do, sir?"

Nevada stepped over the threshold and stifled a yelp. Papered walls, carpeted floor, walnut furnishings, and a toilet stand fitted out the room, while a wide bed covered with what appeared to be stiff silk stood off to the side. "It'll do fine, thanks." He reached into his pocket and withdrew a gold piece.

The clerk shrank back. "No, sir. We don't accept gratuities. My employer pays me quite handsomely, but thank you. Do you have any bags you'd like brought up?"

Nevada shook his head. "I have a saddle bag and bedroll down at the livery. I'll be buying a change of clothes before I eat supper."

"Very good, sir. And we can draw you a bath, if you'd like."

"Fine." Nevada waited till the man left the room, closed the door behind him, then walked to the bed. He sank onto it. *Springs. A real spring mattress.* It had been years since he'd been surrounded by such luxury. He didn't know if he'd be able to sleep on this kind of softness after the nights spent on the hard ground and narrow cots, but he sure aimed to try. He grinned. This was nice. Real nice.

Then his smile faded, and he yanked his thoughts back from where they'd started to drift. No amount of comfort was worth returning to the life he'd led. No. He'd promised Mama years ago he'd not get into trouble. He hadn't kept that promise in the past, but he meant to now, no matter how much his own ranch might tempt him to earn money in a way dishonorable to his family.

* * * * *

Christy rushed into a room off the kitchen following the wails. Joshua had stopped at the door to the dingy bedroom and stared at their mother, who'd flung herself across the narrow bed shoved up against the wall. Christy urged him into the room with her eyes, but he drew away. She turned her back on him and walked to the bed, sinking down beside her prostrate mother. "Ma, it's Christy. I got Joshua's telegram asking me to come, and I just arrived. What's wrong?"

Her mother didn't appear to take notice of her question but lay facedown, groaning and weeping. Dark red hair now peppered with gray had come loose from the knot at the back of her head. Christy could only see the side of her mother's face, but she winced at the deeply etched lines on her cheeks and forehead. How could she have aged in such a short time?

Suddenly the weeping changed to a deep cough. Christy stared at her ma, then over at Josh, who'd straightened from his stance against the doorframe. Fear and desperation chased across his countenance, and he backed away. "Joshua, come help me." Christy lifted her hand and waved him forward, but he continued his slow exodus. "I said, come help me. I need to know what's wrong."

He shook his head. "I don't want to catch it."

"Catch what?"

"Consumption. I won't touch her."

Christy gasped and took a step back, then shame washed over her. Her mother's cough racked her body, interspersed with her sobs. She lifted her hand to her mouth and the paper she'd been clutching drifted to the floor. Christy bent over and retrieved it, certain the telegram must have brought on her mother's weeping. She smoothed out the creases and stepped closer to the tiny window set high in the wall. By its trickle of light she read:

Logan gunned down in Albuquerque. Stop. Man named King done it. Stop. Send money for burial. Stop. Cousin Jake

"What is it?" Joshua peered in through the open door. "What's it say?"

"It's Logan."

"Pa? What about him?" The fear was evident in Joshua's expression.

"He's been shot."

"How bad is he hurt?"

She raised eyes swimming in tears to meet her brother's. She herself felt no love or sorrow for the dead man, but she knew what the news would do to Joshua, and her mother's grief was palpable. "I'm sorry. He's dead."

The young man emitted a cry like a wounded animal and fled from the house. The flimsy front door slammed behind him, and Christy heard footsteps outside the window racing away. That was so like Joshua. Fight or flee, the two options he typically chose. She sighed, suddenly ashamed. She hadn't cared for Logan Malone, but he'd been a part of Joshua's life for several years, and her brother had grown attached to the man. Even if Joshua was nearly twenty years old, he had the right to grieve like anyone else.

Christy turned to her mother, who still had her face buried in a pillow spotted with dirt. But the sobbing had lessened.

"Ma?" Christy touched her gently. "Come on. Sit up, now. We need to talk."

Ivy Malone groaned and rolled over, her back toward Christy. "Go away. I want to be alone."

Christy hesitated, torn between insisting her mother get up and deal with what had happened and wanting to protect her from more pain. Ma had always been the strong one of the family and rarely exhibited much emotion other than anger when one of her children stepped out of line. To see her this way left Christy shaken and unsure. "All right. I'll see if I can find something to fix for supper."

She moved away from the bed, wanting nothing more than to wash her hands. In fact, a bath sounded wonderful. Getting this house in order, bringing her trunk from the livery, and finding something to eat all pressed in at once. But first she'd better discover if there was a place to sleep.

Christy wandered through the kitchen and into the small front room. A crude table shoved against one wall, a threadbare sofa, and an upright chair comprised the furnishings. Not even a rag rug covered the dirty wood floor. She grimaced. No way would she ever walk barefoot in this place. A movement in the kitchen caught her eye, and she turned. A long-tailed mouse skittered across the floor and disappeared in a hole at the base of a wall. Christy gritted her teeth. Or was it a rat? If so, thankfully it was a small one. She hated those filthy creatures. Securing a cat moved to the top of her list.

A glance determined that the sofa would serve as a bed, but she sincerely hoped there might be somewhere else in the house to sleep. Moving to a boardinghouse might be a better option, and she could visit during the day to care for Ma. After all, Joshua would be home during the night, even if he did spend his days gambling in a saloon. He had to sleep sometime.

Further investigation led her to one more room not far from her mother's, just as tiny and dirty as the rest of the house. It appeared to be where her brother slept, as his clothing was strewn across the narrow bed and floor. An hour later she'd picked up and folded the last of the somewhat clean clothes, pitched the rest in a corner for scrubbing, swept the floor, and stripped the bed of the disgusting linens. Her arm throbbed and pain shot down to her fingertips, but she couldn't have rested in that filthy room. She made her decision. Josh would have to sleep on the sofa if he expected her to stay.

No sound emanated from her mother's room, so Christy could only hope Ma had dropped into a restful sleep.

Consumption. The word made Christy tremble. This house would need a thorough cleaning, but she couldn't tackle another chore with her injured arm. Exhaustion and pain swamped her already. She wandered into the kitchen and opened a cupboard door. Her heart sank. Almost empty. Three tins of beans, a sack of flour, salt, rice, and little else.

There went more of her tiny stash of money in her trunk.

The padding of feet on the wood floor turned her around. Ma stood with her hand braced against the doorframe, her face pale and drawn. "Christy? When did you get here?"

Christy rushed forward and wrapped her arms around her mother, giving her a gentle hug. Ma stiffened in her embrace and

Christy released her, stepping away. "I've been here for over an hour. I came into your room earlier. Don't you remember?"

"No. I didn't see you there. You sure?"

"Yes, Ma. You'd just read the telegram the boy delivered." She said the words slowly, wondering what effect they might have.

"Telegram?" Ivy gripped the doorframe and frowned. Her body started to shake, and she bent over, coughing and gasping for breath.

Christy supported the slender woman and urged her forward until they reached the sofa. Her mother sank onto the lumpy surface, the coughing spasm finally ending. "Thank you. What's this nonsense about a telegram?"

"You don't remember, Ma? Cousin Jake sent word about Logan."

"Logan is comin' home soon as he finishes minin' that gold strike he's workin' on." Ma settled against the sofa and closed her eyes.

"No, Ma. The telegram said Logan was shot in Albuquerque, and they need money for his burial." Christy sat down beside the older woman and frowned. Surely she'd read it, or she wouldn't have been wailing and crying when they arrived.

"I don't believe it for a minute. Jake is wrong. Logan is alive and comin' home soon with plenty of money." Ivy shook her head stubbornly. "Jake always was a fool with not enough sense to shake a stick at."

Christy stared, not sure how to respond. Her mother was obviously ill. Maybe she couldn't deal with the situation, and the possibility her husband was dead. She forced herself to relax. "Whatever you say, Ma. Are you hungry? I didn't see much food in the pantry."

Ivy wagged her head. "Not hungry. Where's Joshua? That boy was supposed to bring his winnin's home. He been here yet?"

Christy shut her eyes as despondency rolled over her. She'd so hoped somehow that Ma would have changed since her last visit when Ma, Logan, and Joshua lived in Sacramento. After her mother married her third husband, Logan, they'd moved from one mining town to the next over the next few years, dragging Joshua with them. Tombstone was only one of many attempts to get rich at either gold mining or gambling, whichever hit first. Problem was, they were always chasing a golden rainbow that had yet to pan out.

"He was here for a while, but he left. He didn't say anything about winning any money." Best to keep the episode at the saloon to herself, Christy decided. "Joshua said the cash Logan left you is gone. I thought Logan hit a nice little pocket of gold and left you plenty to live on."

Her mother frowned. "Joshua promised he could increase what we salted away, but I think he lost most of it. I put some aside he don't know about, though. And don't you be tellin' him, neither. It's all the food money I got left."

"Don't worry, Ma, he'll not hear it from me." She felt sick to her stomach. Ma had never been able to stand against Joshua's wheedling when he needed money to gamble. Why Ma allowed him to tag after Logan and sit at a poker table at the age of sixteen, she'd never understood, but her brother's fascination with the game had only increased since. She doubted the stash would last long. "How about you let me take care of it for you? In fact, if you'll give me a little now, I'll go to town and buy some supplies so I can fix us a decent meal."

Ma twisted her lips to the side and seemed to study on the idea for several moments, then pushed to her feet. "I'll give you some, but you can't take charge of the rest. You stay here. Don't want nobody knowin' where I keep that money."

"Oh, Ma." Christy blew out a hard breath. "I won't touch your money without permission."

"Don't care what I think I know. I keep that money in a secret place, and I ain't tellin' where it is."

"Fine. I'll sit right here."

"No. You step outside so you can't see what room I go in." Ma waved toward the door. "Go on now, scoot."

"Will you be all right if I walk to the livery and ask them to deliver my trunk?"

"Why wouldn't I be all right? I'm here every blamed day alone, ain't I? Not like you been around to care for your ailin' ma before today."

Christy winced and walked to the door. There was no sense in answering. Her mother had already turned and headed for the kitchen.

Christy had hoped when she'd left Last Chance that she might start a new life and find some happiness. Now she stepped outside, not looking back. She couldn't see anything resembling happiness in this place and doubted she ever would. Maybe she'd made the wrong decision in coming to care for Ma. After all, Ma didn't act as though she cared to have her around. Returning to Last Chance and the warm acceptance of friends sounded mighty appealing about now.

Chapter Seven
....

Christy stepped into the livery stable. No one in sight. Strange. She was certain the stage driver stated someone would be here all day so she could retrieve her trunk. He'd said the OK Corral Livery, and the sign outside clearly proclaimed this to be the correct location. A horse whinnied, and a pungent odor drifted from one of the stalls. She wrinkled her nose. A few steps took her to the back of the building. "Anyone here?"

The large door on the front trundled open, and someone stepped inside. "Help you, Miss?" A slender, stooped man shuffled out, a pipe clenched between his teeth. A young boy about ten years old followed. The man pulled the pipe from his mouth and grinned. "Never smoke it in here. Don't want no fire, no sir. You lookin' to rent a buggy?"

Christy shook her head and found her voice at the same time. "No, thank you. I came in on the stage. The driver told me he'd drop my trunk and bags here."

"The one that got robbed?"

"Yes."

"Shore, all the bags from the stage are here that ain't been picked up yet." He pointed with the stem of the pipe to a dark corner on a small platform, then turned to the boy and leaned over, whispering something. The boy scampered out of the stable. The hostler flashed a grin. "Name's Charlie."

"Christy Grey. Happy to meet you. Do you think you could deliver my things for me?"

"Let's see if we can find the right one first." Charlie plucked a lantern off a nail and scratched a match against the wood. He lifted the glass chimney and placed the blazing match against the wick, then replaced the chimney. "There we go. What's she look like?"

"Oh, my trunk?" Christy suppressed a smile. "It's about this wide"—she spread her arms—"and dark gray with black bands."

"Here she is." Charlie stooped over and latched hold of the leather strap on one end and tugged. He emitted a grunt and yanked a little harder. "What you got in there—a boatload of books? It's heavy."

At that moment the young boy raced back inside panting. "Uncle Charlie, the marshal is here. I got him, like you asked."

Startled, Christy turned toward Charlie. The marshal? Why would the livery man think he needed to call an officer of the law? "Could you see that my belongings are taken to my mother's home?"

"Sure. Give me directions, and I'll be happy to oblige." He waved toward the tall man with the badge. "Reckon the marshal needs a word with you first."

"Ben Sippy, ma'am." The marshal held out his hand, and a grin warmed his solemn features. "Nothing to worry about. I just have some questions."

"About what?" She gazed into the soulful eyes nearly covered by the brim of his hat. A mustache dropped down on each side of his cheeks, reaching almost to the edge of his chin.

The marshal withdrew his hat. "Are you the lady who came in on the stage that was held up?"

Christy's heart rate picked up at the man's words, suspecting what might be coming. "Yes."

"I hear you were shot during the fracas. You see the doc when you got to town?"

"It was a flesh wound, and Doctor Goodfellow tended to it. It's sore, but I'll be fine."

"Good." He hesitated, twisting his hat in his hands. "What can you tell me about any of the men who robbed the stage?"

"Very little, Marshal Sippy. The shooting started, the stage rolled to a stop, and I was wounded. My attention remained on my injured arm from that point forward."

"Do you mind if we step over to the doorway, Miss? It's a mite dark in here, and Charlie's stirring up dust dragging your trunk."

"Certainly." She allowed him to escort her to the gaping doorway. The street bustled with activity even though it must be near suppertime. People exited the newly erected city hall and hurried down the steps, and wagons rolled past carrying supplies. "I really must get home to my mother. She's quite ill and can't be left alone for any length of time."

"I understand. Now, tell me what the outlaw looked like who tended your arm. I spoke to the driver and two of the other passengers who confirmed one of the robbers took you into a stand of brush. The others weren't able to see any distinguishing characteristics, but they know he removed his mask."

"Yes, but I really can't tell you what he looked like. He tied up my wound, put his mask back on, and disappeared. I can't give you any more information, Marshal." She wrapped her fingers over the throbbing wound above her elbow and grimaced. "Other than it's bothering me right now, and I'd like to go home."

He nodded, his eyes crinkling against the shafts of sun glinting off a nearby window. "All right. Maybe once the pain subsides, your memory will be a mite more clear, Miss…?"

"Grey." She didn't care to offer this man more. Right now she simply wanted to escape.

"May I inquire where you might be staying?" He hitched at his holster belt and the Colt .45 shifted.

"With my mother and brother. My mother's name is Ivy Malone, and her house is on Toughnut Street, around the corner from Second."

"Your brother wouldn't be Joshua Grey, by any chance? Likes to frequent gambling halls and get into fights?" He peered at her, clearly watching for her reaction.

"I can't speak to the fighting, but Joshua is my brother. Why?"

"No reason. Just getting the lay of the land." He placed his hat back on his head. "I'll be stopping by tomorrow to visit, Miss Grey, and see if your memory has returned."

Christy paid Charlie and gave him her address, then hurried away, eager to escape the marshal's intuitive gaze. She hadn't seen the man who'd tended to her wound since arriving in town and sincerely hoped he'd decided to move on and not stop in Tombstone. It wasn't her nature to break her word, but even if she hadn't given it, something in the man's riveting eyes would have compelled her to silence. Not from fear, either. His heartfelt appeal and explanation tugged at her heart. She shook her head and frowned. Another man gone bad.

She cut down Fourth Street and landed on Allen Street, a block away from the Golden Eagle Brewery and the Oriental Saloon. A burning desire to see if Joshua sat at a table turned Christy in that direction. She made it half a block before slowing her pace. What would she do when she arrived? Storm inside and grab him by the ear and drag him out? No. He wouldn't tolerate interference again, and besides, Ma was alone at the house. She made a decision and swiveled, running smack into a woman hurrying the opposite direction.

Christy staggered backwards, but the young lady grabbed her with strong hands, keeping her from sprawling on the boardwalk. "Oh my. Thank you." Christy straightened and peered at her rescuer.

A deep red cape slung around the girl's shoulders did a poor job of covering the cleavage beneath. Long crystal earrings dangled from under the pale blond hair hanging in neat ringlets, and the indecently short skirt ended at her calf instead of her ankles. Her face flamed and then paled at Christy's perusal. She drew herself up and tilted her chin. "I beg your pardon. I wasn't watching where I was going." The blond moved to pass Christy on the outside of the walkway.

Christy reached out and touched the girl's arm. "No, I'm sorry. It was entirely my fault. I'm thankful you were quick-witted enough to keep me from falling."

The girl waved a hand at her dress. "Nice ladies like you don't talk to my ilk. You'd best move on before someone hears you."

"It's no one's business who I speak to. Besides, I'm the last person in this town who would judge you, or your occupation." Christy smiled and tipped her head to the side. "What's your name?"

"Why? You going to try to get me in trouble with my boss?"

"No, I wondered, that's all." Christy extended her hand. "I'm Christy Grey, and I'm new to Tombstone."

The young lady gave a harsh laugh and ignored the gesture. "You *must* be new in town to talk to me. I'm Sara."

"Sara what?"

"Just Sara. I haven't used my last name for a while, and I don't aim to start now. No sense in shaming my family."

"Ah. I understand." Christy stepped up against the wall of the City Bakery, her mouth watering at the heavenly smells wafting out the door each time a patron entered or exited. She beckoned for Sara to join her. "We'd best step out of the way. With the number of people visiting this place, we could get trampled. Do you have time for a cup of coffee and a sweet?"

Sara shook her head. "I have to get to work. I had an errand to run and need to get back. If I'm late, my boss will skin me alive."

"Do you mind if I ask where you work?"

"The Oriental Saloon." She lifted her chin and narrowed her eyes. "Sorry you asked me?"

"No. I used to work at a place like that, years ago." Christy barely suppressed a grimace. Sara's words about her boss brought back harsh memories. She hurt for this girl who didn't look a day over seventeen. From the hard set to her jaw she'd seen plenty she shouldn't and probably endured more hardship than most women twice her age.

"You?" Sara's mouth dropped open and she stared. "I don't believe it. Are you one of those do-gooders, out to save saloon girls from going to perdition?"

Christy chuckled. "I'm afraid not, although I must say it's a high calling."

"You mean it? *You* worked at a saloon?" Sara crossed her arms over her middle.

"I did, for longer than I'd care to remember."

"How'd you get out?"

Christy leaned against the brick building. "My sister had a baby, and when he was only two years old, she died. His pa took him to California, and when he was three, I was sent to steal Toby from his pa."

Sara gasped and covered her mouth with her fingers. "I declare. I think you're stringin' me along."

Christy shrugged. "I don't even know why I'm telling you this, but it's true. I ended up getting hurt. The very people I was sent to destroy forgave me and offered me a new start. Believe me when I say I understand 'nice women' shunning you—and me, the way I was back then."

Sara reached out her hand. "I think I'd like that handshake now, if you don't mind. I'm so pleased to meet you, Miss Grey."

"Christy. It's just Christy." She smiled and extended both arms. "And I'd prefer a hug."

* * * * *

Sara Darnell glanced back at the beautiful, auburn-haired woman walking the opposite direction. Sudden longing rose in her chest for things that used to be and no longer existed. Hard to believe someone like Miss Grey—or Christy, as she'd insisted on being called—would admit to having a less-than-desirable background. Sara tugged her cape closed over her scanty attire as a gust of wind caught the edges and almost tore it from her body. She surged forward toward the only home she could call her own—the Oriental Saloon.

Her stomach churned, and a sour taste lingered in her mouth. *Home* used to be a word she loved, but no longer. Not since the Apache attack, when her entire world had changed. A shudder shook her frame, and she stuffed the gruesome memories to the back of her mind, determined not to look back.

What would have happened if she'd gone into the bakery with Christy and sat like a lady having tea and a pastry? Probably at best Townsley would fire her for not showing up, and at worst...well, she didn't care to think of that option, either. Better get to work and forget a kind person like Christy Grey existed in this raw town. No sense in mooning over a life she couldn't have. It would only increase her misery.

* * * * *

The next morning Nevada stepped outside the door of the Grand Hotel. The early dawn light bathed the street in a kinder glow than it had appeared last night. Nice to wake in a comfortable bed and know you didn't have to cook your own vittles. But it was time to move on and find a cheaper place to stay. His money would soon be gone if he stuck around here.

He'd seen nothing of Jake or the other two outlaws who'd held up the stage. If they were smart, they'd stay away from town. He took off his hat and slapped it against his leg, then plunked it back on his head. Might be solid advice for himself, as well, but he'd be jiggered if he'd leave town for something he'd not even done.

A rooster crowed somewhere in the distance, and he heard the sounds of mining not far away. Strange. This town had mining tunnels right behind some of the buildings and interspersed among the wood shacks they called homes a block or two from here. In fact, they'd even dug underneath some of the businesses. Miles of tunnels ran under most of the town, from what he'd heard.

Before long, he'd need a job. He hated sitting around all day doing nothing. All he knew was horses and cattle, but heading out on trail drives didn't appeal at the moment.

However, there was always the past—what had come before—what he'd planned to do with his life in his earlier years…

Nevada shook his head, disturbed at the memories. He'd never return to being *that* person again. After all, God had failed him in the past when he'd committed his entire future to Him, and Nevada didn't plan on setting himself up for the same type of pain. No. The past was better left alone.

He struck off down Allen Street for the livery stable. The OK Corral Livery, if he remembered correctly, lay a couple of blocks away on Fremont Street. Thankfully it was quiet this time of morning with only an occasional wagon rolling down the dusty avenue and a couple dozen people moving in and out of various businesses along the way. He spotted a large, one-story adobe boardinghouse on the corner of Fourth: the Russ House. From all appearances it was clean and respectable, with a wide, open patio off to the side. Hopefully it wasn't a bordello. Nevada stopped at the door and hesitated, then pushed it open.

A woman who appeared to be in her midthirties looked up from her perusal of *The Tombstone Epitaph* spread out on the low counter.

"May I help ya, sir?" The words were spoken with a soft Irish lilt, and large, dark eyes peered over small spectacles balanced on her nose. The attractive woman didn't stand much over five feet tall and had to look up to meet his gaze. "Did ya need a room?"

"Is this a hotel or a boardinghouse, ma'am?"

Nevada surveyed the room that appeared more like a parlor than a front office. The furnishings were tasteful but not gaudy and made him feel right at home. A piano sat in the far corner with a sofa and two wingback chairs grouped around a potbellied stove. He doubted the stove was used more than two or three months out of the year, but it gave the room a nice touch, along with the braided rugs covering the floor.

"Boardinghouse and restaurant. Were ya lookin' to stay only one night, then? I can direct ya to some clean hotels in town." She stood on her tiptoes and pointed out the window. "There's the Cosmopolitan around the corner on Allen Street, and—"

"No need, but thank you, and sorry to interrupt." Nevada smiled. "I hoped it might be a boardinghouse. I need some place for at least a couple of weeks, maybe a month or more. Is it all right if I don't give you an exact amount of time I plan on staying?"

"Certainly, sir. We rent our rooms by the week or the month, yer choice." She reached under the counter and withdrew a book, sliding it toward him. A pen lay in the open fold. "It's five dollars per week or sixteen per month. Comes with breakfast, and supper in the evenin'. Ya fend for yerself at dinnertime."

"Thanks. I think I'll start with a week and see how it goes." He dug into his pocket and pulled out a couple of gold coins, tossing them on the counter. "You do the cooking?"

"At times, but I also have a man who slings some of the best grub west of the Mississippi. He used to cook in a fancy French restaurant back in St. Louis."

"Aunt Nellie?" A little boy dashed into the room and skidded to a stop next to the proprietor.

"I'm talkin' to someone now. Ya need to wait yer turn, all right?"

He dropped his chin. "Yes, ma'am."

Nellie stroked his hair. "Me sister's boy." Her accent crooned the words. "Oh, a couple of other things ya should know about my place." She leaned over to the boy's level. "What ya needin', lad?"

He stood on tiptoe and whispered in her ear. She nodded, and he ran off, giggling. Nellie turned back to Nevada. "Where were we? Ah, yes. The rules. If ya don't care for 'em, yer welcome to change yer mind."

Nevada lifted one shoulder. "I doubt there's much you can tell me that will make me back out, especially after hearing about your cook."

Her expression softened. "Well, then, here it is. No women in yer room and no smokin' in there, either. I run a clean place and want to keep it that way. Also, from time to time I use a room or two as a hospital, since this town hasn't seen fit to build one yet. I do charitable work and often take in someone who needs a home for a short time. When a sick person is here, I ask my boarders to be courteous and not shout in the hallways or common rooms." She waved toward the piano. "And yer welcome to play if yer able, or if ya have friends visitin' who want to use the piano."

"I think I can abide by those rules, Miss."

"Oh, and my name is Nellie." She pointed at the sign hanging outside visible through the front window. "Nellie Cashman, late from Tucson and before that, Alaska."

"James King, Miss Cashman, but my friends call me Nevada." He took the proffered hand and shook it. "Alaska, huh? I'd have thought Ireland from the accent."

She emitted a tinkling laugh. "Sure now, I was raised there, although I try not to let it get out of hand." Nellie looked him up and down. "Yer a right strappin' specimen of manhood. Will ya be workin' while yer visitin' our fair town?"

Nevada chuckled at the woman's blunt remark, but there wasn't a hint of a flirtatious tone in her voice, and her manner was all kindly solicitude. "Yes, I hope to. If I can find a job, that is."

Her gaze sharpened. "What type of work might ya be lookin' for? I could use a handyman around the house a few hours a week, if ya know how to swing a hammer and use a shovel. In fact, ya could work off part of yer board, if yer of a mind to."

"That would be fine, although I'm hoping to also find something that includes working with horses."

"Ah, I might know just the thing. The smithy across the street from the OK Corral hurt his leg a week ago Saturday. Good man. Got kicked, I believe, and he's hobblin' around a bit until it heals up. He can hammer out the horse shoes, and do some of his other work, but he's havin' the dickens of a time standin' for long periods and doin' the nailin'. Might ya have any skill with shoein'?"

Nevada felt a surge of hope for the first time in days. "I do. I'll go talk to the man. Do you happen to know his name?"

"Sure do. John Draper. He's an honest man and a hard worker. Tell him I sent ya, and he'll probably put ya to work."

"Thank you, Miss Cashman."

"Nellie. No one calls me Miss Cashman. It's just Nellie." She started to turn away and paused. "I almost forgot. This time of day he's probably at the Oriental Saloon gettin' a bite to eat. They serve a fine sandwich, and he's partial to the steak."

"Thank you, Nellie." He turned and reached for the doorknob.

"Would ya like to see yer room before you go?"

"If it's all the same to you, I'd like to head over there straight-away. I'll bring my things with me from the hotel and be back for supper, if not before."

"All right then. Godspeed."

Nevada hurried out the door and stepped into the dusty street. A wind had picked up, blowing fine grains of mixed sand and dust, along with tumbling weeds and bits of paper. Music poured from a saloon up the street, and a man's raucous laughter floated from an open doorway. Time to see what his future might hold over in the Oriental Saloon.

Chapter Eight
....

Christy braced to meet her mother as she walked up the path to the house after her morning trip to the store. Shifting the burlap bag of food momentarily to her injured arm, she winced, then moved the bag back to her other arm. Ma's mood seemed to change as fast as a lightning bug. You could never tell what it would be—mellow, sour, or somewhere in between. Hopefully finding the money yesterday that she'd tucked away so they could buy groceries would help improve her frame of mind.

The memory of her mother's loss smote her, and a lump formed in her throat. What kind of pain must Ma be enduring at the death of her husband? Even if the man was basically no good, he'd treated Ma decent much of the time. Too bad he was the only man in Joshua's life during his teen years, though. Now that Joshua was nineteen he figured himself a man and wanted to be tough like Logan. Christy felt a deep stirring of fear at what may lay ahead for her brother if he didn't change.

Her visit to Doctor Goodfellow first thing this morning had brought a sense of relief. She'd avoided infection and the deep tear in her arm seemed to be healing nicely. He'd placed a fresh dressing on the wound and instructed her to keep it covered for a few more days, but the pain had almost abated.

Her mind drifted to the man who'd bandaged her arm during the robbery. Something about his eyes as well as his actions said decency resided in him, and he'd insisted he wasn't part of the outlaw gang. She doubted that was the truth, as the other robbers accepted his presence. But his touch had been gentle, and he'd not cast an offensive glance her way. Christy pushed open the door of their small house. She'd kept her word and not described him to the marshal. There was nothing more to do.

Ma swung her feet to the floor and struggled to stand, but a coughing spasm hit and held her captive.

Christy rushed to her mother, who was hunched into a ball. She looked so small and fragile, and her entire body shook. "I'll get you a glass of water."

She hurried to the kitchen and searched the cupboards for a container of water. Nothing but a dirty slop bucket. All the water she'd brought yesterday had been used for cleaning. Hastening to her mother's room she surveyed the area. Her gaze lit on a porcelain jug. She lifted it and sniffed. *Eww.* It reeked of spirits. She set it back down and turned away, then spied a small pitcher on the floor by the bed. Gingerly she lifted it to her nose. No smell. Clutching it tight, she ran to the kitchen and poured it into a glass. Water. It didn't appear to be terribly fresh, but it couldn't be helped.

Ma's coughing spell had eased, and Christy pressed the glass into her hands. She took a sip. "Thank you, girl. I'm beholden to you."

Christy sank onto the sofa beside Ivy and wrapped her arm around the older woman. "I've missed you, Ma."

"You too, Christy girl." Ma patted Christy's hand and mustered a smile. "More than you'll know." Then the smile faded, and she stiffened her spine. "That's enough mollycoddlin'. Where's Joshua?"

"I was hoping you could tell me. He ran out of here yesterday without saying a word. Where does he usually go when he's upset?"

Ma grimaced. "To the bar. Like Logan always did." She scowled. "I loved that man, but when it came to whiskey and gamblin', he was worthless for anything else. I've fretted over your brother somethin' fierce. Don't want him endin' up like Logan, lyin' dead in some street."

Christy sucked in a sharp breath. Ma remembered. Maybe she'd only needed time to come to terms with her husband's sudden passing, and now she'd adjust. If only they could get her well and over this bout of consumption. Heaviness tugged at Christy's heart, and worry gnawed at her stomach. Had she ever heard of anyone recovering from a case as bad as Ma's?

She shook off the thought. No sense in borrowing trouble. Making another trip to see Doctor Goodfellow would be her first order of business. "Joshua has a good head on his shoulders, Ma. He'll be home as soon as he works out his grief."

Ma needed medicine and proper care, and Christy planned to get it, whatever the cost. Too bad she hadn't thought about it when the doc tended to her arm.

A tap sounded at the door, and Christy turned her head. Joshua wouldn't knock, and they hadn't ordered anything. Her trunk had already been delivered the day before. She pushed to her feet and glanced at her mother, but she only shrugged.

A peek out the window revealed Marshal Sippy waiting outside, his hand resting on the butt of his pistol. Christy hesitated, then pushed open the door. "Good morning. I'd ask you in, but my mother isn't well."

He swept off his hat and tucked it under his arm. "No problem, Miss Grey. I'm sorry to intrude, but I had another couple of questions, if you don't mind."

She stepped outside and eased the door shut behind her. "I suppose I can spare a moment or two."

A wagon rumbled past, heavily loaded with silver ore, the long team of mules straining at the harness. Her eyes followed what must surely be another prosperous find as it disappeared down Toughnut Street. If only she had a small portion of what they brought from the mines, her mother could have proper care. Maybe Josh wouldn't even feel the need to gamble if they lived in a nicer home and didn't have to scratch for everything. An instant later she shook off the thought as useless, knowing they'd never achieve anything close to wealth in her lifetime.

"Miss Grey?" Marshal Sippy shifted his weight from one boot-clad foot to the other. "About those questions?"

"I'm sorry." Christy turned back to the man.

"Your arm. Is it improved today?"

"Yes, I'm happy to say it's better. Still painful, but not bothering me quite as much."

"Good. Now, on to the reason I'm here. I'd like to get a description of the man who bound your wound during the holdup."

Christy crossed her arms over her chest. "Like I told you before, Marshal, I can't do that."

He narrowed his eyes. "Can't? Or won't?"

"Does it matter?"

"It does to me."

"All right then, won't." She met his eyes squarely. "I made a promise, and I'm a woman of my word."

A startled expression crossed the marshal's face. "What kind of promise would that be, if I may be so bold?"

"He told me if he took off his mask to tend my arm, I had to promise not to betray his identity to the law. Of course, I had no idea who the man was and couldn't give you a name, regardless. Any number of men have the same build and hair color. So I can't see a description would do you much good, even if I was willing to break my word and give it to you, which I'm not."

"I see." His shrewd eyes assessed her, and he seemed to come to a decision. "I suppose you won't tell me if you've spotted him, or any other men from the outlaw band, since you've been in town."

She shook her head decisively. "No sir, I will not." She hesitated. "But I'll not withhold any information about the others who took part. I can honestly say I've not seen them since it happened."

"I appreciate that, but why are you willing to protect a criminal? No one will think worse of you if you don't keep your word to a man who held up the stage." He gestured at her arm. "Not to mention shooting you."

Christy frowned, not caring for the direction the conversation was taking and determined to set the marshal straight. "He wasn't there when the shooting happened and had nothing to do with it. I saw him come out of the brush after the stage halted and we'd disembarked. Besides, he assured me he had nothing to do with the robbery."

"Ha. A likely story. How many outlaws do you know who admit to their crimes?"

"I can't say, Marshal, as I don't typically associate with outlaws."

The man had the grace to duck his head for a moment. "Sorry, Miss. That's not what I meant." His jaw tightened. "But it's a fact. These men all swear they're innocent."

She shrugged. "I suppose. But there was something different about him, and I half believed his story. He claimed he'd fallen in with the group the night before while looking for a meal and a place to sleep. Said he had no idea they planned to rob the stage."

"If that were true, then why did he approach the stage wearing a mask?"

Christy's heart skipped a beat at the question she'd asked herself more than once. "I can't answer that."

"Exactly." His lips stretched in a grim smile. "I suppose I could take you in and arrest you for obstructing justice." He scratched his chin, then held up his hand when she started to protest. "But I won't. I don't think the citizens of Tombstone would look too kindly on a young lady being kept in the same jail cell as some of the riffraff this town affords." He plunked his hat back on. "I'll bid you good day for now, but if you have a change of heart for any reason, I'd appreciate a visit to my office."

"I'll keep that in mind. Good day, Marshal." Her heart pounded in her throat, but she kept her expression neutral. The last thing she wanted was for this man to know he'd struck a nerve with the threat of being hauled to jail.

* * * * *

Sara flitted from one table to the next, serving drinks and trying to avoid the pawing hands of the drunken miners and gamblers. When she'd agreed to take this job, she'd been told serving drinks would be her only obligation. That didn't last long. Now her skin crawled, and she felt dirty all over—and used in a way she tried to forget.

Not that she hadn't met decent men in this place. A couple of them had even proposed marriage. She'd been sorely tempted to take them up on the offer just to get shut of this life, but something held her back. Maybe it was fear of the unknown, or a longing for the love and security her ma and pa had with each other...whatever the case, she hadn't accepted. A tinge of regret tugged at her heart, but she pushed it away.

She stopped next to a table of five black-frocked gamblers, all intent on their cards. Most were older men, but one stood out from the rest—a handsome young man with deep auburn hair and kind eyes. He'd spoken decently to her in the past, and the times Townsley sent him to her room the first few weeks, he'd been tender and caring, a contrast to the men who'd come after. She'd never forgotten his name—Joshua. Sara set the drink next to his elbow.

He glanced up, and a warm grin crinkled his face. "Thanks, Miss. What do I owe you?"

"Nothing. It's on the house since you fellas been playin' so long." She met his gaze. His smile reached to the green depths of his eyes and warmed her sore heart.

* * * * *

Nevada pushed through the doors of the Oriental Saloon and scanned the room. Why hadn't he thought to ask Nellie what the blacksmith looked like? With so many miners and laborers in town, it might not be easy to spot the man. The bartender should know John Draper, though, if he came here for a sandwich on a regular basis.

A young woman with blond hair and clothes leaving little to a man's imagination sidled up. "Hey, mister. Want me to bring you a drink?"

She looked about the age his sister Carrie had been when she'd run away from home. Carrie's hair was a shade darker, but she was pretty like this girl. What was a youngster like her doing in a low-down joint like this? Probably the same thing Carrie had done—while looking for something different than what she'd had at home, she'd gotten trapped. "No thanks, Miss. I'm looking for a man."

She shrank back. "You gonna shoot somebody?"

"Don't worry." He shook his head. "I'm hoping to find me a job, that's all."

"The boss might be hirin', I'm not sure. Want I should call him for you?" She turned wide, darkly fringed eyes on him. "Or, if you're lookin' to get a job at the tables, Morgan or Wyatt can help you. They're in charge of the games around here."

Nevada tried to control the shock that shot through him. He'd seen Wyatt Earp once in Dodge City but hadn't realized he and his brother had moseyed out this way. Where Wyatt was, Doc Holliday was sure to be. A quick look around the place satisfied his guess as correct. The nattily dressed gambler with the black, flat-crowned hat and dark suit faced the door two tables away, his eyes intent on the men sitting across from him. A glass of whiskey sat near his left hand along with an open bottle, and his right clutched a hand of cards. He lifted his arm, placed his sleeve across his mouth, and smothered a cough. Nevada had heard the rumors about Holliday being ill, and from the sound of things it could be consumption, a disease running rampant these days.

He turned to the girl standing patiently for an answer. He couldn't get over how much she reminded him of Carrie. "What's your name, Miss?"

She scrunched her brows. "Sara. Why do you ask?"

"You remind me of someone."

Sara batted her eyelashes. "I've heard that line before. Sure you won't buy me a drink?"

Nevada pressed a silver dollar into her hand. He'd already wasted enough of her time, and most of these girls only got paid for the number of drinks they hustled. "No. Sorry for taking your time. I'm looking for the blacksmith. Man by the name of John Draper. You know him?"

Her countenance fell. "Yeah, I know him. He's over there at the bar. The big gent with his sleeves rolled up above his elbows. Lots of muscles."

"You take care of yourself now, you hear?" Nevada gave the girl a gentle smile and moved away. He swung his gaze to the man at the bar wolfing down a sandwich.

"Hey!" A man's voice at a table close by froze Nevada in his tracks. He slowly swiveled to see the young fellow who'd rushed from the saloon yesterday glaring at the slick-looking gambler sitting across from him.

"You've cheated one time too many, mister." The young man threw his cards on the table.

The hum of voices quieted. Only the shuffle of feet and the

scraping of chairs could be heard as men cleared away from the area where the two sat.

"No man calls me a cheat." The gambler's tone was even and unhurried. It appeared he'd played this hand more than once in his life. "Back down and walk away."

The young man pounded his fist on the table. "No, sir. I saw you slip a card from the bottom of the deck when you dealt that hand." He jumped to his feet and pushed back the tail of his jacket. A gun showed beneath the fabric, and his hand moved toward the butt.

Too slow.

Nevada's eyes darted to the gambler, who sat unmoving. Wasn't he going to draw?

Suddenly, a gun blasted from beneath the table and the shot caught the raging man in his thigh, causing his body to jerk. He withdrew his gun from the holster and started to lift it, but the still-seated gambler raised his from beneath the tabletop and calmly pulled the trigger one more time.

Red blossomed on the young man's shirt, high up in his chest. He gazed at his opponent with wide eyes and stood without moving for several seconds, then slowly toppled onto the table. His body hit hard, scattering the chips and cards across the floor. Then he rolled off the edge and landed with a thud on the carpet.

Men raced forward, and voices babbled around the room. A man wearing a fringed buckskin shirt strode forward and bent over the prone form. "He's alive." He straightened and stared at the gambler. "I'm Buckskin Frank Leslie. The town council granted me the power to make arrests in here as I see fit. Let's see your gun, mister."

"It were a fair fight, Frank." A bearded miner stepped forward and motioned at the man on the floor. "He called this gent out. Said he was cheatin' and went for his gun. Then this 'un shot him."

Buckskin Frank turned to the knot of men standing nearby. "That the way it happened?"

"Yep. Pretty much," a chorus of voices responded.

Leslie gave a curt nod. "Anyone know where this fella lives? He's bleedin' all over the carpet, and we need to get him outta here. The boss ain't gonna like this."

A voice called from a short distance away, "Name's Joshua Grey. Lives with his ma back of town on Toughnut Street."

Nevada peered at the man who'd spoken, memories of his own mother returning. This boy's ma would be waiting for her son to return. "I'll take him. Help me get him up."

The man shook his head and backed away. "No thanks, mister. I don't want nothin' to do with him. He's trouble."

A heavy hand landed on Nevada's shoulder, and he pivoted. The blacksmith, John Draper, stood beside him. "I'll help with the boy. Horse kicked me not long ago, but it won't stop me from helpin' to carry him. I've met his ma, and she's a decent woman. Let's get him home."

Nevada stepped forward, then turned his attention on Buckskin Leslie. "Can you send someone after the doc and direct him to the Grey home?"

"I can."

"Thanks." Nevada looked at John Draper, then gestured at Joshua Grey lying still on the floor. "Let's see if we can get him home to his ma before he dies. She'd probably like the chance to say her good-byes."

* * * * *

Sara stood riveted to the floor as the bloody scene played out before her. The young man with the warm smile and gentle touch looked to be near death. Why had he pushed that gambler so hard and egged him into a fight? She'd seen that trick before—hiding a gun under the table and waiting for the other fellow to draw, then shooting him down. She gripped her hands in front of her waist and stared at the room, appalled at how quickly the men returned to their drinking and games of chance.

What was wrong with these people? She shuddered, suddenly afraid the same thing could happen to her. Not that she'd be shot, but that a hard crust might form over her heart and she'd quit caring about others. In this business it served a woman to grow a thick skin and not allow anything to penetrate—not sympathy, love, or what appeared to be genuine caring.

The other man who came in asking for a job—the one who helped carry out Joshua—he'd also been kind, pressing a dollar into her hand and refusing to flirt or buy her a drink.

But she couldn't stop thinking about Joshua...*Grey*. Shock coursed through her veins as she realized the significance of that name. Could he be related in some way to the compassionate woman who'd spoken to her on the street not long ago?

A prayer welled up from her spirit but got caught in her throat. She hadn't prayed since Ma and Pa were killed in the Indian attack. How many desperate, pleading prayers had she sent heavenward as she lay hidden in the brush outside their small shanty, watching the horrible events unfold? God hadn't answered, but for some reason she still had hope He'd see fit to answer now. For the young man with the kind eyes, and for the woman who might belong to him in some way. *Please, God, even if You can't save me from this life, reach out Your hand and save the ones who've shown kindness to me.*

Chapter Nine

A loud rapping rattled the front door of Ma's house, and Christy pushed to her feet. She'd gone to town yet again and hauled back two buckets of water. A young neighbor girl had spent the last two hours helping Christy scrub down the kitchen and had gone home happy with money jingling in her pocket. A small price to pay for cleanliness.

Joshua had been gone for so long. If only he'd return, she'd send him back to town for a barrel. She hated having to purchase water. In Last Chance water was plentiful, either in the clear mountain creeks or the wells people dug on their property. Here it cost three cents a gallon. Hopefully Ma didn't have any expenses besides water and food.

Ma walked into the room and headed to the door. "Better not be that scoundrel from the bank pestering me about money again. I'll have to shoot me a banker if he don't leave me alone."

"Ma?" Christy was puzzled. "What banker? Why's he pestering you?"

The knock grew more insistent, and a man's voice penetrated the thin wood. "Anyone home? We got Joshua here, and he's hurt pretty bad."

Ma gasped and clutched her chest. She drew in a hard breath, and a ragged cough tore from her throat.

Christy flew to the door. Joshua hung limp, upheld by a man on either side. Blood covered the front of his shirt and oozed from a gash in his thigh. "Hurry. Bring him inside." She ran to the kitchen for rags. *Blast it all!* Only a small amount of clean water left in the bottom of the bucket.

She raced back into the room and watched as they lowered her unconscious brother onto the sofa. "Someone...please send for the doctor. I don't know anything about injuries like this, although I know we've got to get the bleeding stopped."

The large-boned man, whose voice she recognized as the one who spoke through the door, stepped forward. "Already sent for him, Miss. He should be along shortly. What you want I should do?"

"Help me get his shirt off so we can see the wound." She started to unbutton the front but could barely see the buttons for the blood. A tremor shook her, but she pressed on, determined to save her brother if she could.

"Allow me, Miss." The other man who'd helped carry Joshua bent over the sofa and slipped a knife under the edge of the damp fabric. He ripped it all the way up the seam to the collar and split that, as well. A flick of his fingers and the shirt fell away from Joshua's chest.

Christy gasped at the sight, and her head started to spin. She had to get hold of herself. This was no time for weakness. How many times in the past had she been forced to help with some beat-up, drunken patron at one of the saloons where she worked? But this wasn't just some patron—this was her brother and, for all she knew, he was already dead.

Strong hands gripped her and gently moved her aside. The stranger took the rags she'd tossed onto the back of the sofa and knelt on the floor. He worked quickly, making a compress and dipping it into the bucket of water, then cleaning her brother's damaged flesh.

Christy turned and looked for her mother, as Joshua appeared to be in capable hands, at least for the moment. Ma sat huddled in a chair with tears coursing down her cheeks. Two quick steps and Christy arrived by her side. She bent over and wrapped her good arm around her mother's shoulder and squeezed. "He'll make it. He's a fighter."

"Joshua is my baby. I can't lose another child, Christy. I already lost Molly." A deep groan ending in a wail shook the older woman's body.

"The doctor will be here soon, and those men are doing all they can to save him." She nodded toward the two bent over the still form on the sofa and dropped her voice. "Do you know who they are? They knew where to bring Joshua. Are they friends of his?"

Ivy shook her head and leaned it against the high-backed chair. "The big man with his sleeves rolled up is John Draper, the black-smith. I don't know the other one." She sniffled.

Boots thumped on the porch and Doctor Goodfellow hustled into the room, his presence bringing hope to Christy's heart. She hurried to his side, not wanting to miss anything he might say.

The doctor shot her a glance and then stooped over the sofa, running a keen gaze over the unconscious man. "I see you've stopped the bleeding. How about the one in his leg?"

John Draper wiped his hands on a rag. "It'll have to be dug out. The one high up on his chest don't look so good."

The other man rinsed his hands in the bucket and wiped them off. "Is this all the water you've got, Miss?"

For the first time Christy really looked at him, and as she did so, her heart plummeted to her stomach, leaving her feeling sick. *The man from the stage holdup—the one who tended my arm.*

Somehow she managed to catch herself before the words tumbled out that would cause her to break her promise. Did he recognize her? She peered at him, then met his gaze squarely and saw no flicker of awareness. Her chest heaved in relief. "Yes. I was going to ask Joshua to have a barrel sent over when he got home, but…" She bit her lip.

"Yeah." He nodded. "Any neighbors you can borrow a bucket from?"

"I don't know anyone. I just arrived yesterday.…" Her words trailed off as she realized what she'd revealed.

His eyes moved swiftly from her face to her arm. A hint of knowledge sparkled in their depths. "I see. I'll head to town and bring some back then." He turned and grabbed the handle of their bucket and disappeared out the door.

Christy watched him go, certain she'd never see him or her bucket again. He'd realized who she was, even with her sleeve covering the bulky dressing. The man wasn't stupid. No doubt as soon as he'd saddled his horse, he'd be on his way out of town.

* * * * *

Nevada hurried up the street still clutching the bucket, his mind swimming with what he'd learned. *The woman on the stage.* Why hadn't he known as soon as he'd heard her voice? She was more beautiful than he'd expected, although his imagination had created a number of pretty faces. She recognized him—that was apparent from her shocked look. He'd almost laughed out loud at her wide-eyed surprise, for the pure joy of finally discovering her identity.

Another thought struck him, and he slowed his pace. *There's no guarantee she didn't break her word and alert the law.*

What should he do now?

His decision was swift. *Get the water and return.* After all, that's what he'd promised to do, and he wasn't going back on his word, no matter what.

If the marshal came calling, Nevada would figure that out when the time arrived. Problem was, even though he hadn't been part of the robbery, he couldn't prove it.

But running would solve nothing. He'd been down that path years ago when he'd walked away from what he believed to be his destiny. If only God hadn't taken Marie, his life would be so different now. Just as the woman's life back at the house would surely change if Joshua died.

What was this Joshua Grey to the woman with the deep auburn hair and mesmerizing green eyes? Friend, sweetheart, brother? She looked to be closer to his own age than the injured man's, but what did he know? He'd reached the advanced age of twenty-nine and only been close to one woman besides his mother and sister. What was she doing chasing Joshua from the saloon the day she'd arrived? Trying to make him come home?

Nevada jogged across the street and headed to Nellie's boardinghouse. Too bad he didn't know where the source of water was for this town, but he knew Nellie wouldn't mind him using her pump and filling his bucket.

A few minutes later he headed back to the sad-looking house on Toughnut Street, balancing his load off to the side and walking carefully. By the time he arrived at the door he'd sloshed only a small amount. He heaved a relieved sigh when he stepped inside the door and set the bucket down.

He glanced around the silent room. Voices echoed from somewhere back of the crude kitchen beyond the open archway. John Draper appeared at the entrance to the living area. He gave a brief nod but no smile lit his broad face. "You got the water. Good. They moved him to a bedroom."

Nevada jerked his chin toward the back of the house. "Want me to take it back there?"

"No. Miss Grey said if you returned with it, to set it to boiling." He gestured toward the potbellied stove in a corner. He looked Nevada up and down. "Why'd she think you wouldn't come back?"

Nevada leaned over and grasped the bucket handle, needing time to think. So it was Miss Grey, and she didn't expect him to come back. Interesting. For sure she'd pegged him for the man who'd bandaged her arm. Apparently she didn't think much more of him now than she had the day they'd met. "Can't rightly say." He headed toward the stove.

Keeping his back to the blacksmith he poured the water into the pot on the floor and lifted it onto the hot surface. "So she's Miss Grey, huh? Know her first name?"

"Yeah, Christy. 'Pears she's come to care for her ma, since she took sick. Good thing she got here when she did, what with her brother gettin' shot and all."

Ah, so Joshua is her brother. Nevada felt relief at hearing that. "The mother is sick? Know what's wrong?"

John shook his head. "Naw. Heard her cough a couple of times."

Silence fell as the men stared at the water, waiting for it to heat. Nevada thought over what he'd learned. Miss Grey had been summoned, probably by her brother, to help with the care of her mother. A racking cough broke the silence, and Nevada turned to look. No one appeared, but the coughing didn't cease for several minutes. He'd heard that sound before, and a tremor of dread coursed up his back.

He pitied this family. They had a lot to deal with. Even if the young man brought it on himself by calling the gambler a cheat, no one deserved to die by taking a bullet in the gut.

Was Joshua Grey right with his Maker? Nevada lassoed his thoughts. He'd given up worrying about other people's souls years ago, and it wasn't his place to pick it up again now. He turned to the blacksmith, anxious to talk rather than think. "I came into the saloon to find you before the shooting started."

Clearly, Nevada's words got the big man's attention, because he tensed. But he didn't reply.

"Miss Nellie over at the boardinghouse sent me."

John grinned. "You know Nellie?"

"Met her today. Nice lady."

"The best. She's doin' wonders for this town. Takes collections from miners, gamblers, and such, and helps those in need. She even went to the jail to pray with some men condemned to hang."

Something tugged at Nevada's heart, but he pushed it aside. "Sounds like I picked the right place to stay."

"So why were you lookin' for me?" John crossed his arms over his muscular chest.

Nevada stood eye-to-eye with the man, but Draper probably outweighed him by fifty pounds. He grinned. "Hoping you needed a man who's handy around horses."

John's stance relaxed. "You want a job?"

"That's the idea."

"Well, why didn't you say so?" He reached over and clapped Nevada on the back. "What's your name, son?"

"Nevada." He bit out the word, not eager to share more at the moment.

"Good handle. You ever shoe a horse before?"

Nevada gave a wry smile. "Way too many of them, my friend."

John threw back his head and laughed, then sobered quickly. "Sorry. Forgot to keep my voice down"—he gestured toward the end of the house—"but I know what you mean when you say too many horses. Come by tomorrow and we'll talk over hours and such. Wonder what's happenin' with the doc?"

Nevada shrugged. "No telling. Hope Grey pulls through, but he didn't look good."

"Yeah. Too bad for the family."

"Do you mind if I slip out of here? Maybe you could tell Miss Grey and her mother I hope Joshua recovers."

"Got things to do, huh?" Draper rubbed the stubble on his chin.

"Something like that." Nevada raised his hand in a friendly salute and headed for the door. As he closed it behind him, he heard the pad of light feet. Part of him wanted to go back and take another look into those beautiful eyes, but he squelched the urge. No. The best thing he could do was stay out of her sight before she changed her mind and turned him over to the law.

* * * * *

Christy walked through the kitchen and entered the front room. Just as she'd expected. The blacksmith stood over the pot of water on the stove, and the other man still hadn't arrived. *Wait a minute. Pot of water?* How did that get here if he hadn't come back?

She stepped closer to the front window and peered outside in time to see the man striding down the walk. She gaped at John Draper. "He brought the water?" It sounded stupid even to her ears, but thankfully the big man was too much of a gentleman to comment.

"Yes, ma'am. 'Bout fifteen minutes ago. Got the water to boilin', and we jawed for a while, then he said he had to leave. Told me to say he hoped Joshua gets better." He stepped away from the stove. "Gettin' a mite warm. Fire will probably feel good later this evenin' after the sun goes down, though."

She nodded absently, only barely taking in his last words. He'd brought the water back and stayed. He could as easily have left town, or at the least left the bucket and disappeared to wherever he was staying. She lifted her chin and stared at John. "Did he tell you his name?"

John scratched his head and thought for a moment. "By crickety, I don't think he did, other than Nevada. And I didn't think to ask for more. Guess I'll find out tomorrow."

"Tomorrow?"

"He's comin' by my shop so we can talk about work."

"Work?" She kept repeating everything the man said like a woman who'd lost her way. Well, maybe she had. "He's going to work for you?" Something akin to excitement stirred in her heart.

"Said he would. Told me he knows how to shoe a horse, and I need somebody bad. Glad to have the extra pair of hands and a strong back, leastways until my leg heals." He gestured at his shinbone. "Speakin' of which, it's gettin' plumb sore. Think I'll head home if you don't need any more help."

"Thank you for everything. Forgive my manners. Would you like something to eat before you go?"

"No thanks, Miss. You look plumb tuckered out. How's young Grey? He gonna pull through?"

"Doc says it's too soon to tell. If he does, it's going to take steady nursing."

"Ah, well, I expect you're good at that." He plucked his hat off the nearby table and slipped it onto his head. "I'll pray for him and for your ma. Sounds like she's havin' a rough go of things."

"That's kind of you." Christy walked him to the door and shut it carefully behind him. *Prayer.*

The thought hadn't even occurred to her. After all the church services she'd sat through in Last Chance, you'd think some of it might have rubbed off, but she'd never seen prayer do much good. Maybe her family roots ran too deep. Gambling, shooting, working in saloons, and all the rest that came along with her heritage. She'd hoped moving to Tombstone would give her a new start. A scan of the disheveled room made her groan. What a foolish thing to expect. Nothing had changed in her family, and she doubted it ever would.

Chapter Ten

....

Nevada grasped the fetlock joint on the mare's front leg and lifted, but she didn't budge. "Come on, girl." He pinched the tendons above her hoof, leaned against her forearm, and lifted again. This time the horse's foot came off the ground easily. He grabbed the long file and rasped the curve of the mare's hoof wall, shaving off enough to get it level and ready for the shoe.

John Draper swung his hammer against the red-hot shoe, shaping the curve to the right fit. He held it up with his tongs and inspected it. "Good enough, I guess."

Nevada tossed John a grin. "Nothing's ever just good enough with you, John. After working here for a week I've figured that out. It's perfect or not at all."

"Customers deserve to get my best work." The blacksmith dipped the shoe in a bucket of water and left it for a full minute before pulling it out and handing it to Nevada. "Should fit now."

Nevada put four nails between his teeth and placed the shoe against the horse's hoof, holding her leg between his tightly clenched knees. She gave a sharp jerk and he braced himself, holding firm until she quieted. "Whoa there, mare. Easy now." The words came out between tightly clenched teeth. The last thing he needed was to suck a spike into his throat.

When the mare relaxed, he picked up his hammer with one hand and withdrew a nail with his other, keeping the mare's leg steady with his clamped knees. A few taps and all four nails were in. Another couple of minutes and he'd have the sharp points clipped off, if she didn't decide to jerk her foot away again and rake him with the sharp points. He winced, remembering his early days of shoeing and the deep gashes he'd received when an unruly stallion did just that.

Lowering the hoof to the ground, he gave the mare a break before he moved on to the next foot.

John hobbled over and looked down at the pair of shod front hooves. "Nice work. Sure glad you hit me up for a job last week. Not sure what I'd done if you hadn't showed up."

"I hate sitting idle. I'm not crazy about town life, but I'm thankful for the job."

He knew the reason he hadn't shaken the dust off his feet and hightailed it out of Tombstone. Christy Grey. As much as he'd like to disappear from sight and find a job on a ranch, he couldn't forget the agony shining out of Christy's green eyes when she'd first seen her brother lying near death. She'd not told his secret, and he was grateful. No way could he leave town without finding a way to help her.

"You hear anything more about Joshua Grey?"

"He pulled through. That's all I know."

"I'm glad. Maybe I'll stop over and check on him. See if his ma needs anything."

A glint sparked in John's eye. "Good idea. They don't have an able-bodied man in the house now, and his sister is new to town."

Nevada ran his hand down the mare's back leg and pinched the tendon above the fetlock joint. This time her foot came up without protest. "Good girl. You're learning fast."

John sank down onto a low stool with a grunt and extended his bum leg in front of him. "Gets better one day, and hurts the next. How about you come to church with me and the missus this Sunday?"

Nevada kept his back to John, not wanting to hurt the man's feelings. He had no desire to attend Sunday services now, or anytime in the future. God was not high on his priority list anymore.

His new boss didn't seem to notice the lack of an answer. "Reverend Endicott Peabody's quite the preacher, even if he only has a tent to preach in. Sure will be nice when they finish buildin' the church he's raisin' money for."

"I didn't realize they were building one. Where at?"

"Over on the corner of Safford Street and Third." John puffed out his chest and grinned. "It's gonna have a bell tower with a cross on the top. St. Paul's Episcopal is what she'll be called."

"Sounds fancy."

"Peabody's a blamed good man, if you ask me. Stands up for what he believes and ain't afraid to say what he thinks."

John's words rankled Nevada. He'd stood up for what he believed once upon a time, then lost sight of it all. Now he didn't know what was truth and what wasn't, and no longer cared to find out.

"Haven't heard a sermon yet that didn't mean somethin' to me and the missus," John continued. "Yes, sir, he sure packs a wallop. If you can't come this week, maybe you'll find the time the following Sunday." He pushed to his feet and walked to the forge, lifting a shoe from the pile and bringing it back to Nevada. "Check her out and let me know what she needs."

Nevada placed the shoe against the hoof. "This one looks good the way it sits. Don't think you'll need to shape it."

"Good." John flexed his arms and grinned. "I think my arms are gettin' plumb tired out with all this work I'm havin' to do with you here."

Nevada stifled a laugh. "Right. I've been pushing you hard, Big John." He stuck four more nails between his lips and bent to his job.

"I was gettin' downright lazy before you came along. Couldn't do much shoein' on my own account. Figured I'd go out of business with all my customers skedaddlin' to my competition. 'Course, I coulda retired early."

"Ha." Nevada withdrew a nail and hammered it in. "You'll retire when you're six foot under. I can't see you sitting on the front porch gabbing with the other old coots." He gritted the words between clenched teeth.

John scratched his head and grinned. "Sounds mighty peaceful and appealin' sometimes. But you're right. Ain't no life for the likes of me. I need to keep busy." He shifted his leg and winced. "Sure hope you can stick around until this leg is strong enough for me to start shoein' again."

"I'll be here unless something happens I'm not expecting."

As soon as the words were out, Nevada regretted saying them. He could almost feel John's curiosity, even with his back turned, but the big man didn't reply. Nevada finished the hoof and set it down, then turned and faced the man who was quickly becoming a friend. Might as well come right out and say what was on his mind.

"I need to level with you first, John, and then you can decide if you care to have me stay."

* * * * *

Christy opened the cupboards in the kitchen. She wanted to stomp her foot and shout at someone. But who? Her injured brother, hanging between life and death for the past week, who had gambled their money away? Or her seriously ill mother, who'd allowed him to do so? Regardless of who was at fault, the state of the pantry wouldn't change without a source of income. Joshua seemed to be out of mortal danger now, and Ma's coughing had eased some. Christy had known since her arrival she'd have to find a job if they were going to keep eating. Now she shut the cupboard door with more force than necessary and went in search of her mother.

Ivy sat in a rocker beside her son's bed watching him sleep. The fever had broken, and Doctor Goodfellow seemed to think they'd avoided gangrene. Christy shuddered, knowing infection would mean certain death if it traveled through his chest. What might have happened if the blacksmith and the stranger hadn't brought him home and summoned the doctor?

She'd hadn't learned Nevada's last name and hadn't yet figured out what manner of man he might be. She'd been so convinced he'd helped rob the stage and would soon disappear. Then he arrived at her mother's door carrying her brother and returned with water when she'd assumed he'd light out and wouldn't look back. He realized she'd recognized him, that was certain, and he had no way of knowing she'd continue to keep her silence.

Something in his eyes when he'd gazed at her had sent a shiver of anticipation straight to her heart. No hint of accusation or censure shone there but rather warmth and almost a touch of humor. More than once she'd found herself hoping he'd return to check on Joshua but realized there was no real reason he should.

She took a step forward and touched her mother's hair. "Ma?"

"Yes?" Ivy didn't turn her gaze away from her son, and her listless voice didn't evoke any hope in Christy's heart.

"Will you come out to the front room and talk, so we won't disturb Joshua?"

"I suppose." She gripped the arms of the rocker and moved with the slowness of an old woman, instead of the forty-nine years she'd seen. With a sluggish, dragging gait she followed Christy out of the room and sank onto the sofa in the living room. "What you want, Daughter?"

Christy pursed her lips, wondering where to begin. Best use the example Ma had always set and get right to the heart of the matter. "We're broke, and the food is almost gone."

A weary expression crossed Ma's face. "I know. But we been here before and survived. Somethin' always seems to work out."

"Not this time, Ma. Logan isn't coming back, and Joshua won't be making any more quick money at the poker table." Her voice came out harsher than she'd planned.

Ma winced and a hard light entered her eyes. "What you want me to do about it? Go to work?"

Christy jerked like she'd been slapped. Why didn't her mother ever choose to think the best of her, instead of the worst? All her life it had been this way. Molly and Joshua could do no wrong in her eyes, but Christy never seemed to measure up. Maybe that was one reason she'd run away and gotten her first job at a gambling hall. The manager had made her feel like somebody important—a desirable woman who mattered. Now she knew that was only an act and all he'd cared about was lining his own pockets. But at the time she'd believed it and basked in the feelings of acceptance and approval.

"Of course not. I know you're not well. I thought I'd start looking for a job today, if you're up to caring for Joshua. I'll come back and check on you often, at least until I find something. And maybe I can work a half day to start with, until he doesn't require as much care."

Ma's eyes seemed to brighten, and she leaned forward a little. "You still have your looks. It wouldn't be hard for you to get on at the Golden Eagle or the Oriental. I hear tell they're goin' to open a fancy place soon at the other end of town called the Bird Cage Theater. Gonna have playactin', singin', and such like. Should bring in a pile of men wantin' to wet their whistle and talk to a pretty girl. I'll bet all of those places pay good money and they're always lookin' for help."

"Ma!" A shaft of pain bit deep into Christy's insides. "I'll never work in one of those places again."

"You ain't suited for anything else, Daughter. What you think, you're gonna get some highbrow job and be a fine lady?" Ma bit the words out and nearly spit them on the floor. "You're a Grey, and nothin' more. You was born poor, and you'll die poor. Ain't nobody in town who knows our family is gonna give you a job."

Christy felt as though she needed to bolt outside to the privy and empty her stomach. She'd always known her mother didn't think highly of her, but she'd had no idea to what degree. "I worked at a boardinghouse in Last Chance. I'll check some of those and see if I can't find something. I'm sure I'll find work before the day is out." She forced herself to paste on a smile and pushed to her feet. "Now do you think you'll be all right here with Joshua while I'm gone?"

"I'll be fine. I been takin' care of myself and you kids all the times we didn't have a man in the house and did just dandy."

Christy turned away before her mother could see her expression. Those times had been few and far between, but she didn't care to think of that. She'd decided long ago to either honor her mother or stay clear of her. Right now she didn't have the option of staying clear, so honor won out. "I'll be back as soon as I can."

Ivy waved her hand in the air. "Don't matter. We'll get along. And remember, if they won't take you at those boardinghouses, you ask around at them fancy saloons. Shouldn't be hard to get on." She stood and walked out of the room to where Joshua lay, not looking back.

Christy plucked her hat off the peg behind the door and settled it on her head. Slow anger welled up inside, causing her hands to shake. She should have stayed in Last Chance, where people respected her. Over the past four years she'd earned a place for herself there, and most of the folks in town had even forgotten her background. Of course, there were still a handful of uppity women who put their nose in the air when she walked by, but the majority of the people were kind. Had it all been an act? Could her mother be right? The Malone name didn't demand respect like some did, and apparently neither did Grey, but surely they didn't deserve the disdain Ma painted them with. She wondered what her mother had been through since arriving in this town. Joshua probably hadn't helped, what with stirring up trouble and getting into fights.

She grasped the doorknob and opened the door. Enough worrying over what hadn't happened and probably wouldn't. Her saloon days were behind her, and she'd have a job before this day was out. Somehow she'd find a way to prove to her mother she was a woman to be proud of—and certainly fit for more than the life of a dance-hall girl.

* * * * *

Nevada slapped the mare on the hip. "There you go, girl. All done." He swung the gate of the corral shut behind her and turned to face his boss.

John Draper shifted his weight on the stool and leaned against a post. "So you're on the run after shootin' a man in Albuquerque. You wanted by the law?"

"No. There was a witness who said he'd tell the marshal the other man drew first."

"That the first man you've had to kill?" John's eyes penetrated deep into Nevada's soul.

Nevada's gut clenched, and a light sweat broke out on his forehead. "Wish I could say he was, but I can't."

"Don't worry, I won't ask how many. Not my business. What a man is now is what matters to me, not what he's done. Besides, you don't appear to be a killer, or a man who hunts trouble."

"No, sir. I don't like to think I am." Nevada met John's eyes squarely.

"Ah-huh. So why you think trouble keeps huntin' you, then?"

"Wish I knew the answer to that." Nevada bit back the words he'd almost let slip about the events of his past. No. John didn't need to be burdened with things that couldn't be changed. Nevada had buried that old life so deep he never wanted to resurrect it.

Chapter Eleven
....

Christy departed the third boardinghouse and as many hotels, her steps dragging. She'd left home with such high hopes for success but had been met with discouragement at every turn. Most of the places had all the help they needed, but two had looked at her askance when she mentioned her name and politely turned her down. Ma was right—apparently their family didn't command much respect in this town.

She hurried across the boardwalk, head down and deep in thought. All of a sudden she came up against a person's chest. A pair of strong hands grasped her upper arms and steadied her before she fell.

"Whoa there. What's the rush?" Gordon Townsley, the manager from the Oriental Saloon, retained his grip on her arms.

Christy took a step back and tried to smile. "I apologize. I wasn't paying attention to where I was going."

"Are you staying here?" He waved a hand at the sign hanging above the door.

"No. Looking for a job." Her heart sank. She wished she could drag the words back. This man didn't need to know her business.

"Hmm. I might have something available." He raised his hand before she could speak. "Just listen. I'm not suggesting anything improper. You could run one of the gaming tables and no one would bother you. Doc Holiday or Wyatt would see to that."

"I'm sorry. No." Christy started to turn away.

Townsley stepped in front of her. He dropped his voice low and met her eyes. "You may not get a lot of job offers, Miss Grey. Your stepfather didn't have the best reputation before he was run out of town, and neither does your brother."

"Run out?" Christy drew herself up and frowned. "You're mistaken. He left to care for a mining claim."

"That what your mother or brother told you? He may have done so, but that's not the only reason. He was caught cheating at cards more than once and got rough with one of the girls down at the Golden Eagle when he'd had too much to drink." Townsley paused to tip his hat at a lady who passed. "The owner there doesn't much care for men who rough up his girls, so they threw him out. Malone came back roaring mad and shot up the place. The marshal told him to leave town or get thrown in jail." He glanced at the door of the boardinghouse. "Word travels in this town, and your brother didn't fall far from the tree, even if he isn't Logan's blood."

"I'm sorry, but I really need to be going." Christy picked up the hem of her skirt and stepped off the boardwalk.

"Don't wait to take me up on my offer, Miss Grey. I can't promise how long I'll have it available."

The soft words barely reached Christy's ears, but they pursued her down the street like hounds. Why would that man consider offering her a job at his saloon? He had no way of knowing her background, and she certainly didn't dress like a woman who'd work in one of those places. Her pace slowed. Joshua? Would he talk about her past? She hated to think it, but her little brother's jaws flapped when they were better kept shut.

* * * * *

Nevada stepped out of the livery and sauntered down the street, rubbing the ache out of his right arm. Too many months had passed since he'd swung a hammer for any length of time. His rumbling stomach reminded him he'd better find something to eat. Since Nellie only served breakfast and supper at the boardinghouse, he'd gotten used to stopping at one of the small restaurants along Allen Street for his noontime meal.

A flash of dark auburn hair caught his eye as a woman wove through the men crowding the sidewalks. Most of the miners took their dinner into the mines in a pail and didn't venture out until the end of their shift, but there were still plenty of people on the streets. He peered ahead and quickened his step, hoping to catch another glimpse of the woman. He'd seen plenty of blonds and brunettes in this town, and even a few gals with raven-black hair, but not an abundance of redheads. Excited anticipation tugged at his heart as Christy Grey's face flashed through his mind.

Half a dozen long strides brought him within sight of the young lady and his pulse quickened. Should he accost her on the street, or would she think him rude for doing so? Nevada had never followed through on his plan to stop at the house and inquire as to her brother's condition. He plunged forward and fell in beside her. "Miss Grey?" He kept his voice low so as not to startle her.

A rapid intake of breath indicated her surprise, but she slowed her pace and turned. "Yes?" Recognition flashed in her eyes and she halted. "Oh. It's you."

Nevada's stomach tightened at the apprehension in her voice. "Miss Grey, I'm not here to bother you. But I hoped you'd allow me to inquire after your brother's health."

The firm set of her lips softened. "I see. Thank you for asking. The doctor thinks he'll pull through. He's talking some and able to eat soup and bread."

"That's fine." Nevada struggled to think of something else to prolong the meeting. "Are you and your mother getting along all right?"

"Yes. Why do you ask?" She tilted her head to the side.

"I heard her coughing the day I was there. It didn't sound good."

Christy nodded. "You're right. Ma's been ill, but I hope she's improving." Her voice quivered. "She's getting more rest since I arrived."

"I'm glad to hear it." He paused, then plunged forward. He'd held on to this question for as long as he could, and now it was time for an answer. "Why did you do it?"

Her eyes widened. "I beg your pardon?"

He touched her arm and drew her into the lee of a closed doorway, out of the press of streaming humanity. "Why didn't you turn me in to the marshal?" He dropped his voice and allowed his eyes to scan the area, but no one seemed to pay them any attention. Men hurried by, and a woman scolding her fussing children disappeared into a nearby store. "I know you recognized me from the stage."

"Yes, I did, not long after you walked into our home carrying Joshua." She shrugged. "I gave you my word, and I won't break it."

"Even if it gets you in trouble?"

"It won't. The marshal questioned me, but I haven't told him anything. Besides, you didn't harm me or the other passengers, and you helped my brother. I'm sorry you felt the need to rob the stage, but I won't go back on my promise."

Frustration swelled in his chest and Nevada clenched his hands. "I told you. I had nothing to do with the robbery. I fell in with those men the night before when I needed a place to bed down. That's all. I didn't want to start shooting for fear more people on the stage would be hurt, so I took the mask and slipped it on. Besides, I saw you were hurt and hoped to help."

Christy frowned. "I'd like to believe you after all you've done to help. But either way, your secret is safe."

Shame burned in Nevada's mind that this woman would doubt his word and think him the type of man who'd rob others. Bad enough that he'd been forced to shoot men in self-defense, but thievery was something he'd never stoop to. "I hope someday I can prove you're wrong."

"Someday? I assumed you'd be leaving Tombstone. In fact, I was rather astounded you decided to take a job with the blacksmith and stay."

Nevada gritted his teeth to keep from saying something he shouldn't. "I'm sorry I haven't been by to offer my assistance since your brother's unfortunate accident." He pushed the words through clenched teeth, then forced himself to relax. "If there's anything I can do to help, please let me know."

She seemed to waver, then slowly shook her head. "Thank you. I'm sure we'll be fine."

Something in her tone caused a flicker of doubt to ignite in his mind. "Please. With your mother ill and brother recuperating, I'm sure you're busy. Might I bring you a barrel of water or any other supplies?"

She reached for the cloth pouch dangling from her wrist. "A barrel of water would be wonderful, if you find you have time."

Nevada held up his hand and took a step back. "No need for pay. It's the least I can do after the injury to your arm. By the way, has it fully healed?"

She reached up and touched the spot above her elbow. "It's fine now. Once the bleeding stopped and the flesh started mending, I only had to deal with the soreness."

Silence settled around the spot where they stood. Nevada wished he could find a way to delay the meeting, but nothing came to mind.

Christy dipped her head. "I'd best be getting back home. I've been gone long enough, and Ma will worry."

"Do you have anything I can carry for you?" He looked askance at her empty arms, wondering what brought her to town.

"No, thank you. I came hoping to find work." She gave a small smile. "Maybe tomorrow. Good day."

Nevada squared his shoulders. "I'll bring the water over straightaway."

"Please don't rush. Finish whatever brought you to town."

He watched her walk down the boardwalk until she disappeared around the corner headed for Toughnut Street. His appetite had fled, and only one desire consumed his attention—finding out where water could be purchased, hiring a wagon, and taking it to

Christy Grey's home. Something in her determined tone when she mentioned getting a job tugged at his heart. She needed a champion, and considering all she'd been through since arriving in this town, he'd like to take on that role. He grinned as he headed the opposite direction. It might be a nice change from the part he'd played for the past few years. A nice change, indeed.

* * * * *

Christy hurried past the open door of the last saloon she had to pass on Allen Street and averted her gaze. Four steps on up the walkway and two more to swing around the corner before she could draw a breath of relief. Time to get home. This day was wasted, and Ma probably needed her by now.

Nevada presented a challenge to her thoughts that would keep her awake at night if she wasn't careful. She'd never felt an attraction to any man since Ralph died, and if she were completely honest with herself, she'd agreed to marry Ralph only because of his love for her. Having someone of her own had been a draw, and Ralph was a decent man who always treated her with kindness, but she'd not been strongly attracted to him.

But Nevada was different. The man had a rugged strength about him that drew her in spite of her attempts to hold herself aloof.

Hard footsteps slapped the boardwalk behind her and a man's deep voice called out, "Christy? That you?"

Dread knotted her stomach and she halted, then slowly turned. She should have kept going. Nothing good would come of this meeting. "I'm sorry. Do I know you?" With a lift of her chin she stared at the man, praying he'd decide he'd made a mistake and scurry back to the saloon.

Instead, a broad grin split his whiskered face. "Sure you do. I'm Ben. I used to come see you dance down in Sacramento, and you always served me drinks."

Christy forced her voice to remain calm. "Sorry. You must have the wrong person."

"No, ma'am. I'd know your red hair and pretty face anywhere. You gonna be working at one of the joints here in town? Let me know, and I'll spread the word to my friends."

"Pardon me, but I need to get home."

She spun around and hurried up the street, holding her head erect. Her insides roiled. It had been over five years since she'd worked in Sacramento—for that matter, in any saloon in the West. Who'd have believed she'd stumble across someone who'd recognize her in this booming mining town so far from California? She wouldn't run from her past, but she'd be dad-blasted, as Alexia's uncle Joe used to say, if she'd allow anyone in the present to force her back where she didn't care to go.

Chapter Twelve
....

"Christy!" Ma's voice smote Christy's ears like the harsh clang of a dinner bell, making her cringe.

"I'm in here." She smoothed the blanket over Ma's newly changed bed with satisfaction. The house might not be much to boast of, but at least this room shone with cleanliness. "Don't get up. I'll come out as soon as I check on Joshua." But Christy couldn't help but ache for her ma. She'd been feeling poorly again, and her cough had grown worse.

Christy shoved the door open leading into Joshua's room, the one she thought she'd be using before he was shot. She'd been sleeping on the sofa for the past five weeks, and her back paid for it daily in aches and pains. Her younger brother slept facing the door, and the lightweight sheet covering his torso didn't show the usual evidence of fitful tossing. Relief and gratitude swelled in her heart that God had answered her prayers. She hadn't been sure He would, with the way she'd always ignored Him, but Joshua being alive and not losing the use of his arm or his leg was nothing short of a miracle.

Stepping around the corner into the living area Christy winced. During her growing-up years the house had been properly kept, but since Ma's illness she'd relaxed her standards. Shoes lay where they'd been kicked in the middle of the room, a blanket had been tossed on the floor, and a dirty plate sat on a small table strewn with newspapers and a coffee cup. Ma's dressing gown was stained where she'd apparently spilled some of the strong brew.

Ivy pushed to a sitting position and grimaced. She struggled to take a breath, and harsh coughs poured from her throat. Christy could see a noticeable weight loss since she'd arrived in town. Of course, it didn't help that Ma had lost her appetite with the advent of the hot weather. May was well upon them, and the temperatures often soared into the high eighties. The wind still kicked up a fuss on a regular basis, but it only blew warm, dust-laden gusts over the town. Occasionally a whirling dervish touched down, tearing the roofs off the flimsy canvas-covered shanties and sending items flying down the streets.

The dressing gown clung to Ivy's spare frame, and beads of perspiration dotted her forehead. "It's almighty warm in here." She swiped at her forehead with the back of her sleeve.

"Let me get you a cool cloth and a glass of clean water. I'll be right back."

Christy hurried to the kitchen, thankful once again for Nevada's kindness in bringing that first barrel of water over a week ago. Since then he'd deposited two more at the back door within easy reach of the kitchen and never once allowed her to pay. She'd not been able to entice him into the house to meet her mother or stay for a cup of coffee, and she admitted to feeling a twinge of disappointment. Slowly her opinion of the man was changing from distrust to growing respect.

Christy stepped outside. She lifted the lid on the barrel and drew back in surprise. He'd come again, and she'd not been home.

Regret pierced her heart. She looked forward to those brief meetings when Nevada delivered the water and felt sick she'd missed him this time.

The noise from the mining claims on the hillside behind Toughnut Street floated clearly on the spring air. A steam engine ran twenty hours a day pulling carts full of rock and ore from the depths of the mines. On the far side of the house, men's voices, rumbling wagons, and the occasional laugh of a woman or child could be heard. This town rarely slept, and Christy found it a difficult transition after the quiet of Last Chance.

With a full glass of water in one hand and a cool, damp cloth in the other, she returned to her mother's side. Leaning over, she pressed the glass into Ivy's hand and gently wiped her forehead. Ma closed her eyes and gave a long sigh. "You're a good girl, Christy. I know I don't tell you often, but it's the truth."

Surprise and pleasure shot through Christy. Rare was the day her mother praised anyone. She could count on two hands the times she'd heard words of love or appreciation from her parent. "Thank you, Ma." Her voice cracked, and she tried to steady it. "Did you need anything else?"

"Yes. We need cash money, and soon."

The words struck Christy like a physical blow coming so close on the heels of the affirmation she'd longed to hear. She'd looked for work several more times with little success. Gordon Townsley's offer had returned to her mind more than once, but she'd been successful in dismissing it. "Do you have any more hidden for groceries?"

Ma shook her head. "Used most of it. While you were away this mornin' I had a visit from the banker." She scrunched up her face.

"Mean-hearted little man. He said if I don't catch up on my payments by the end of this month he's takin' the house and sellin' it."

Christy sank onto the far end of the sofa and struggled to take in her mother's words. "You're that far behind? I thought Logan left you enough to pay this house off. Surely you didn't give all the money to Joshua?"

The older woman pursed her lips. "Thought he'd do well with what I gave him, so I kept enough for a few months' payments. Haven't made one for over four months now."

Christy gasped. "Four months? I'm surprised the bank hasn't forced you out already."

"You have to get a job, Daughter."

"I've been trying." She pushed the words out between cold lips.

Ma peered at her. "You know what I mean. I got to have medicine, Joshua needs good food, and we can't live on the streets. Set your stubborn pride aside and work at a saloon. It's good pay, and we'll get by till Joshua is up and around and can go to work."

Christy sat up straight and strove to maintain a respectful tone, although what she wanted to do was rail over Ma's foolish use of money, not to mention any expectation her son would get a real job. "I'm not going to work in one of those places again. I'm done with that life."

"No one said you had to do it long. I'm askin' for your brother's sake, if you won't do it for mine." Another bout of coughing shook her slender body and she covered her mouth with a soiled handkerchief. "Just till somethin' else comes along, that's all."

Shame hammered at Christy. Was she being proud and selfish, refusing to take work that would put money on the table and keep the banker away? Did she have the right to refuse the job when her mother and brother needed better care than she could provide? "I'll think about it, but not until after I've tried one more time. I won't see you or Joshua go hungry, or without medicine."

Ma raised watery eyes to Christy's. "I'm ashamed to put this on you, girl."

Christy patted her mother's hand. "It's all right, Ma. Surely something else will come along. God couldn't be so cruel as to not provide for us some other way."

* * * * *

Nevada hadn't eaten all day, and it was well past time for the noon meal. He'd taken a barrel of water to Christy's home and been disappointed at not finding her there. No one answered the door when he knocked. He'd left it on the back stoop and slipped away so as not to wake her mother if she slept. He'd been lucky to see Christy the first couple of times he'd brought water, but it had been three days since the last delivery and he'd hoped to speak to her this time. Maybe find out how her job hunt was coming and ask about her brother. Too bad he'd missed her. Hopefully that meant she'd found work.

Now that he'd finished up a few odd jobs for Nellie at the boardinghouse and John didn't need him for the rest of the day it was time to find some food. He stood outside a restaurant debating with himself, his mouth watering at the fragrances emanating through the open door. The large number of patrons inside made him hesitate, but the odor of frying beef urged him forward. He swung the door open and paused. Tombstone's marshal, Ben Sippy, sat at the counter dipping his spoon into a bowl. Nevada backed out of the door, his stomach rumbling in protest.

A few long paces took him up Allen Street and he halted outside the Oriental Saloon. He hadn't been inside since the day Joshua was shot, but he remembered John talking about the excellent food they served. A push of the door and he stepped inside, allowing his eyes to adjust to the light.

Someone stopped beside him, and a sweet fragrance tickled his nose.

"Hi, Cowboy. Haven't seen you in here for quite a while." Sara, the girl he'd spoken to the day Joshua Grey was shot, stood beside him. She leaned closer, her smile suggestive and simmering with something he didn't care to define. "What can I get you to drink?"

"Nothing, thanks. Maybe a bowl of stew or a sandwich. Whatever the house is serving."

"No whiskey or beer?" Sara asked.

"No. Just something to eat."

Her hands went to her hips. "We get paid by how many drinks we sell, mister. The boss frowns on girls who serve a meal without a drink." Fear flashed across her face. "I don't care to make him angry, know what I mean?"

"Fine. Bring me a whiskey and when I leave, you can toss it."

Disbelief colored her voice. "You'd do that for me? Spend money and not get anything out of it?" A frown transformed her countenance. "Don't think you'll get cozy with me, Cowboy."

Nevada gave a slow, lazy smile. "I wouldn't think of it, Sara. Not that you aren't an attractive young lady, but I only came in for food, not...companionship."

Her stiff stance relaxed and she nodded, then hurried away.

He made his way to a table and sank into a chair. Sara's presence in this place was a bit of a puzzle. She didn't seem to fit. Sure, she was pretty enough to draw the attention of any man hungry for female company, but she didn't have the hard edge most women working in places like this acquired. Maybe she was a new addition to the saloon. A shaft of unease speared his heart as he once again noticed the strong resemblance between Sara and his sister Carrie. She'd escaped a hellhole of a saloon barely in time before her life could be ruined.

A scuffle on the far side of the room near the foot of the stairs turned his attention that direction. Buckskin Frank Leslie gripped Sara's arm, then shoved her toward another neatly dressed man wearing a black broadcloth suit. Leslie's voice rose above the ongoing hum in the room. "Do what the boss pays you to do, girl. This man wants an hour of your time."

Sara tried to shake the hand off her arm. "I don't feel good, Frank. My stomach's been sickly all morning. Please don't make me."

The dark-frocked man drew her close. "Come on, darlin'. I'll make you forget all about your troubles."

A coarse laugh echoed from someone sitting at a nearby table. "She's a sweet one, mister. You picked a winner."

Nevada shoved back his chair and pushed to his feet, pity for the girl's plight mingling with disgust at the man gripping her arm. He wove his way toward Sara, unable to ignore her obvious distress.

Buckskin Frank Leslie, a well-known gunfighter currently working as the law enforcement for the Oriental, stepped in front of him. "Where you headed, mister?"

Nevada rested his hand on the butt of his gun. "Looks to me like the young lady doesn't care to do any entertaining today."

Leslie shook his head and hitched at his gun belt. "Not your business. The girls know what's expected of them. Leave it be if you don't want trouble."

Nevada's body tensed and he stared into the man's eyes, assessing his options. He'd love to walk over and separate Sara from her customer. This girl's situation shouted for intervention. He'd been in more fights than he cared to remember, and he gave a half shrug. What was one more?

He drilled the man with a hard stare. "You know, I've never much cared about getting into trouble. Like I said, the young lady isn't feeling well. Why don't you let her go to her room and rest?"

"Can't do that. The boss don't like slackers. She's got to earn her keep."

"Fine." Nevada dug into his pocket and removed a wad of bills. "How much?"

Frank Leslie's eyes narrowed. "For what?"

"To outbid the other gent."

"Ha. So that's the way the land lies, is it? You jealous?" Frank shot the other man a look and turned back toward Nevada. "Ten dollars should do the trick."

"Hey!" The dapper man holding Sara's arm lifted his voice in protest. "I already paid you. She's mine." He jerked the girl against his chest and glared.

Leslie snatched the bill out of Nevada's extended hand. "Not tonight, she ain't. You come back another time, and we'll set you up."

"No, sir. I demand my rights."

"Now ain't that funny? Your rights, huh?" Leslie wrenched Sara out of his grasp. "Charlie?"

A burly man stepped forward out of the shadows. "Yeah, boss?"

"How about you escort this gentleman to the door?"

"Sure, boss." Charlie pushed the sleeves of his shirt up to his elbows and grinned. "Be happy to."

"Now wait a moment. You can't treat me this way!" The blustering protest was cut off by a shove to the center of his back.

"Out you go, mister." The strong-armed man collared the customer around the neck and forced him toward the door.

"How about my money?" the customer whined.

"We'll hold it for you till you come again. Or if you care to behave yourself, we might allow you to visit one of our other girls."

"But I want Sara!" The man wrenched out of his captor's grip and turned fierce eyes on Leslie.

"Too bad. She's done spoken for tonight." Leslie rolled the ten-dollar bill in his fingers and grinned. "Don't be such a bad sport. Tell you what. You keep hollerin', and Charlie here will toss you out in the street. You behave yourself, and I might set you up with a drink on the house."

"Only one?"

Leslie's grin faded. "Maybe you'd prefer the street."

The man shook his head. "I'd appreciate that drink very kindly." He shook free of the hand gripping his arm.

"Good enough." Leslie motioned to his employee. "Tell the bartender to pour our friend a whiskey." He turned toward Nevada and beckoned to Sara. "She's all yours, mister. For an hour. You want her longer, you'll have to pay double."

"How much for the night?" Nevada glanced at the retreating form of the disgruntled customer.

"We don't usually allow gentlemen to spend the night with our girls." He eyed the roll cradled in Nevada's hand. "But maybe this once..."

Nevada grunted and pressed a wad of bills into the eager man's hand, then turned toward Sara. "Want to show me your room, darlin'?" He hated the pretense, but saving this girl for even one night made it worthwhile.

He knew from his sister's experience that many of these girls and women fell into the trap of prostitution when they had no other options, while others chose the lifestyle for the amount of money it brought. He imagined Sara to be one who'd not had a chance. She certainly hadn't seemed too happy at the request to entertain yet another visitor in her room.

She turned an apprehensive gaze his way and took a half step back. "I'm—I'm awful tired."

Frank Leslie let out a roar and sprang forward, raising his hand. "This man paid good money for your time. No more bellyachin', you hear?"

Nevada stepped between them and gave a disarming smile. "Don't worry. I'll show her who's boss."

He took Sara's arm and drew her within his embrace, then turned and ushered her up the stairs. Hair prickled on the back of his neck. He felt eyes watching his exit. As he turned to scan the room, his gut clenched into a knot. Christy Grey stood beside Gordon Townsley, his arm casually draped across her shoulders.

Chapter Thirteen

....

A shudder passed over Christy as Nevada followed Sara up the stairs. His eyes had mirrored a flash of shock before he headed up behind her. Had he felt guilty she'd caught him in the act of accompanying a girl to her room? Disappointment sat like a lump of sourdough in her stomach, but she shoved it away. Nevada's choices were none of her concern, but she hurt just the same. Of course, she'd started to grow attached to Sara and hated seeing the young girl used in such a fashion, so her feelings had little to do with the handsome cowboy.

It took several seconds before she awoke to Townsley's arm draped across her shoulder. Reaching up, she shoved it off and stepped away from Townsley's side. "If this is the way you plan to act, Mr. Townsley, then I don't care to take the job after all."

An emotion bordering on irritation lit his features before it was replaced with calm agreement. He nodded. "As you wish, Christy. It's all right if I call you that? We don't stand on ceremony here, and our patrons like to use the Christian names of our employees."

She hesitated, then slowly gave one nod. "Fine. But I'll not have men handling me, or it will be a very short term of employment."

His eyes narrowed for the briefest of moments before a wide

smile stretched his lips. "I think that's what drew me to you in the first place, my dear—your strong spirit. You didn't wail or carry on even though you'd been shot and were in obvious pain. Now you come in here like a queen and start setting the rules." He gave a sharp bark of a laugh. "I like that, I surely do." He touched her arm and gestured toward the roulette wheel. "That's where you'll be working. Do you think you can handle the men who play here without too much trouble?"

Christy fell into step beside him, her gaze trained on the spinning wheel. "I'm familiar with the game, but I'm concerned about the men. You said Doc Holliday or Wyatt keep an eye on things, correct?"

"Yes, and I assure you, nothing will happen. I'd like you to start tomorrow afternoon. Does that work for you?"

"Yes." She noticed three more scantily clad women serving drinks to the patrons. "How many girls do you have working, and do they all live here?"

His eyes focused intently on her. "Why do you ask?"

She shrugged. "I like to get acquainted with my surroundings so I can do a good job. You know, in case a gentleman inquires after one of the ladies." The words tasted sour on her tongue, but she forced them out anyway. Her meeting on the street with the blond Sara had left an impression of a young woman working hard to cover a life of pain and confusion. Well she knew the plight of these women, and she intended to uncover all she could about the "ladies" who worked here.

"Ah, I see." He gave a sly smile. "You don't seem the type to be interested in their profession." He swept a probing gaze over her face and allowed it to drop a few inches before returning to meet her eyes. "Unless I miscalculated, my dear."

Christy took a step back and frowned. "No, you did not, and I'm sorry I asked."

"No need, and I apologize for the insinuation. Please, let's start over, shall we?" Gordon tipped his head toward a table. "We serve excellent coffee and sandwiches."

"Thank you, but I really must get home to my mother and brother." She plunged back into the subject still close to her heart. "I met a young woman named Sara. Has she worked here long?"

Townsley's expression smoothed and he turned away, but not before Christy recognized an emotion common to his sort burning there. Lust. If Sara had caught the man's eye, she could be in more danger than Christy realized.

* * * * *

Nevada dragged a hard chair from the vicinity of Sara's bed and planted it in front of the door, then sank onto it, keeping his eyes fixed on the agitated young woman standing in the far corner. "I'm not going to hurt you, Miss."

A hollow laugh broke from her throat. "Sure. That's what they all say. Somehow I thought you were different. I guess I was wrong."

"I'm staying right here and not moving."

Nevada eyed the girl, sick to his stomach at what she must be going through. Fear, apprehension, and disgust all flitted across her expressive features. How many men had entered this room with less than honorable intentions? He'd itched to throw a gun on Frank

Leslie earlier and take Sara out of this mess. At the least, he'd like to throttle Gordon Townsley within an inch of his life for forcing this kind of life on any young woman.

"What do you mean, stayin' there? What do you want from me?" She grew even more agitated.

"Nothing," he said calmly. "If you want to sleep, I'll sit here and make sure no one disturbs you." He folded his arms across his chest and tipped the chair onto its back legs, hoping to put her at ease.

"But you paid to spend the night with me."

"Yeah, so I did. And that's what I aim to do, right here in this chair." A gentle smile curved the corners of his lips. "You can do whatever you see fit."

A *whoosh* of air left Sara's lungs, and she collapsed onto the edge of the bed. A tear trickled down her cheek, then she dropped her face into her hands and sobbed. "Why? You don't know me. Why would you care?"

The question set Nevada back. How much should he tell her? It only took a second to decide honesty might be the best route if he hoped to convince her of his good intentions. Otherwise, she'd probably lie awake all night figuring he'd change his mind. "I guess partly because you remind me so much of my little sister."

Sara sniffled and stared at him. "I beg your pardon?"

"She ran away from home when she was about your age and ended up in a similar situation. I found her and took her back home. Thankfully, she's married and happy now, but it could've ended a lot worse."

"So you paid Frank extra to spend the night with me because of your sister?" Sara's eyes clouded with confusion.

"Yeah. And because I didn't think you cared to spend an hour in the company of the man I outbid." He gave a rueful smile. "'Course, you might not want to spend it in mine, either, but I don't aim to take advantage of you."

"I see." Her tense shoulders relaxed. "I've never met anybody like you. Except maybe..." Her features took on a dreamy quality for a moment. "There was a young man who used to come in..."

"Ah." Nevada nodded. "He doesn't anymore?"

"No. He got shot awhile back, and I haven't seen him since."

Nevada let the legs of the chair thump onto the floor. "Was he gambling when it happened?"

"Yes. The other man pulled a gun under the table, but they said it was a fair fight. I never heard if he died or not."

"He didn't."

She leaned forward. "You know him?"

"I do. His name is Joshua Grey."

"Grey. I've heard that name before."

"Yes," Nevada said, "he has a sister who came to town a few weeks ago."

Her expression cleared. "I wondered. I didn't realize she was his sister. She stopped and spoke to me on the street. Right out in the open where people could see and she didn't even mind." A shake of her head sent the blond curls bobbing up and down. "Most ladies in this town go out of their way to walk around me, but not her."

Nevada didn't answer, but warmth crept through his body and penetrated his heart. Somehow the knowledge of Christy's kindness to this girl didn't surprise him at all.

* * * * *

Christy arrived at work the next afternoon, dreading the thought of starting this job. She couldn't get the image of Nevada walking behind the young saloon girl out of her mind and had barely slept last night.

Her gaze swept the room, praying he wouldn't be here. Should she go straight to the roulette wheel and announce herself to the person manning it, or find Townsley first? Straightening her shoulders, she marched around a table of men playing poker, sweeping her full skirt out of the path of a slightly inebriated man tottering toward her. The last thing she needed was someone stepping on her hem or spilling his drink on her second-best dress.

She neared the roulette table and waited, glancing around. No sign of Nevada, but none of Townsley either.

"Miss Grey?" A hand touched her arm.

Christy jumped and turned.

Doc Holliday stood close by, wearing a serious expression. "Mr. Townsley is in his office and asked me to escort you there."

"Good. I was hoping he'd be here." She followed him through the crowd toward a back corner under the stairs and waited while he rapped on a closed door.

"Come in." Townsley's voice penetrated the wood.

Holliday gripped the knob and swung open the door, then turned to go.

"Thank you." Christy's soft tone halted him midstride.

He smiled, then disappeared into the melee of men.

She stepped over the threshold but left the door ajar. "I'm ready to start work, Mr. Townsley."

A cloud swept across his face. "It's Gordon, remember?"

Without waiting for a reply, he stood and came forward. His eyes traveled over the modest, dark-blue gown with pearl buttons running up to the simple collar, and ruffles at the wrist. "I'll require one adjustment before you start."

She looked down at her clothing, her heart sinking. In the years she'd worked in saloons she'd never seen any of the women dressed like this, but she'd hoped her new boss might allow her a little decency. "I won't dress the way your other girls do, so don't bother to ask. It invites undue attention from men I'd prefer to avoid."

"I understand, but I can't have you dressed like some school-marm, either. We'll have to come to an agreement if you plan to work for me." He stepped out of the office and beckoned to a young woman with light blond hair walking by with a tray of drinks balanced on the palm of her hand. "Sara. Get those to your customers and come right back. I have a job for you."

Her skin drained of color. "It's too early to take anyone upstairs, Mr. Townsley. I just started working, and it's only the dinner hour."

His expression tightened. "You misunderstand. I simply want you to take Miss Grey…er, Christy…up, and show her one of our more modest gowns."

Sara's gaze shot to Christy. "Oh. Yes, sir. I'll be right back."

Christy's heart sank. This was the girl she'd tried to befriend and the one who'd gone upstairs last night with Nevada. It was obvious Sara was shocked to see her and probably wondered why she'd fallen so low as to take a job at this place. Right at the moment she wondered the same. Her fingers trembled, and she curled them into a fist, hoping to still them. All she wanted was to walk out the door and not look back.

A few minutes later Sara returned. "I'm ready to go now, Mr. Townsley."

"Fine." He turned to Christy. "And please let your hair down." He held up a hand as Christy opened her mouth to protest. "I'm allowing you to work the roulette wheel and wear modest clothing. Humor me by wearing your hair down."

It wasn't a request but rather a firm command. His eyes didn't hold even the hint of a smile.

Christy's hackles rose. She'd been told what to do too many times by saloon owners and managers and had learned to hate it. But Ma and Joshua's faces rushed to her memory, along with the cupboards bereft of food. "I suppose I can do that."

"Good. And in return, I'll give you an advance against your wages." Gordon jerked his head toward the stairs. "Don't worry, Christy. I think you'll find we're easy to work for here at the Oriental."

She wound her way through the tables following Sara as the girl dodged outstretched hands and calls for more whiskey. She didn't look left or right but kept her gaze fixed on the staircase at the far end of the long room. As they mounted the steps, Christy drew abreast of the young woman. "Thank you for showing me the way. I hope your pay won't suffer as a result."

Sara turned. "What do you mean?"

"Don't you get paid by the number of drinks you sell?"

"Ha. That and a lot more." She pressed her lips together and looked away.

"I'm sorry. I didn't mean to pry." Christy fell silent as they made their way to the top and down a hallway. The life of a saloon girl might only be serving drinks, but too often it extended beyond those boundaries. She had an uneasy feeling Sara had experienced things she didn't care to dwell on. Christy had been lucky over the years—the places she worked hadn't pressed her into taking men to her room. Some of the girls did it for the money; others because they'd lost all hope of making anything of their lives and quit caring. But she'd always known that lifestyle wasn't for her and she shunned it. Bad enough serving drinks and fighting off uncouth men without offending them. Making a cowboy, miner, or gambler angry because he couldn't touch you or haul you upstairs could get you fired and thrown out on the street. She'd had to learn early how to sweet-talk the men but not give them anything more.

Disgust filled her. It was all she could do to not turn and stalk back down the stairs and home.

Sara pushed open a door of what appeared to be a storage room and walked inside. "This is it, ma'am." She swept her arm toward a row of dresses on the far wall, a curtain draped across a corner for privacy. "I'll show you what we've got and let you try on what you'd like."

"It's Christy, not ma'am. And I hope it's all right to call you Sara?"

The tension eased from the girl's expression. "Shore, I'd like that…. What're you doin' here? In this place, I mean? You told me that time on the street you used to work someplace like this, but you seem like such a lady. It don't make sense to me."

Christy moved to the row of gowns hanging on pegs. The last thing she wanted was to share her troubles with a stranger, but she didn't care to hurt the girl when she appeared generally confused.

She plucked a royal blue dress with a softly rounded neckline off a peg and held it in front of her. The sleeves came to her elbows and a bow-covered bustle in the back fell away into a flared skirt ending in a short train. The fabric was silky and the waist tiny—this would certainly be a form-fitting gown, but decent in all respects. She raised her eyes to meet Sara's. "This will do if it fits."

Slipping behind the curtain she hung the gown over the back of a chair. She unbuttoned her dress and stepped out of it, then handed it around the curtain to Sara. "I don't mind answering your question, if you'll answer one of mine."

Silence filled the room for several heartbeats, then Sara's soft voice answered, "Ask yours first and we'll see."

"What brought you to this town, and to work in this place?" Christy fastened the cloth-covered buttons up to within a couple of inches of her collarbone and smoothed the fabric of the skirt. The gown was something a lady would wear to a ball, not a gambling den, but she shouldn't be surprised based on the piano, velvet drapes, and highly polished walnut bar downstairs. The owner of this place apparently wanted to exude an air of luxury and wealth, and this outfit certainly fit the bill.

Christy shoved aside the curtain and stepped out, watching for Sara's reaction.

The girl's eyes widened and her lips formed a silent O. She beamed and clapped her hands. "You look beautiful!" The smile faded. "You might want to wear the other one, though, if you don't want men grabbin' at you."

"Mr. Townsley assured me that won't happen, and besides, I can take care of myself where men are concerned."

Sara's lips tightened. "That's what he told me when I came too."

Christy inhaled sharply. "Told you what, exactly?"

"That he wouldn't let men bother me none." Her slender frame quivered. "But it didn't last long."

"So when you said it was too early to take a man upstairs...does Townsley force you to entertain men in your room—against your wishes?"

Sara tucked her chin against her chest. "I don't think..."

A hard rap sounded at the door. "The boss wants you downstairs, Sara. Says yer takin' too long. Get a move on it."

Sara's chin jerked up. "We're comin' straightaway. Miss Christy just finished dressin'."

"All right then, I'll let him know." Footsteps grew fainter as he traveled away from the door.

The girl turned toward Christy, real fear in her eyes. "Please, are you ready to go? We can't keep Mr. Townsley waiting any longer."

Christy nodded and adjusted her hem. "I'll leave my other dress here and come back to change before I go home."

She longed to wrap her arms around this waif and take her away, but that wasn't possible. The house was too crowded as it was, and they didn't have enough money to feed their family, much less a stranger. But she didn't intend to let this subject drop. She'd find out what brought Sara to the point where she had to work in such a place and see what she could do to protect her while she stayed—which might not be long if the hints she'd gotten from the girl were true.

She knew fear when she saw it, and it didn't come from being a minute or two later than expected. Something was up, and Christy would get to the bottom of it, if it was the last thing she did.

* * * * *

Early the next morning Sara sat on the edge of her bed and gripped her stomach. The smell of food wafted up the stairs and drifted under the edge of her door. Hunger should be tugging her downstairs, but revulsion took its place. The night manager had insisted she entertain yet another visitor to her room and he'd been rougher than most. She rubbed the bruised flesh of her upper arms and winced. A sudden queasiness shot her from the bed and sent her racing for the chamber pot in the corner. She knelt on the floor and retched. When she finished, she sat back on her heels and whimpered. This was the fifth time in the past two weeks she'd been sick.

Sara had a horrible, sinking feeling she knew what this meant, and it wouldn't be good. Girls in her condition got sent to a doctor who had no scruples, or they ended up in the street if not discovered before it was too late. Horror and shame threatened to suffocate her. All her life she'd wanted nothing more than a good man to love her and a family of her own. Never had she imagined she'd find herself in such a compromising position because of events beyond her control. Right now, all she wanted was her mother…and a way to escape.

* * * * *

Nevada pushed away from the supper table at the Russ House the following night and sighed with satisfaction. Nellie told the truth about having a good cook. He'd have to straddle his horse and ride herd a few hundred miles or he'd be too soft to do much. The menu had quite a variety on a Sunday, when the dining room was open to the public. They had their choice of roast duck, mutton, short ribs, or pork with sides of applesauce, mushroom sauce, biscuits, three types of vegetables, and a table full of desserts. His favorite had drawn him for seconds—green apple dumplings—but the pie, New York plum pudding, and cake had been just as tempting.

His thoughts turned from food to the last time he'd been in the Oriental Saloon. For the past three days he'd resisted the temptation to swing by and see if Christy were there. She mentioned she'd been looking for a job, but he'd never believed she'd stoop so low....

He jerked back hard on his thoughts before they could run away with him. There was no proof she'd taken work there, and besides, it wasn't his place to judge. What's more, he hadn't lived any kind of clean, upright life for the past few years. But she'd seemed different somehow than the other women he'd met in those joints. With her ma sick and brother hurt, maybe she didn't have a choice. He shoved away from the table, a sudden thought propelling him to the kitchen doorway.

Nellie stacked dirty dishes next to a large pan of steaming water, her sleeves rolled up to her elbows. She reached up with the back of her hand and pushed away a stray curl drooping over her forehead. "What can I do for ya?"

Nevada leaned his hip against the doorjamb and stuffed his hands in his pockets. "I know you've got a great cook, but you still seem to have a lot of work to do."

"Yes, it does get to be a bit of a pull at times, but I'll make it." She blew at the curl, but it didn't budge.

"I have this friend...." Maybe he should have checked with Christy first. After all, she might be working at the Oriental now and be happy with her new job. He shook his head and pushed on. "There's a woman I know who might need a job. I don't know if you want to take someone else on, but I thought—"

"Ya were right to ask. It's a wonder I've kept me sanity these past couple days with things bein' so busy and all." Her Irish brogue thickened. "Men comin' and goin' at all hours with the different shifts at some of the mines, and all the cleanin' and bed changin'."

He straightened, new hope surging through his heart. "So you might want her to come by?"

"Send her if she's interested. I'd be happy to chat with the lass." She returned to her work.

"Thanks, Nellie. You're the best." He turned to leave, then swung back around. "I don't know the lady well, so I'm not sure if this would suit her, but she mentioned she was looking for a job."

"Happy to oblige. Get along with ya now, so I can be done for the night."

He walked out of the kitchen, hope bubbling in his heart. If things worked out, Christy Grey might be here in the next couple of days. Maybe God cared a little bit after all. Of course, he hadn't bothered to pray about this, and didn't really want to, but he was willing to toss God some of the credit just the same.

Chapter Fourteen

....

Nevada placed the hot horseshoe on the anvil and hammered it into the desired shape, wishing John was here. His boss was feeling poorly but insisted he'd return tomorrow to help get caught up. Nevada didn't care so much about the extra work, but he'd sure like someone to talk to. He'd gone to the Oriental twice in the past three days since talking to Nellie. He'd tried more than once to talk to Christy, but Doc Holliday stood between her and the crowd and frowned on any man who attempted to get close. Part of him rejoiced that she had a protector from the throng, but frustration rode him hard that she'd taken a position in a saloon.

And here he'd thought God might care about one small aspect of his life. Right. He couldn't remember the last time God had intervened in a meaningful way.

He tossed the hammer to the side and set down the horseshoe. A variety of sizes lay in a neat stack where he'd placed them, and he'd earned a break. A black horsefly buzzed around his head, and he swatted it away. The chair John used was perched too close to the fire for comfort. The closing days of May had brought soaring temperatures. The middle of the day often hit ninety. Nevada hated working over the hot fire hammering out shoes.

Drawing the chair into the deep shade, he sank down for a few minutes of rest, his mind returning to the problem before him. Was this about his desires and needs, or Christy's? He'd like to see her working at Nellie's place, but what if Christy didn't care to change jobs? Besides being beautiful she had integrity, something he valued above most other character traits. She'd kept her word and not turned him over to the law, not even after Wells Fargo offered a reward for the capture of the gang. She could've made some easy money, but apparently it hadn't tempted her.

A sound at the open door turned him toward it, his back stiffening. His hand slipped toward his gun but fell back into his lap as John limped into the yard. "What you doing here, man? Your wife was supposed to keep you home in bed."

"Aw, shucks. I'm not that poorly to stay abed all day. Needed some fresh air." John drew in a deep breath through his nostrils and grinned. "Love the smell of hot metal and horses." He rubbed his hands together and sank into a nearby chair. "Smells like cash money to me."

Nevada chuckled and shook his head. "Good thing I'm done for the day, so you won't be tempted to tire yourself more."

"Thought you might like some company. We talked awhile back and I been studyin' on some of what you told me."

"About what?" Nevada put his feet up on a nail keg and leaned back.

"After you shot that last fella, you said you got sick to your stomach and wanted to quit."

"Yeah. More than anything."

"So what you wantin' to do instead? Got any plans?"

"I'd like to have my own ranch and maybe a wife and kids someday, but I can't see that happening."

John plucked a piece of straw from a nearby bale and put it between his teeth, wallering it from side to side. "Why not? You're a handsome young fella. Can't see you'd have any trouble findin' a woman willin' to marry you."

Nevada exhaled. "Don't think a decent one would want me with my past."

"Mind tellin' me how it all started? Just so I have a handle on things, if you know what I mean."

"Sure." Nevada placed his foot on the bottom rail of the corral fence and draped his arm over the top one. "It's not something I talk about, but I trust you, John."

"And I won't betray your trust, son."

"I know." Nevada had tried to bury the past and leave it there, but somehow it always managed to rise from the dead and track him down. Maybe bringing it out in the open and facing it would make a difference somehow. "Years ago I was engaged to a wonderful young woman. We planned to marry as soon as I graduated from seminary."

"Seminary? You're a man of the cloth?" John's leg propped on the bale of straw thumped to the ground as he sat upright and winced. "Ouch. Guess it's not doin' as good as I thought."

Nevada grinned. "You're just getting old and soft."

John flexed the muscles in one of his huge arms and grinned. "I can take you any day, young man. Now get on with your story."

Nevada's smile faded as the memories rushed back. "That was my plan. Mostly attending seminary was my parents' idea, but I didn't have anything else pulling at me. It was as good a job as any, so I applied and got accepted."

John frowned. "That's not a good reason to enter the ministry. You got to believe in God your own self and want to serve Him with your whole heart. Otherwise, the job will eat you up and spit you out."

"Yeah. Well, I believed in God and even loved Him—to some degree. And I thought it was a good calling." The old familiar anger stirred in his heart, and he dropped his head to keep it from showing. "Until God took my Marie."

"Took her, you say? How's that?"

"Pneumonia. She died shortly after."

"Ah, too bad. I'm sorry. But what's that have to do with killin' a man?"

Nevada felt the pain that had dulled over the years but never quite disappeared. He'd often wondered what life would have held for him if Marie had lived. "I left seminary."

"To take a church?" The blacksmith scratched his head.

"No. That was the last thing I wanted. God didn't care enough to save Marie, and I didn't want to serve a God who'd take a beautiful young woman with her whole life ahead of her. I walked away. Then my younger sister left home when she was sixteen, yearning for adventure. She landed in a dance hall and gambling den. I found her there two months later."

"Ah. Now the picture is takin' shape." John wagged his head. "You took her back home?"

"Yes. But not until I shot the man who abused her when he drew on me. After that, I didn't figure God would want anything to do with me, even if I wanted to return to Him. So I got a job riding herd on a cattle drive from Texas to Colorado. A man in one of the towns recognized me as the one who'd shot my sister's boss and called me out. Told me to shoot or die. I decided to shoot. I'm not sure why I'm still alive. He got his gun out first, but he shot too fast and his bullet missed. Mine didn't."

"So things went south from there, I take it?" John shifted his weight on the stool and massaged his leg.

"Yeah. I figured I'd better start practicing my draw if I wanted to live. It's a good thing I did. But I hated the life and still do. There's nothing about it I want any part of—not the killing, the reputation, or the constant moving from place to place."

"What now? You stayin' here or movin' on again?"

"I hope to stay, but I don't know. I've been saving money for years and have a pretty decent stash put aside for a ranch. I'd planned on buying something around Albuquerque, but that didn't happen."

"Someone else call you out?"

"Yes. I told him to back down. Begged him to walk away. But they never listen. They're so sure they'll be fast enough." Nevada shrugged. "What they don't realize is what kind of life they'll inherit when they kill me. It's not something I'd wish on anyone."

"Where does God figure in all of this?"

Nevada scowled. "He doesn't. Not as far as I'm concerned, anyway. He's not done me any favors over the years."

"I think you're missin' a mighty important fact, son."

"Yeah? What?"

"You're still alive." John let the words linger on the air for a moment before he continued. "That's not a coincidence in my way of thinkin'. I'd say God's got some kind of purpose for you, whether you like it or not. Maybe it's time you started ponderin' that and gettin' your life in order."

Nevada dropped his feet from the nail keg and stood. "I'm alive because I'm faster with a gun than anyone who's challenged me." He picked up a horseshoe. "We've jawed long enough. I'd best get back to work."

"Thought you said you was done with work."

"I've got some things I can do, if it's all the same to you."

John pushed to his feet and stretched. "Sure. Guess I'll mosey on home and see if the wife's missed me yet." He walked toward the door, then turned. "Want you to know I'll be prayin' for you. God ain't done with you yet." He walked out the door and didn't look back, but a jaunty whistle drifted in through the doorway.

It had been years since Nevada had prayed, and he wasn't sure he even remembered how. He didn't care about himself at the moment, no matter what John said, but something about Christy's plight urged him to try. How many times in years past had he begged God for an answer that would only benefit *him*? Grief washed over his heart, and he dropped his head into his hands. He needed to set aside his desires and petition the Almighty for someone else.

"God, if You still care, would You help Christy? I'm not asking for me, but because I'm concerned about her. Please." He raised his head. It was the best he could do, but a gentle peace touched his spirit.

* * * * *

Anger clogged Christy's throat, and she allowed the emotion to swell. "Get off me, you drunken lout." She gripped the roughened hands of the miner latched around her waist and tugged, but they didn't loosen. Gratitude toward Gordon Townsley for convincing her to wear high-heeled shoes swamped her. She lifted her foot and came down hard on the man's instep. He let out a howl, dropped his arms, then fell to the floor, unable to stand in his inebriated state.

Buckskin Frank Leslie bent over the prostrate man and jerked him to his feet, pinning his arm behind him. "Sorry, Miss Christy, for not gettin' here sooner. I'll have one of the men walk you to the wheel from now on if you need to leave."

"Let go a'me. I ain't gonna hurt the lady. Just wanted a little kiss, that's all. Ain't that why you got these girls?" the man blubbered as the grip on his arm tightened.

Leslie shook his head and shoved the man toward the door. "You're not welcome here anymore, mister. Take your business somewhere else." A hard push and Leslie delivered the miner outside. He turned and made his way back to Christy. A wide space had formed around her, and Doc Holliday stood at her side. "It won't happen again, Miss."

"Thank you." She turned away, clutching her hands in the folds of her skirt to hide their shaking. The past week manning the roulette wheel and fending off the advances of drunken miners had been harder than she'd expected. Old emotions of revulsion threatened to choke her. Disgust at the position she'd agreed to take in this place grew daily. Sure, either Doc or Wyatt, or one of the other gun hands like Frank Leslie, hovered on the fringes most of the time, but there was always at least one episode per day when some man pushed the limit.

The doors opened again, and Christy glanced that direction, wondering if the miner had decided to try again. A familiar figure stepped through, and Christy's pulse quickened. *Nevada*. He'd pulled his flat-brimmed hat low over his forehead, but she could still see his eyes searching the room, peering into every corner. He carried the look of a careful—or a hunted—man. She'd seen it before over the years. Someone who had no cares entered with long, free strides, heading directly for the bar or game table of their choice. Others, like Nevada, lingered and made sure of the room before stepping too far inside.

She hadn't seen him for several days, other than at a distance a couple of times while working the wheel. Part of her hoped he'd decided to leave town, but an even stronger part prayed he hadn't. She detested being drawn to an outlaw, and worse, to a man who frequented women of the night. His gaze moved from the bar to where she stood. Their eyes met above the heads of the seated gamblers. A hot jolt struck her in the chest. Something danced in his eyes that she couldn't quite fathom. It took an effort to tear her gaze away and turn back to the job at hand. What was he doing here? At least one time she'd sensed him trying to approach her, but her bodyguards had kept the space around her clear.

Christy turned to Doc and touched his arm.

The slender man bowed. "You need something, Miss?"

"Yes. That man across the room took my brother home when he was injured." She struggled with an excuse she could give that would convince the gambler to allow her a few minutes with Nevada. "He's come to our house to check on him and bring water a couple of times, and I think he may have a message from my mother. Do you mind if I speak to him briefly?"

Holliday looked across the room to where she indicated and stared at Nevada for several long seconds without speaking. His hand slowly dropped to his waist and settled an inch away from his gun.

Prickles ran up Christy's spine and she stood still, almost not daring to move. Finally, she stepped closer to Doc. "He's all right, I promise."

The man relaxed and his arms dropped to his sides. "Go ahead. I'll be right behind you."

Christy felt the gunman's presence as she wove between the tables toward Nevada. She took a quick look over her shoulder and saw Doc positioned a couple of yards back, his hands folded across his belt. Stopping in front of Nevada, she looked up into his eyes, her heart racing. The man had strength in his face and in the set of his shoulders. Not only physical strength, but something deeper— she was drawn in spite of herself.

Nevada glanced around before returning his attention to her. "I was hoping you'd find time to let me speak to you, Miss Grey."

"In here, it's Christy. Is something wrong at home? Did you bring word from my mother or brother?"

He appeared startled. "No. Did you expect me to?"

"I thought…" Christy swallowed and tried to gather her wits as she continued to gaze into those dark depths. "Since you were bringing us water, I thought maybe my mother had sent a message."

"I didn't see her. I rarely do." He folded his arms across his chest. "I came to tell you I found you another job, if you want it."

She stiffened and resisted the urge to look behind her. The noise level was too high for Doc to hear their conversation, but she kept her voice low in case. "I have a job."

"I know, but I figured, well…maybe you might be looking for something else."

"Like what?" Hope that he that he cared surged inside, but she pushed it down. "I've been everywhere in this town and couldn't find work." She waved her hand at the noisy room. "I don't entertain men, but what I do pays well enough. Apparently I'm not suited for much else."

She hated the sarcasm that tinged her voice. At least she hadn't been forced into what Sara and some of the other girls were expected to do. Not yet, anyway.

Nevada narrowed his eyes. "I don't agree. You're an intelligent woman."

Christy emitted a grim laugh. "Thanks, but business owners care about reputation over intelligence." She raised her chin and met his gaze squarely. "Besides, shouldn't you be offering this job to Sara?"

"Sara?" He frowned. "I don't get it."

"I saw you escort her to her room the first night I was here." Christy watched his face, certain she'd see guilt or shame flash across it.

He held her gaze without wavering. "Yes, I did. But nothing happened."

She sniffed. "Of course it didn't." She gave a wry smile. "Most men would brag about their conquest, but not you. Always the gentleman, as well as the liar. First you're not an outlaw, even though you're present at a stagecoach holdup, and now you simply escorted a girl to her room after outbidding another man for her favors. But nothing happened." She smirked. "Right."

"Ask her." He folded his arms across his chest.

"What?" A slight shock coursed through her at the blunt words. Where was the cocky attitude she'd expected, if not embarrassment or confusion?

"Ask Sara. She'll tell you I didn't touch her."

"Then why…?"

"To keep that low-down scum from bothering her. She was ill and in obvious distress."

"So you came to her rescue like some gallant knight?" Christy struggled to keep her voice from shaking. Everything in her wanted to believe him, but she'd been fooled before. Five years ago a handsome face and smooth manner had nearly destroyed her. Not this time. She clasped her hands so tightly her nails dug into her skin.

He shrugged. "Something like that." And then he grinned. "Like I said, ask Sara. For now, I want you to know there's a job waiting for you at the boardinghouse where I'm staying if you want out of this place."

Her heart did a somersault—his cocky grin and lifted brow gave him a rakish air. He'd be hard for any woman to resist, no matter how hardened she'd become. She gave a slight shake of her head. "I doubt they'd employ me."

"This place would. It's called the Russ House. It takes boarders and also has an excellent restaurant. "

"I stopped and spoke to the cook. He said they weren't hiring."

"He's not the owner. Nellie Cashman is, and she told me she could use more help."

Christy closed her eyes for a brief moment, then opened them. "She wouldn't hire me."

"Yes, she would."

"If Miss Cashman knew who my stepfather was, or where I'm working now, she wouldn't."

Nevada's jaw set in a stubborn line. "It won't matter to her. This woman is different. She helps people in need all the time, even the women in the red-light district. Besides, anyone can tell you're a lady, no matter where you work."

Joy bubbled in Christy's spirit, and she wanted to laugh out loud. Right now she didn't know whether she wanted to hug the tall man standing so straight and proud in front of her, or shake him. Red-light district, indeed. Then she remembered his words. She might have a job and could leave here forever—start fresh in a reputable business.

Then a flash of gold caught her attention. Sara walked across the room, a tray of drinks balanced on her hand. Christy's heart sank. "Please thank Miss Cashman for the offer."

Nevada followed her gaze. "It's Sara, isn't it?"

Her throat pinched closed, and tears welled up. "I'm not sure I can leave her here alone." The words came out in a whisper. "She's so young. I don't know her story but—"

"Christy." A firm voice spoke behind her and she whirled around. Gordon Townsley stood with his feet planted wide and fists resting on his hips. "You are neglecting your duties. I don't pay you to stand around fraternizing with the customers." He jutted his chin toward Nevada. "Especially when they're not paying ones."

It was all Christy could do not to quit on the spot, now she knew another job waited outside these four walls. She bit her lip and glanced at Sara as she walked by again. "I apologize, Gordon. I'll be right there." She turned her back on the manager and smiled at Nevada. "Thank you for bringing me word."

Townsley stepped to her side and held out his arm. "Allow me to escort you back to your table, Miss Grey." His stiff voice left little doubt as to the state of his mind.

She touched her fingers to the fabric but refused to hold on to his arm. This man didn't own her, and she wouldn't allow him to think he did. All she wanted right now was to get out of this dress and into her own clothing. March out this door and not look back.

But if she left, Townsley would make sure she never got close to Sara again. No, she'd bide her time a little longer and pray somehow her luck would turn.

* * * * *

Nevada watched Christy walk beside Townsley to the roulette wheel, wishing there was more he could do for Christy and Sara. Two lovely women, both trapped in a situation not of their liking, and more than likely, not of their choosing. He scanned the room, wondering what to do now. Head back to the Russ House and see if Nellie needed anything done? Or hang around here in case he might be of use to Christy or Sara?

A movement across the gambling floor caught his attention and he stared, not certain he believed what he saw. A big-boned man with a scar on his cheek pulled out a chair and sat at a table with another man already seated—two people he had reason to remember. He tugged his hat down over his eyes and sauntered closer, making sure to stay out of their line of sight. Curiosity nudged him on and he settled into a chair sitting back to back with Jake, the leader of the gang who'd robbed the stage.

At first the scraping of chairs, clink of coins, and low voices of gamblers playing poker and faro at nearby tables drowned out any hope of hearing the conversation behind him. He'd noted the intensity of the two men as he'd approached the table and hoped their focus would stay on whatever drew them here. After several minutes, Nevada tipped back his chair and managed to block out the noise surrounding him. He narrowed his concentration on the outlaw now less than a foot away.

A fist slammed down on the adjoining table, and a voice rose in irritation. "I don't care what you think, Jake, I need more money. This town's eatin' up every dime I got from the last job."

"Quiet." Jake hissed the words. "I've got somethin' in mind, but you got to keep shut about what I tell you. I'll need another man in on the job."

"Good." The first outlaw grunted his satisfaction. "I'll find somebody. When you gonna pull this off?"

"The shipment comes through in about ten days or so. Tell your friend to get in touch with me here, or over at the Golden Eagle."

"So what are we hittin'? What's my cut?"

Nevada strained to hear the answer, his pulse racing. If he could stop what appeared to be yet another holdup, he might be able to walk around town without fear of arrest. If either of these two were picked up for the stage robbery without his intervention, they might decide to implicate him in the deal.

Sara appeared next to his chair, carrying a tray laden with drinks. "Hi there, Nevada." A shy smile lit her pretty face. She leaned over and lowered her voice. "I know you don't drink this stuff, but I thought you might want to have a glass in front of you, just the same. The boss don't like it when men sit around takin' up table space without buyin' anything."

He tipped his chair forward and stifled a groan. Not the best timing. "Sure. Give me one of whatever you've got there." He dug into his pocket and pulled out a coin, tossing it onto her tray. "Thanks for watching out for me, Sara."

"Anytime, Cowboy." She set the glass of amber liquid in front of him and moved away.

The scrape of chairs at the adjoining table caused him to moan. He'd missed the chance to hear their plans. If he'd understood correctly, Jake hung out here and at the Golden Eagle, and wanted to meet the new member of the group. Looked like he'd have to frequent this saloon for the next few days and hope he could figure out what they were up to.

* * * * *

Christy had worked a longer shift than usual, hoping she'd find a moment with Sara. Finally it came. Most of the customers had cleared out, and the bartender bent over a table on the far side of the room, scrubbing it down. Doc Holliday, Frank Leslie, and Gordon Townsley were nowhere in sight when Sara started across the room and headed for the staircase.

The girl walked like a woman three times her age, her slow gait and slumped body indicating her fatigue. She didn't look back at the room but gripped the banister and hauled herself up the first step.

Christy moved swiftly to cover the distance and walked up beside her, touching Sara's hand.

The young woman gave a sharp start and recoiled. She turned frightened eyes on Christy, then released a sigh. "Oh. It's you."

"I'm sorry I worried you." Christy drew back a bit. "I wanted to tell you something, if you have a minute?"

"I'm awful tired." The dark circles under her eyes gave truth to her words.

"I won't keep you long."

"All right." Sara waved at a table below the staircase. "Did you want to sit?" Exhaustion tugged at her features.

"No. I'll walk you up, if that's okay?"

Sara hunched a shoulder. "Sure."

They traversed the stairs in silence and continued down the hall till Sara stopped outside a door. She turned weary eyes on Christy. "I need to ask you somethin' important."

"Of course, what is it?"

"Your brother, Joshua." Sara clasped her hands in front of her waist and twisted her fingers together. "Is he gonna be all right?"

"You know Joshua?" New interest sharpened Christy's gaze.

"Yes. He and I…that is…" A rosy blush colored her cheeks. "He used to come in and see me. He was the first man Townsley sent up for quite a while and…" She sighed and dropped her eyes.

Christy touched Sara's hand. "You care for my brother?"

The girl nodded without looking up.

"Does he feel the same?"

Sara risked a glance, then shrugged. "I thought so at the time, but I don't know for sure. Will he live, do you think?"

Christy's mind raced at this new revelation. Sara and Joshua. Tendrils of hope wove their way through her heart. Joshua had never been responsible for anyone or anything. Maybe caring about Sara would be good for her brother. "Yes. The doctor believes he'll make a full recovery."

"Good." A smile flashed across Sara's face, then disappeared. "What did you want to talk to me about?"

Christy extended her hand, wanting to hug the girl, but let it fall. She had no idea how her gesture would be received. They'd had so little time to talk since she'd arrived here. "To let you know I'm here for you. I want to be your friend, if you'll let me."

Sara's eyes turned wary. "Why? I'm not important."

"That's not true." Christy shook her head. "Like I told you when we first met, I understand and I care. That's all."

"You don't even know me." Sara reached for the door handle and gripped it tight.

"I know I don't, but I want to, especially if you care for Joshua." Should she tell the girl about the job offer? Practically every moment since Nevada shared the news with her, she'd thought about it, and wondered if there was any way Sara could work there too. Christy hesitated, then plunged forward. "I've been told about another job that doesn't require working a gaming table or serving drinks. Maybe I could ask if the owner would hire you too."

Sara released a sharp laugh. "Won't happen, Miss Christy. I got a bad reputation in this town. Men talk, you know." She dropped her gaze to the floor and scuffed a toe against the polished boards. "Thanks for askin', but I think I belong here."

Christy knew that look and her heart hurt in a way it hadn't in years. She'd seen her sister Molly give up after being subjected to men like the ones running this saloon. Why, even though she was a strong woman herself, she'd been prone to spells of doubt and despondency, wondering if there would ever be a way out. "I'm not in a hurry to leave, either. If I can help you in any way while I'm working here, I'd like to."

Sara gave a sharp bob of her head. "I don't know what kind of help you can give me, but I could use a friend. Thank you." A wistful look crossed her solemn features. "He said the same thing."

"He?" Christy's mind drew a blank. Could Sara be referring to her boss, Gordon Townsley, or someone else? Surely she couldn't mean...Nevada? Her thoughts raced to the claim he'd made about helping Sara. She'd tossed it aside at the time, assuming it to be yet another excuse for poor choices.

"The cowboy who stayed in my room that night. He came to protect me." With those words, Sara slipped inside her room, closing the door softly behind her.

Christy turned to go, alarm warring with elation in her breast. Nevada had told the truth. More than anything she wanted to leave this place and start over in a decent establishment. She wasn't even sure why lending a hand to Sara felt so important, but the emotion wouldn't be denied.

A picture of Joshua flashed before her mind. Rescuing Sara might convince her brother to make a decent life for himself, if he actually cared for the girl. Christy would have to find a way to get the young woman away from here first, although right now she didn't see how that could happen. She'd commit to staying at the saloon if that's what it took.

Her heart told her she'd chosen the right path, no matter how much it might hurt her to do so.

Chapter Fifteen
....

Christy slipped upstairs at the end of her long workday, wanting nothing more than to change from her gown and into her own simple attire before heading home. Three weeks of working in this place had dragged beyond measure. If only she could accept the offer at Nellie's boardinghouse, but that position must surely be gone after a week and a half. She blew out an exasperated breath as her thoughts turned to Sara. Gordon Townsley or one of his strong-armed men made sure the girls didn't interact during work hours, and it wasn't often Sara was around when Christy's shift ended. She'd barely spoken to the girl beyond an occasional sentence, but from what she'd been able to tell Sara didn't appear happy.

Christy paused outside Sara's room, wondering if she dared knock. The young woman had looked tired and almost bedraggled recently and could easily be sleeping. Christy moved on, but a disturbing noise slowed her pace. Sobs emanated from the other side of the door.

Christy retraced her steps, all hesitation gone. She rapped lightly and waited, then tried again a little harder.

A muffled voice came from the far side. "Go away. I'm not workin' now."

Christy dropped her hand to her side. "It's me. Christy. I won't bother you if you're tired."

Footsteps drew close and the door swung open. Sara peered out, her eyes swollen and red, with traces of tears still evident on her cheeks. She shook her head. "I'm sorry. I thought—" Another sob choked off her words and she stepped back, motioning Christy inside. "Please."

As soon as the door shut behind her, the dam broke. Sara flung herself at Christy as tears rained down.

Christy led the young woman to the edge of the bed, but Sara recoiled. They moved to the small settee pushed against the wall and sank onto the firm surface. "There, there. It can't be as bad as all that." Christy patted her shoulder, knowing full well her words were hollow. She'd seen some of the men the girl was forced to entertain and could only imagine the horrors Sara had endured.

Sara grabbed the hem of a skirt draped over the arm of the settee and wiped her cheeks. "I'm afraid it is. Worse in fact." She stood and dug through a drawer in the nearby bureau, withdrawing a handkerchief and blowing her nose.

Christy waited for her to return to her perch, then stroked the girl's blond curls. "Can you tell me what's bothering you?"

Sara's face crumpled again, but she forced herself to sit straighter. "I think—" She sucked in a deep breath. "I'm not sure how to say this." A faint flush crept into her cheeks. "I've been sick in the mornings for a while now."

"Do you need a doctor?" A faint sense of alarm shot through Christy.

Sara was quiet for a minute, then said, "I don't think so. Not for a few more months, anyway."

Comprehension dawned on Christy, and she leaned against the back of the settee, feeling as though she'd been walloped. "Oh, my. Oh, my!"

"I don't know what to do."

"Any idea when your little one will arrive?"

Sara winced and dropped her head. "I'm not sure, but I think maybe around Thanksgiving."

Christy jumped to her feet. "We have to get you away from here. You can't keep allowing these...*men*"—she spat the last word—"to paw you every night."

Sara shrank back as though she'd been slapped. "It don't happen every night, Miss Christy. Besides, I got nowhere else to go."

"Do you have any family who would take you?" Christy tried to calm the outrage swelling in her breast. She'd frightened the girl and possibly hurt her, which certainly wasn't her intent. How many times in past years had she seen this same scenario play out? Too often for her peace of mind.

Her head still bowed, Sara remained quiet for several moments, then murmured a soft negative. "They're all dead. 'Sides, they'd be so ashamed if they knew what I stooped to." A whimper stole past her parted lips. "I'm glad my ma didn't have to see me here. It would break her heart. There ain't nobody who cares anymore, not even God."

"I didn't mean to upset you," Christy soothed. "I know what happens to you isn't your fault." She stroked the young woman's hair.

Sara raised eyes that looked older than her seventeen years.

"Some friends I love very much told me something that might help. They said God always hears us, no matter what our circumstances, if only we'll call out to Him." Somehow speaking the words out loud made them feel real for the first time. Christy's heart beat faster, and a new sense of hope rose in her spirit.

Sara bit her lip. "That won't work for me. You got no idea some of the things they make me do here. I'm dirty, like an old dishrag left to mold next to the slop bucket. God won't take notice of me."

"But that's where you're wrong." Excitement colored Christy's voice, and she leaned forward, tucking a strand of hair behind Sara's ear. "Jesus loves everyone. Did you know He forgave the men who nailed Him to the cross? He said they didn't understand what they were doing."

"He did that?"

"Yes, I read it in the Bible."

Sara's shoulders slumped. "But I guess that's different. No reason for Him to forgive me when I knew it was sin to come to a place like this."

Christy struggled to find the words to explain. This was all so new to her. She'd heard sermons preached over the years but hadn't taken in a lot of what was said. She searched her memory in hopes of finding something to help. "You didn't have a choice, Sara."

"Don't matter. I still sinned."

A phrase Christy had heard popped into her mind. "Sara, none of us are perfect, but God loves us the way we are. He's the only one who can change us." Christy suddenly realized all the words she'd spoken to Sara were actually directed at herself. All these years she'd thought she had to be perfect to accept God's love. She thought she needed to clean up her life before God would want anything to do with her. Peace swept over her heart. All this time she was the one needing to be redeemed. In trying to help Sara, a door had opened in her mind and God's truth rushed in.

Sara looked confused. "Then why are you here?"

"What do you mean?"

"You told me that day on the street you used to work someplace like this years ago and you'd changed. If you believe all that about God and forgiveness, why did you come here? This is a bad place, full of sin and darkness. And believe me, Gordon Townsley won't keep you safe from it forever."

The room seemed to whirl as the starkness of her question left Christy speechless for a minute. Finally, she said, "My family needs the money." She whispered the words, but they left her feeling hollow inside. Had she tried hard enough to find something else, or had she returned to the one thing she knew because it was easy? Or could it be Ma's lack of belief in her that convinced Christy she'd never rise above her family name?

She'd fallen into the same trap many women had over the centuries—allowing someone else's poor opinion and circumstances to dictate her actions.

Christy wanted to rail against the injustice of this young woman's plight, while her intuitive side wondered if there could be a deeper reason she'd landed here. She touched Sara's cheek and turned the girl toward her. "Forgive me. I know you need money too."

Sara twisted her lips in a half smirk. "Yeah, that's what sends most of us girls to these places."

Christy leaned forward. "I think there's another reason I came that I'm beginning to understand. There's a lot I still don't know about God and the way He works, but I think He may have sent me here for you."

Sara's eyes widened. "What do you mean? He wouldn't do anything like that for me."

"But He would. I never saw it before. I always thought God forgave *good* people, but a friend told me He came to save sinners. I've seen and done some bad things, Sara—worse than what you've been through. All the things my friends told me are true. I didn't understand before." She shook her head. It had taken so many years of ignoring God, but He'd finally gotten her attention through this young girl. "God loves you. He really does."

Another thought hit harder than the first. "Sara." The word came out in a startled gasp. "God didn't send me here just for you, but for me too."

"Huh?"

Christy wanted to laugh with delight. "He loves me too. All this time—He's loved *me*." She felt a sense of wonder at the flashes of revelation bombarding her mind. She'd never accepted this truth in the past, always believing God's forgiveness and love were meant for people better than she.

"I'm tired, Miss Christy, and I don't feel so good." Sara clutched her hands to her middle, and beads of sweat broke out on her forehead.

Christy's stomach knotted with fear, and she jumped to her feet. "I'm going for the doctor. Come on, let's get you in bed."

"No. It'll pass; it always does. Please help me get under the sheet." A tear trickled down Sara's pale cheek, and her hand shook as she closed the neck of her dressing gown. "And if God loves me like you say He does, then I sure hope He'll keep men away from my room tonight." She stretched out on the bed with a sigh. "Oh, and Miss Christy?"

"Yes, dear?"

"There's something I should tell you."

Christy sank onto the edge of the narrow bed and picked up Sara's hand. "Only if you want to."

"I think your brother might be my baby's pa."

* * * * *

Hurrying across the darkened street lit only by the gas streetlights, Christy peered behind her, half afraid she might be followed. One of Townsley's thugs gave her a hard look as she exited Sara's room and made her way to slip into her own dress. Something had to be done about the girl's plight, and she could think of only one person who might help. Nevada. Thank God he'd told her he was living at the Russ House. Hopefully he wasn't frequenting a saloon tonight, and she'd find him at home.

Christy's mind kept trying to grasp the import of the news Sara had shared. She shouldn't be surprised at Joshua's actions and felt pity for the young woman. Learning that Sara had been with Joshua a number of times before any other men approached her and counting the months since then gave truth to the suggestion that the baby could be Joshua's. This revelation only deepened Christy's resolve to help Sara escape the degrading life she'd apparently accepted. She could only pray Nevada would be willing to help.

She turned off Allen Street and started down Fifth, walking past the now darkened Adolf Cohen's Clothing Store and an assortment of small shops until she reached the one-story adobe building on the corner of Fifth and Toughnut Street. Lights blazed from the windows of the Russ House, casting a welcoming glow. The fragrance of fine food wafted out the open front door, making her stomach grumble. Her mother would probably be worried and more than a little crotchety at her delay in arriving home, but she'd have to understand this once.

Pushing open the heavy door, Christy stepped into the wide foyer. She'd never been inside this new business. Her gaze strayed off to the left and a little beyond at the dining room, where a couple of young women cleared tables and swept the floor.

One of them made her way across to where she stood. "The dining room is closed, Miss. Do you need a room for the night?"

"No. I was wondering if…" She hesitated, suddenly struck by the inappropriateness of asking for one of the male boarders. "Would the owner be in by any chance?"

"Miss Cashman? Yes, ma'am. Would you like me to fetch her?"

"Thank you, I'd appreciate that." She stood by the front counter and waited, wondering what the woman who ran the place would be like.

Heels tapping across the floor alerted Christy of someone's approach. A diminutive woman entered the room, dark hair parted in the middle and piled on top of her head, blue eyes sparkling with warmth, and a smile that immediately put Christy at ease. She was as pretty as a Victorian cameo, and not many years older than herself. "Meg tells me ya asked to see me. I'm Nellie Cashman. How may I be of help?" Her words had the soft lilt of the Irish.

Christy released the breath she'd been holding and returned the smile. "Miss Cashman, I'm happy to meet you. My name is Christy Grey, and I—"

Nellie gave a small squeal of excitement and stepped forward, extending her hands. "Yer the young woman Mr. King mentioned might be wantin' a job. Oh, my. Yer lovely, and I'd be most pleased if you'd join us. And it's Nellie, not Miss Cashman, if ya please." She gripped Christy's hands in her own. "Is that why you've come to me, darlin'?"

"Well..." Christy's head swam from the onslaught of words headed in a different direction than she'd expected. She hadn't thought of the job when she'd come. The only thing on her mind had been saving Sara before something worse befell her. "I'm sorry. Mr. King?" She shook her head. "I don't know anyone by that name. I was hoping to see Nevada."

"King is his last name, dearie. James King. You didn't know?" The blue eyes peered intently at her.

"No." Something worrisome niggled at Christy's memory, but she pushed it aside for later inspection. "He introduced himself as Nevada, nothing more. It's important I speak to him if he's in and it's not too late." Sudden shame sent a flood of warmth to her cheeks as she realized she'd not expressed appreciation for the job offer. "And please forgive me for my thoughtlessness. I'd like to come another time and talk with you about accepting the job, if I may."

"Certainly, I'd love that. Now, let me see if Nevada is in his room." She bustled away, disappearing down a hallway on the right side of the entrance.

A few minutes later the woman reappeared with Nevada walking behind her. Nellie stepped aside and allowed him to pass, then excused herself and turned back the way she'd come.

Nevada didn't appear as though he'd been sleeping, but he rubbed his jaw and eyed Christy speculatively. "I'm surprised to see you here. You told me last time we spoke you didn't want to quit working at the saloon."

Christy gripped her hands in front of her waist. "I'm considering taking the job, but I came to see you, not Miss Cashman. It's about Sara," she blurted out.

His expression didn't change. "Can't say I'm too surprised. Something happen over at the Oriental?"

Christy's heart dropped to her stomach. She hadn't thought this through before coming. How could she tell a virtual stranger that a young woman they both barely knew was with child? That wasn't something a lady discussed with a man. Of course, she'd never claimed to be anyone special, and this situation demanded a different response than what society might expect. "Sara told me tonight she's in a family way…and it's possible the baby is Joshua's."

Nevada's jaw clenched. "Ah-huh. Does Townsley know?"

"I don't think so. I'm the first person she's told, but she's been sick in the mornings and wasn't feeling well when I left this evening."

"So it won't be long before he guesses."

"Yes."

Silence fell over the room as they stared at each other for several long heartbeats. Nevada was the first to break it. "What do you want to do?"

"I hoped you might help me get her out. I don't know how Townsley will react to her quitting, and she may need an escort."

Nevada leaned his hip against the doorjamb and crossed his arms. "Any idea where she'll go when she leaves?"

Christy bit her lip. "I haven't thought that far. My mother's house is tiny, and I've been bunking on the sofa, but I'll sleep on the floor if need be."

"There might be another solution." He gestured down the hall. "Take the job you were offered and move your family here."

"Here?" She frowned, not understanding why he'd suggest such a thing. "We have a home. But if Miss Cashman would consider allowing Sara to stay for a short time…"

"From what I've seen of Nellie, she's more than generous to those in need, and I'm guessing she'd welcome Sara. I'll be happy to ask her tomorrow." A warm smile reached his eyes and he clasped her hand, giving it a gentle squeeze. "Partners?"

A surge of blood leapt to Christy's cheeks and her fingers tingled. "I'm sorry?" She slowly withdrew her hand, amazed to discover a feeling of loss when she'd done so.

A spark of amusement glinted in his gaze, and a deep chuckle rolled out. "Don't worry, I'm not asking you to rob a stage with me. I meant partners in breaking Sara out of the Oriental Saloon as soon as you think she's willing to leave."

"Oh. Of course." She raised her palm to her hot cheeks and turned away, trying to quell her rapid breathing. "I'll talk to her at work tomorrow." She half-turned toward him again. "You can stop by if you'd like, and I'll try to speak to you. But if not, I'll get word to you at the blacksmith shop."

"All right. Good night…Christy."

She hurried out the door, her emotions doing battle with the feelings evoked by the way Nevada said her name. The warmth of his touch and caring in his voice almost drew her back. But Ma and Josh would be worried, and there was no time to dally. She'd done what she'd come for and enlisted his help.

James. How strange he went by *Nevada* instead of his given name. What had Nellie called him? *James King.* What a nice name.

She stepped off the boardwalk and hurried across Toughnut

Street toward her mother's small home. Then it hit her. No wonder his name was familiar. The telegram sent by Logan's cousin announcing he'd been shot had pointed at a man named King as the shooter. All this time Nevada claimed he'd been set up by the outlaws robbing the stage and pretended to care about Sara, when he'd been a gunfighter. She'd promised herself she'd never be duped by a man again and look what happened. He couldn't lie himself out of this one, no sir. No matter what her step-father had been, he didn't deserve to be gunned down in cold blood.

Chapter Sixteen

....

Nevada strode down the boardwalk late the following afternoon, intent on seeing Christy if he had to fight his way through a line of bodyguards. Holding her hand for even a brief moment last night had reawakened a longing for companionship he'd thought long dead. Not since the carefree days spent with his fiancée years ago had he been stirred in such a way.

He dodged a fast-moving team pulling an empty wagon and nearly collided with a man. A quick sidestep and he avoided plowing into him, but not before he got a glimpse of the shadowed face—Jake, the leader of the outlaws who'd robbed the stage. Nevada pivoted to watch the man as he moseyed across the street and entered the Golden Eagle Brewery, one of the swankiest saloons in town. He wavered for only a moment, casting a look at the Oriental Saloon on the corner across the street from the Golden Eagle. His business with Christy would have to wait a little longer.

Pulling open the heavy, solid-wood door, Nevada stepped inside the smoke-filled room, allowing his eyes to adjust to the dim light. Billiard balls clicked off to his immediate left and he glanced at the players, scanning their faces for the man called Jake. He turned his attention to the right, at the tables lined up against the brocade-covered wall where men sat eating and playing cards, but again, no one looked familiar. At the far end a raised stage with a heavy curtain covered most of the width of the room. Not much chance Jake would've headed that direction.

His gaze took in the most likely spot, the bar lining the wall to the far left. The shelves were stocked with every type of alcohol imaginable, and Nevada was certain most came with a hefty price. These miners and gamblers didn't stint on their liquor.

He walked to the end of the bar and surveyed the length, taking time to examine the features of each man standing or sitting in front of the counter. Not one was the man who'd robbed the coach. A glance revealed a door near the far end of the stage, probably leading into an office. Nevada's eyes narrowed and he took a step toward it, then paused. What was he going to do—ram his way in and demand to know what Jake was up to? Like as not, he'd end up with a bellyful of lead if he tried. No, the best thing to do was wait and hope he'd run across the man again. One thing was certain—the outlaw knew men of influence and had been walking around since arriving in town a few days ago without being caught.

The bartender sauntered down the bar to where he stood. "Hey, mister, what'll it be?" He plucked a glass from under the edge of the counter and thumped it on the smooth surface.

For the first time Nevada truly took in the drinking area lined with men lounging on stools or leaning against the gleaming wood surface. The magnitude and beauty of the carved bar amazed him, and he'd been in many a saloon in the West. Dark cherrywood spanned over half the length of the room, and much of the back piece was mirrored. The scrollwork around the mirrors looked to be hand carved, and a glass-fronted cabinet was built on either side of the centerpiece. Cut glass chandeliers hung from the ceiling, and gas flames worked to illuminate the long room.

Nevada took a half step back and raised his hand. "Nothing for me. Just looking for a friend. I'll be moseying along." Another glance down the length didn't reveal the man he sought, and he turned to go.

A gruff voice behind him spoke barely loud enough for him to hear. "You lookin' for the gent that slipped into the boss's office a few minutes ago?"

Nevada turned slowly, facing the man. His low-brimmed hat almost obscured his eyes, but the light from the room revealed prominent cheekbones and a strong chin. "Who wants to know?"

"Someone who might want to see the feller in question gets his due. That is, unless you're a friend of his."

"Might be, might not. What's he to you?"

The man leaned close and dropped his voice low enough so Nevada strained to hear over the noise in the saloon. "*Not* a friend if you get my meanin', but I won't say nothin' more till I know where you stand."

"You've shown your hand, so I'll lay down mine. He's of particular interest to me owing to a slight problem we had a couple of months ago."

The man jerked his head toward a table and headed that direction, pulling out a chair and dropping onto it. "Name is Tom Parks."

Nevada gave a nod of acknowledgment and extended his hand. "Nevada King."

A knowing light entered Tom's eyes, and he leaned forward, shaking his hand. "Late of Albuquerque?"

"Yes, although I don't plan on spreading it around."

"I heard about the shooting and knew Logan. The world didn't lose much when he cashed in his chips."

Nevada's gut wrenched. The last thing he wanted was to discuss a man he'd been forced to kill. "I didn't know him before he called me out. But you didn't haul me over here to talk about Logan Malone. What's your game where Jake's concerned?"

"Jake?" Tom slapped his leg and chuckled. "So that's the name he's goin' by in this burg, huh? I know him as Charlie Danvers, come up the trail from New Mexico, and before that, Old Mexico."

A scantily clad barmaid approached their table, a grin pasted on her painted face. "What can I get for you fellas?"

Tom quirked an eyebrow at Nevada, but he raised a hand. "Nothing for me, thanks. You go ahead, Tom."

He placed his order and turned back to the table. "I need you to answer one question before I say anything more. Are you the law?"

Nevada nearly choked on a laugh. "Good night, man. I shot a man in Albuquerque and you ask if I'm the law?"

Tom grinned. "Never know these days. Look at Bat Masterson, Wyatt, and Virgil Earp. All of them been in shootin' scrapes, and they've all been lawmen of one sort or another. So you're denyin' it, then?"

"I am. My beef with Danvers is personal."

"Good enough. Would it have anything to do with a certain Wells Fargo shipment disappearing from the stage awhile back?"

Nevada leaned back in his chair. "What makes you ask?"

"Just a hunch. You said somethin' happened between you and him a couple of months ago. A stage got hit around that time and four armed bandits confiscated a shipment of gold. Danvers has been known to hit Wells Fargo shipments and always works with one or two other men, but rarely three. He don't much like to share." He squinted at Nevada for several seconds. "But somehow you don't look the type to be in on that job."

"I wasn't. What's this all about?"

"I got a reason to hunt Danvers I don't care to share yet, but I'd like to see him pay for what he's done. Figured if you're half the man I think you to be, you might like to throw in together."

Nevada looked Tom Parks over more closely, liking what he saw. His hat sat back on his forehead and dark, blue-gray eyes met his squarely. He appeared to be close to Nevada's age, probably nearing thirty, and no trace of dissipation had touched the square jaw and clear skin. Tom might have been a cowboy, a rancher, or some other type of hard-working businessman, but he was no gambler, drunk, or miner. Something in his gut told Nevada to trust him. "You got a plan?"

Tom shook his head, his dismay apparent. "Not yet. I hit town a couple of days ago and been scoutin' around, hopin' to find Danvers. Now that I have, I'll wait and see what develops."

"He's trying to put together another job. I overheard him talking to a man in the Oriental Saloon not long ago."

"Any idea what it might be?"

"No, but I hope to find out."

"Good enough. Where you bunkin'?"

"At the Russ House."

"All right." Tom stood and stuck out his hand. "I'll look you up if I hear anything. Keep your ear to the ground, and I'll do the same. I'm at the San Jose Lodging House, corner of Fremont and Fifth."

Nevada shook the proffered hand and turned to go. Time to see Christy and hopefully help her get Sara out of that miserable place she called home.

* * * * *

Christy paused in front of Ma's house. A lamp glowing in the living area revealed an empty room. She was thankful no one was up and awaiting her return. Joshua grew better by the day but still spent much of his time in bed, and lately Ma's cough had eased a bit. How long that would last Christy couldn't say, but at the moment she didn't require constant care.

Christy pushed open the door—she didn't care for this place. It was too close to the mines and only a stone's throw from the red-light district. Not that she didn't hurt for the women who lived there, especially those who'd hit tough times and were forced to ply their trade from their homes. But the occasional shrieking laughter, drunken men's voices, and the chug of the engines at the mine often kept her awake at night far past the time she should be asleep. She'd never understood how she'd managed to avoid the trap so many of these women found themselves in, but now she realized God had been involved.

Too bad she hadn't gotten a chance to speak to Sara, but she admitted to a certain relief at not being needed late tonight. Apparently Townsley had promised work to a friend and put the man on the roulette wheel halfway through her shift.

Her thoughts drifted back to Sara. If only she had a way of reaching more of these girls—helping them to see there were other options than contracting diseases and dying of pneumonia or consumption in the dirty hovels they called home. But in reality, what choice did they have? She'd heard horrible stories over the years of men selling their wives into prostitution when they thought it would make them big money, and other girls lured by the promise of riches, only to discover the empty, hollow life they'd attained. An occasional woman chose this life and often went on to become a madam, but most grew hard or died young.

Christy knew how difficult it was for these women to gain any kind of respectability. If Alexia and Justin hadn't championed her in Last Chance, and if Miss Alice hadn't given her a job, she'd probably have left town as an outcast and pariah. What hope did a young woman ever have of finding a job to support her aside from the only one she knew? A few girls accepted marriage proposals and found a new life, but from Christy's experience, that could almost be as dangerous as working in a saloon. Most of the men who'd proposed to her over the years were hard-working, but a girl couldn't know what life she was headed for until after she'd arrived.

A footstep from the direction of her mother's room woke her from her thoughts. Ma stood in the doorway holding an oil lamp. Her pallor stood in sharp contrast to the darkness behind her and almost matched the pale nightgown she wore. She stared at Christy, then swayed on her feet.

Christy rushed across the living area and took the lamp before it toppled to the floor, setting it on the nearby table. She placed her arm around her mother and led her toward the sofa, helping her to sit. "Why are you out of bed? Are you feeling ill again?"

Ma covered her mouth with the back of her hand and bent low

over her lap. A long cough shook her body, and she struggled to get her breath.

Christy loosened her hold and headed for the kitchen. "I'll get some water."

"No." Ma's sharp tone brought her to a halt. "I'm all right now. I need to talk to you."

"Can't it wait till morning? You need to get in bed."

When Ma shook her head, Christy settled herself next to her mother.

"No." Ma looked even older than she had this morning, if that were possible. Deep creases ran along her cheeks and carved gouges in her forehead. "That banker came again today." She nearly spat the words. "We have to be out in a week."

"What?" Disbelief coursed through Christy. "But I made a payment right after I started working."

"It's not enough. He said we're too far behind, and he has a cash buyer for the place. Unless we can come up with the same amount his buyer is offering, we can't stay past week's end."

"Does he know you're ill and Joshua was shot?" Disbelief was quickly changing to despair. She'd worked so hard to keep this from happening. Why had she thought, moments ago, she had answers for anyone else?

"He don't care. Said there's lots of hurtin' and sick people in Tombstone, and it's none of his business to look out for them all."

"I'll find a way to get us out of this, Ma."

Trust Me. The words whispered themselves in her mind, but Christy pushed them away. She'd always looked out for herself. Ma had been too busy scrambling to make a living or caring for her husband to think much about Christy's needs, even when she was a youngster. During the years she'd spent working in saloons, Christy had learned to be tough and fight for survival. Only her four years spent under the loving care of Miss Alice, Alexia, and a couple of other close friends had helped soften the crust she'd allowed to grow over her heart.

I can be trusted. Again the words pricked at her spirit and this time she hesitated, turning them over in her mind, recalling the acceptance she'd felt while talking to Sara. Nellie had offered her a job and opened a way of escape—that could've only come from God.

On the other hand, she'd hoped Nevada might be a man she could lean on. But since discovering his last name and the possible tie to the death of her stepfather, she wasn't so sure he could be trusted. In years past, she'd always viewed God as not much more trustworthy than a man, but she'd recently come to understand His love for her. Maybe it was time to trust someone other than herself, and if God was offering, she'd take Him up on it.

* * * * *

The atmosphere at the Oriental Saloon was rollicking this time of night, and Nevada had a hard time pushing through the men grouped around the bar and the various gaming tables. He could see the roulette table, but a man he didn't recognize ran the game. A quick survey of the area didn't reveal either Christy or Sara nearby.

Weaving his way back to the bar, he leaned a forearm on the

polished surface and beckoned to the bartender. The man moved his way. "What'll you have?"

"Where's that pretty little blond named Sara? I'd like to talk to her." Nevada pasted on a sappy smile.

The bartender polished the glass he was holding and set it down in front of Nevada. "Yeah, you and half the town. The boss keeps that one busy." A coarse laugh sprang from his mouth. "Haven't seen her for the last hour or so, if you get my drift." He wagged his brows at Nevada.

"I get it just fine." Nevada's hand snaked out, and he gripped the front of the man's shirt, drawing him close. He waited several seconds until the face only inches from his turned red. "I suggest you watch your mouth if you value your hide."

"What's she to you?" The man gasped out the words.

Nevada shoved him away. "A friend." He reached down and touched the butt of his gun. "Where's Miss Grey? The woman who usually works the roulette wheel?"

The man backed out of Nevada's reach, his eyes growing wide. "Don't know nothin' about her. Boss keeps the men away from her. I think he's got his eyes on her his own self."

Nevada leaned forward, but the bartender scurried away, stopping partway down the bar to speak to a man leaning his elbow against the edge. Words were exchanged that Nevada was unable to hear. The stranger threw Nevada a hard look before sauntering his way.

Swiveling on his heel, Nevada stalked across the room, casting another look at the roulette wheel. Still no sign of Christy or Sara. Something was up and he didn't like it, but starting a fight tonight would only get him thrown in jail. Besides, this place was notorious for keeping an eye out for offenders and barring their entrance at the door. Best to leave now and come back tomorrow.

And in the meanwhile, he'd pray Christy and Sara were safe for the night.

Chapter Seventeen
....

Christy had avoided Nevada for just over a week since discovering his last name, but doubt hammered at her door. What proof did she have that he was the man who'd shot her stepfather, even if he did share the same last name? She'd asked for his help, but when he'd come to the Oriental, she'd ignored his attempts to speak to her.

Sara's situation grew worse by the day, and while Christy had determined to help her on her own, she'd begun to see the foolishness of her decision. Townsley's men kept watch over the girls, and she'd discovered threats kept them from running when they did find time to themselves. Maybe she'd been foolish to judge Nevada without giving him the opportunity to explain.

It wouldn't be long before Sara's condition made itself apparent, and they couldn't take the chance the baby might be harmed. Maybe she could catch Sara today before things got too busy, if the watchdogs in the saloon weren't dogging her trail.

Christy pushed through the saloon doors and threaded her way through the tables, thankful to see the room quieter than normal. There was no sign of Sara downstairs, and Doc Holliday seemed deeply engrossed in a game of cards. Buckskin Frank Leslie wasn't present either, and Christy gave a sigh of relief.

Then someone gripped Christy's elbow, and she whirled around. Gordon Townsley raised a hand in apology. "Sorry, my dear. Didn't mean to startle you. There's been a change of plans for you this evening."

"In what way?" Christy lifted her chin and met his eyes, not allowing the dread rising inside to show.

"I need to keep my friend working the roulette wheel for a couple more days. You'll work the tables." He pasted on a conciliatory smile. "Don't worry. It won't be for long."

Christy shook her head. "I wasn't hired to take drink orders, and I have no desire to do so."

"I'm sorry, but you don't have a choice."

She crossed her arms over her chest. "Of course I do."

"I advanced you more money than you've earned so far. You still owe me for a week." He tilted his head toward the staircase. "You can wear your same dress, but you'll be working the tables." Townsley swung on his heel and stalked off to his office.

Christy's mouth went dry, and her hands trembled. She felt like a mouse caught in the claws of a playful cat. The idea of serving drinks sickened her to the point of feeling faint. Somehow she'd have to get through this week and pay back what she owed, and then she'd be done. Her resolve to help Sara escape doubled, and an added urgency of her own pushed her forward.

She picked up her pace and mounted the stairs, praying she'd find Sara in her room. As she rounded the corner, a door clicked shut and hurrying footsteps came toward her.

Sara stepped into view, and a wan smile lit her tired face. "Christy. You're early. I'll walk with you if you're going to change now."

"Thank you. I was hoping for a chance to speak to you before starting work."

They fell into stride together and passed down the hall, entering the wardrobe room. Thankfully, all the men knew this space was off limits.

"You've got to get out of here, Sara," Christy murmured. "Tell Townsley you're quitting."

"What? He'll never let me."

"What choice will he have if you walk out the door and don't come back?"

"I owe him money. Besides, I think he's had his eye on me for a while now."

"How so? He farms you out to every man with the price to pay."

Sara sank onto a chair, rubbing her belly. "Not lately. He's been turnin' them down and only lettin' me serve drinks. I never thought much of it, but there's somethin' different about the way he looks at me, and it scares me a little. It's not the look of a man who loves a woman, neither. I know that look of love from how my pa used to look at my ma."

"All the more reason to leave." Christy clutched Sara's hand, giving it a gentle squeeze. "I've decided to take the job at the boardinghouse. Townsley says I owe him money, and he wants me to start serving drinks. I'll do it until I can get you out of here, then I'll pay him back out of my wages at the boardinghouse if I still owe him. I spoke to Miss Cashman at the Russ House, and she's a wonderful lady. Nevada thinks she'd give you work, as well."

"Nevada? What's he got to do with this?"

"He offered to speak to Nellie about you. He lives at the Russ House and told me about the job."

A spark of hope ignited in Sara's eyes. "I'll do it. Tonight when I get off work, I'll tell Gordon I'm quittin'. I'll pay him back everything I owe him when I start work somewhere else." She pushed to her feet and held out her arms. "Thank you, Christy, for believin' in me. Maybe somethin's gonna go right in my life for a change."

* * * * *

Sara paced the floor, waiting for Gordon Townsley. A sense of expectancy mixed with dread pounded her emotions, and she gripped her hands, trying to still their shaking. What would she do if Gordon said no? He'd seemed amiable enough when she'd asked him to meet her here, and she hoped that meant he was in a good mood.

A tap at her door made her pause. She reached for the handle and pulled it open, apprehension causing her insides to quiver.

Gordon stood there, hat in his hands and his eyes glowing with something she'd seen too often before. "Hello, darlin'. I've been waiting for you to invite me to your room." He stepped inside and pushed the door shut behind him. "Of course, if you'd waited much longer, I probably would've invited myself." A low, guttural chuckle broke from his throat, and he stroked his chin. "You look particularly fetching tonight."

Sara took a step back, her legs bumping into a chair. She slid around it and gripped the top rail, holding it like a barricade between them. Why hadn't she thought to approach her boss in his office, instead of inviting him here? "I...I didn't ask you here for that reason, Gordon. I want a favor."

"Ah, yes. I do a favor for you, and you do one for me. Is that the way it works?" A playful gleam sparkled in his eyes. "Name it, and I'll see what I can do." He reached for the top button of his white shirt.

"No." Sara held up her hand. "Wait. Please. Hear me out?"

His fingers paused. "Go ahead." The words were uttered in a low, flat tone.

"I want to quit workin' here." She was appalled at the way the words blurted out with little or no finesse. "I mean, I've been thankful for this job and all, but I'd like to quit seein' men and servin' drinks all the time. I'm sick of havin' them paw at me." Her hand went to her abdomen and halted there.

"Quit? You can't quit." He scowled. "You owe me money."

"I know." She reached out a hand, palm up. "But I'll get another job and pay you back. I swear."

"That's right. You will." He grabbed her wrist and yanked her towards him, landing her hard against his chest. "I don't know where you got this crazy idea to leave, but it's not going to happen. You belong to me, and you'd better not forget it."

"You're hurtin' me, Gordon." Sara tried not to whimper, but the cruel grip on her wrist tightened, and she let out a sob. "Please." She tried to pull away, but he simply drew her closer, leaning down his head to capture her lips.

Fury at the loss of her dream exploded inside, and she twisted her head, evading the pressure of his mouth. "Stop it! I don't want you to touch me. Leave me alone!" She pulled back and struck him in the face with the flat of her hand.

Townsley's hands dropped from her body and he cursed—a low, growling curse that frightened Sara more than his recent actions. "Is that how you want this to go?" He drew back his arm and swung it, his open hand connecting with her cheek with a force that sent her reeling against the bed. He took a step forward and stood over her, panting in rage and raining oaths down on her helpless body.

Sara cowered on the bed, covering her head with one hand and shielding her belly with the other. She tasted blood as it oozed from her split lip but ignored the pain. Only one thing mattered right now. "Don't hurt my baby. Please, don't hurt my baby." The words slipped out before she realized she'd released them.

"Baby? What's this about a baby?" Townsley let his arm fall by his side and allowed his gaze to rove over her figure, stopping on her midsection. "I don't believe it."

She avoided his eyes and lay mute, unable to respond.

"If that's true, then we'll get it taken care of quickly enough. Tomorrow I'll have the doctor from the red-light district come by. If you're right and you're carrying a brat, he'll get rid of it fast enough. After that, you'd best change your tune and be thankful for the home I've given you."

He headed for the door but paused and looked back. His voice dropped to a silky whisper. "You'd better remember you belong to me, Sara. And you're going to learn to like it, so help me."

He left the room, and she heard him shout at the top of the stairs, "Leslie! Get up here and guard this door. I don't want this girl going anywhere tonight. And have someone relieve you tomorrow morning. She doesn't leave, and nobody gets in, or you'll be the one to answer for it."

Sara sank onto the bed, total despair swamping her mind. Her palms grew damp, and her stomach roiled. She bolted for the corner and bent over the chamber pot. When the retching abated, she rocked back on her heels and wiped her mouth. Christy couldn't help her, or even Nevada. Not with a gunfighter guarding her door.

She might as well give in to Gordon's demands and end this baby's life. He or she wouldn't stand a chance of a decent existence anyway. Desperate sobs shook Sara's body as she crawled to her bed and threw herself across it. She wasn't sure even God could help her, if indeed He cared the way Christy had claimed. If He did, she'd gladly turn her worthless life over to Him if He wanted it.

She drifted into a troubled doze with a prayer on her swollen lips: *Please, God, save my baby.*

Chapter Eighteen

....

Nevada clenched his hands into fists to keep from grabbing a chair and throwing it through the mirror behind the bar of the Oriental Saloon. He'd been lied to and stalled for the past two hours. After previously paying big money to spend the night with Sara, he'd hoped he could talk to her today or, if necessary, buy his way back into her presence. However, she hadn't come downstairs, and no one seemed very forthcoming when questioned.

He stalked across the room, stopping not far from the roulette table, hoping to catch Christy's eye. Raucous laughter and mixed shouts of glee and disappointment filled the air as the wheel came to a slow stop. What a foolish waste of time and money when so many other things in life mattered more. He wondered how many of these men had wives and children sitting at home, praying they'd not spend all their wages on drinking and gambling. Were babies crying for lack of food because their fathers were too irresponsible to see to their needs?

Right at that moment Christy raised her head from her place by the bar. He'd not gotten close enough to discover why she wasn't working the wheel. Nevada tried to erase his frown lest she think him angry with her. She'd been distant and nearly impossible to talk to since the night she stopped by his boardinghouse. He couldn't imagine what had happened after he'd spoken to her, as things seemed fine when she'd left.

His thoughts swirled, battered by winds of hopelessness as he noted Christy's defeated expression. She gave a slight shake of her head. Had she given up on the idea of leaving this place and taking Sara along? No, he couldn't accept that.

He'd always known someday an end to his life must come, whether by violence at another man's instigation, accident, or sickness. But he'd never considered losing his life to the noble cause of saving another. That time might be here now, and if so, he welcomed it. Another thought stopped him in his tracks. What of his eternal soul, if that were to happen? He'd neglected that side of his life for years, thinking himself invincible. The past few months had awakened something inside. No longer did he think himself impervious to a bullet or immune to sickness or carnage. Death was no respecter of persons, and this could easily be his last day on earth.

Christy balanced a tray of drinks on her hand and headed across the room to a far corner. Her despair had been unmistakable. He dug into his pocket and found a two-bit piece. Time to order a drink and get to the bottom of what was happening here. He half turned to go when a loud shout carried above the din.

"Fire!" A bewhiskered, rough-clad man stood inside the front door waving his arms. The room instantly grew still, and every head in the room turned his way. "It started four doors down at the Arcade Saloon and it's movin' this way fast. The City Bakery is already ablaze. You'd best clear out if you value your hides!" He turned and bolted back through the doors and into the street.

Shouts rang out across the room, and men raced for the door.

A couple of them vaulted over the bar and grabbed bottles, tucking them under their arms.

The bartender reached under the counter and came up with a shotgun, aiming it at the first man's chest. "Put those back where you found 'em, or the fire will be the least of your worries."

The clink of the bottles hitting the shelf was the only reply.

Nevada elbowed his way through the bodies pushing and shoving to exit the room. He peered over the heads of the crowd, praying he'd see Christy's auburn hair. Nothing. The roulette table had emptied, leaving only chips scattered across the surface and chairs tipped over on their sides. The table she'd been serving stood empty.

"Christy!" He raised his voice above the din and tried again, louder this time, with the same result. She'd disappeared. Had she already made her way to the door and headed home to check on her mother? Suddenly he knew the answer. She'd never leave without Sara.

The room quieted as more patrons fled, but with the silence came a new sound—the roar of flames and the creak of timbers. One of the nearby buildings must be fully engulfed. Nevada picked up his pace and raced to the stairs, suddenly thankful he knew the location of Sara's room. The girl should have heard the shouts and surely could see the flames or smell the smoke from her second-story room. Why hadn't she appeared at the top of the stairs?

He took the steps two at a time and met no one coming down. The area seemed to be clear of people. His thoughts went to Gordon Townsley and Frank Leslie, along with the other employees and regulars of the Oriental. Had they all abandoned the building, or were they at this moment digging through offices and safes, hoping to clean out anything valuable they might carry?

Waving tendrils of smoke drifted through the open front door below and found their way up the stairs. He peered down the stairwell, craning his neck to see through a window. Prickles of fear raced down his spine. Sparks flew through the air, and the roof of the building next door exploded in flames.

No wonder the town was ablaze. The temperatures had soared into the high nineties the entire month of June, and the buildings were tinder dry. Most were lumber. Only a handful of the businesses on Allen Street were made of adobe and safe from the flames.

He covered his mouth with his bandana to filter the smoke growing in intensity and stalked around the corner into the hall leading to Sara's room. A woman's cry met his ears just before Christy's distressed face came into view.

She stood in front of a short, stocky man guarding Sara's door. As Nevada drew closer, she turned toward him, tears cutting a path down her cheeks. "Sara's inside." She pulled in a shallow breath and coughed.

Nevada strode up to the man, who stood defiantly in front of the door with a chair shoved under the knob. "Move aside, man. Don't you know the building's about to catch fire?"

"I have my orders. Townsley told me not to let anyone in or out of this door, no matter what. I aim to do my job."

Nevada scowled at the words, incensed at both the order and the stupidity of the man carrying it out. "Even if you burn to death?"

"Fire ain't reached here yet, and it might not. All there is right now is smoke. The boss said stay put, so I'm stayin'."

Nevada tugged the bandana away from his mouth. He motioned at Christy, and she stepped away to the other side of the hall. Then

he turned his attention back to the guard. "Move out of the way, or I'll do it for you."

"Don't think you're man enough to do that, mister."

Nevada didn't take time to reply. He didn't swing his arm back in preparation for a punch. He simply swung it up in a wicked uppercut with as much force as he could muster, connecting with the man's belly.

The guard's breath went out in a *whoosh* and he leaned over, cradling his stomach with both hands.

Nevada followed the blow with another to the man's chin, then shoved him aside. His body crashed to the floor, and he moaned.

Christy rushed forward, grasping the back of the chair and jerking it away from the knob. "Sara? Are you in there? Are you all right?"

Loud coughing could be heard through the wood panel separating them. Nevada grabbed the knob and shook it, but it didn't open. "Stand back, Sara." He waited a moment and raised his leg, then kicked hard with the heel of his boot. The flimsy lock broke free, and the door crashed open, bouncing against the inner wall.

Christy flew across the threshold with Nevada following right behind. Sara raced across the short expanse of her room and launched herself into Christy's arms.

Nevada gripped Sara above the elbow and gave her a little shake. He peered out the lone window. "The fire's on the roof of the building next door and making its way into the walls. It'll only be a matter of minutes before this one's ablaze. Come on, we've got to get downstairs and out of here."

The two women broke apart, and Sara looked wildly around.

"I need to take some things." She snatched at a dress lying discarded on the floor, then ran to the bureau and jerked open a drawer.

Christy followed. "Sara, there's no time. Let's go!"

Nevada herded the ladies out the door and to the head of the stairs, stepping over the body of the moaning guard. He hesitated, then turned to Christy. "Take Sara downstairs and get her out. I'll be right behind you."

Christy turned toward him, her gaze filled with uncertainty and fear. Nevada touched her hand. "Just go. I can't leave this man, no matter what he did." His heart lurched at the caring expression that blazed across her features.

She gathered Sara close to her side. "All right. But please be careful." Her eyes met his, then she turned, pulling Sara toward the staircase.

Nevada walked back to the fallen guard and bent over him. "Can you get up?"

Glazed eyes turned up to meet his. "What's it to you?"

Disgust and anger filled Nevada. How easy it would be to leave this man lying here. If the fire killed him, it wouldn't be his fault. He'd made his own decision to stay, cornering a young girl in a deadly situation. No one would blame him for leaving the fellow to find his own way out of the firetrap.

A memory swirled back, like the tendrils of smoke growing denser around him. Years ago he'd made a promise to God to rescue the perishing. Sure, he'd expected to rescue men's souls from the fires of hell. But apparently God must have meant it literally. He pulled the bandana back over his mouth, then stooped down and grabbed the man by his shirt collar, dragging him toward the stairs.

"You might want to lie here and die, but that's not going to happen if I have anything to say about it."

The man struggled for a moment, then began to cough. He doubled over on his side, retching and gasping. Nevada took shallow breaths as the smoke penetrated his bandana, making his lungs burn. A crackling noise jerked his attention upward. Smoke billowed from a chink in the ceiling and something overhead began to roar.

Nevada bent over and hauled the guard to his knees, then lifted him to the point where he could get his shoulder under the man. With a loud grunt, Nevada strained to push to an upright position. He staggered with his load to the top of the stairs, then leaned his free shoulder against the wall and slowly started to descend. By the time he reached the bottom, his lungs were on fire. It was all he could do not to drop the man and crawl for the door.

The dense smoke in the room made the tables in front of him barely visible. He stumbled through, gasping for air. Since the guard had quit struggling, Nevada could only assume he'd lost consciousness.

"Nevada?" A man's voice penetrated the murky air.

"John? Over here!" Nevada pushed out the words.

Footsteps approached, and an arm flung itself around Nevada's waist. "Here—let me take him." Strong hands lifted the burden off Nevada's back. "Come on, the door's this way."

Nevada followed through the thick haze, his lungs burning and eyes streaming tears. He stumbled against a chair lying prone on the floor and hit his knees, gasping for breath. John disappeared through the open door, but Nevada couldn't seem to force himself up off the floor. Spots of color danced before his eyes, and the crack of breaking timbers barely registered on his hearing.

He forced himself to his knees and pressed the bandana tighter over his mouth with the back of his arm, trying to get at least one breath of air not laden with smoke. Sparks and hot embers landed on his neck and he squeezed his eyes shut, trying to block the burning sensation.

He had to get out of here before the entire building collapsed around him.

One knee in front of the other. Only a few more yards to the door.

His body felt so heavy—barely able to move.

Keep going. Can't stop.

The light from the open door shone in—or was that the flames from the building next door?

Almost there.

No air seemed to reach his lungs, and he struggled to remain conscious. Then blackness swirled around him as his arms gave out and his chest hit the floor.

* * * * *

Christy stood outside the saloon, her arm wrapped around Sara's trembling body, drawing her close. Thank God the girl had gotten out safely. She'd been certain the building would burn down around their ears before they escaped. If Nevada hadn't watched over Sara in her room that night not long ago, he might never have found them in time.

Shouts of men filled the street, and cries of women and children echoed them. People raced past carrying armloads of belongings, and glass crashed as windows were broken in a nearby building. Christy glanced that direction and saw items being tossed out the broken panes into the dirt. Men hurried out of businesses now threatened by the fast-moving fire. It appeared as though the entire block must be consumed, and no telling when or if it could be extinguished.

She couldn't believe Nevada had stayed to rescue the very man who'd put Sara's life in danger. Most people would've left him to burn and never thought twice about the matter. Not Nevada. Christy's heart swelled with admiration. Her gaze sought the open door, wondering what was taking the cowboy so long to exit.

Ah, there. A man carrying another across his back. "Come, Sara. Nevada may need help." She urged the girl forward toward the pair backlit by the fire.

They hurried across the street and Christy looked around, praying they wouldn't run into Townsley. Though she didn't really know the man, she knew his type. He wouldn't hesitate to claim Sara as his property and drag her to whatever hovel he set up until the saloon was rebuilt. In a few more steps they reached the two men, one kneeling over the other lying prostrate on the dirt in the middle of the street. When the man looked up, Christy gasped.

John Draper sat back on his haunches, his body covered with soot and ash. "Miss Christy." He nodded, but his face wore a pained expression. "Glad you made it out of there."

She clutched his arm. "Where's Nevada? He was carrying this man and sent us on ahead. Why isn't he with you?"

John glanced back. "Thought he'd be out by now. I took this feller off'n him. He must still be inside." He pushed to his feet and headed back toward the door.

Men jostled each other to get away from the front of the building. Fire leapt from the second-story windows, and the roof of the saloon collapsed as Christy stared. She jumped to her feet and raced after John, fear dogging her steps.

Please, God, don't let Nevada die. The prayer hammered at her mind, echoing repeatedly as sparks and bits of charred wood fell to the boardwalk.

John disappeared through the open doorway, and Christy stopped on the threshold, horror freezing her feet in place. The velvet curtains, once the pride of the establishment, blazed from floor to ceiling. Flames engulfed the entire bar, and the staircase started to crumble as a timber fell from above and smashed against a step halfway down. How could someone live through this inferno?

Christy took a step back as the heat scorched her, but she continued to peer inside, terrified of what she might see. A gust of wind parted the smoke for an instant, and she focused on John leaning over a still figure. Nevada. She sucked in a big gulp of smoke and retched.

Strong hands from behind gripped her upper arms and drew her away from the doorway. "Lady! Get out of there! What you tryin' to do, kill yourself?" A sooty-faced man in rough miner's garb peered at her from under bushy brows.

She fought against his grip as tears streamed from her burning eyes. "My friend is still in there."

"Well, he ain't gonna live much longer if he don't get out soon. Nobody's gonna go in there, lady. It's too dangerous." He backed away, pulling her with him in a determined grip.

A few seconds later the bent form of John Draper lumbered through the open doorway with Nevada slung over his shoulders. Christy wrenched free from the miner's grip and raced to help him. She clutched Nevada's hand as John crossed the street and moved far from the blazing buildings. He gently laid the cowboy on the boardwalk of a side street. "He'll need water, ma'am."

"Yes, of course." Christy straightened and gazed around, unsure where to turn. What to carry it in, if she even found the precious liquid? This town was burning due to the lack of water. All they had was carried in on wagons in barrels. No water main had been run from the mountains yet, and no streams flowed nearby. The founders had built this city because of the silver and gold mines, with no thought of the life-giving fluid.

She turned to John and beckoned down the street. "His boarding-house is at the end of the next block and Miss Cashman will surely have water. Can you carry him that far?" She knelt beside Nevada and brushed the hair off his forehead. His breathing was ragged and his cough, hoarse.

"Yes, ma'am, I surely can." John leaned back over the prone figure, then stared at Christy. "But where's your young lady friend?"

Christy's heart plummeted. How could she have forgotten Sara and the danger facing her? She pushed to her feet, peering among the melee of people thronging the streets. Standing on her tiptoes, she continued to search. But no one resembling the golden-haired girl stood out in the crowd.

"She's gone. Oh dear Lord, watch over her, please." Christy whispered this second prayer of the evening as despair tore at her heart. A glance at John holding the motionless body of Nevada in his arms gave her renewed direction. She'd have to trust God with Sara and tend to the man who'd saved them both.

"Come. This way." She beckoned to the blacksmith and led the way down the side street toward the Russ House. If it was within her power, she wouldn't lose both of them in one night.

Chapter Nineteen
....

Nevada fought his way through the pain, his lungs burning and his limbs aching. All he could see was blackness, although he could hear a melodic voice singing somewhere in the distance. Had he died in the fire and arrived in heaven? He moaned and the singing disappeared. No. He wanted it back.

"Nevada? Please, you've got to fight. I don't want to lose you."

Had he really heard those words, or were they all part of the dreams he'd been drifting in and out of? Some were nightmares, cloaked with dark figures floating like wraiths, their burning eyes accusing as they drifted past. Others were filled with warmth as a sweet voice called him toward the light. He moaned, struggling to the surface of this newest dream, pulled ever upward into conscious thought by the whisper willing him to awaken.

"Nevada. Can you open your eyes?" Soft fingers stroked his cheek, and then a cool cloth touched his forehead.

His spirit was drawn to that voice like a moth to a flame. A gentle hand gripped his and held it. Warmth passed from his arm and shot straight to his heart. His eyelids fluttered, and harsh morning light from an uncovered window woke him to the reality of the place where he lay. Not heaven, but his room at Nellie's. His tired heart gave a small bound at the vision sitting beside his bed.

"Christy?" The word came out as a hoarse whisper. He licked his dry, heat-chapped lips. "Water."

The auburn-haired angel reached for a glass on a nearby chest of drawers and slipped her hand under his head. She positioned the glass, waited for him to take a sip, then eased him back on the pillow.

"I'm so thankful you're finally awake. You gave us all quite a scare."

"What…?"

"John got you out before the saloon collapsed. The doctor will be back in a moment to check on you. He's been busy all night since the fire."

He passed his tongue back over his lips again. How his throat burned even after the water. "How many dead?" The words came out with a croak.

"Only one we've heard of so far." Footsteps clumped outside the room, and John crossed the threshold of the open door. Christy motioned to the big man. "Nevada's awake. He's worried about how many died in the fire. Have you heard?"

The blacksmith stepped forward to the edge of Nevada's bed. "Just one man, and I'd say it's a miracle for sure." He laid his hand on Nevada's head. "How you feelin', son?"

Nevada raised the back of his hand and covered his mouth only a second before a terrible cough shook his body. After several long moments he drew in a shallow breath. "Hurts like fire."

"Not surprised. You was in that buildin' long enough to burn your lungs to a crisp. If God hadn't shown me where you was in that smoke, you wouldn't be alive." John scowled. "Who was the feller you dragged down those stairs? A particular friend of yours? He got

up off the ground and staggered away without so much as a thank-you-kindly."

Nevada moved his head against his pillow in a weak negative. "No friend. Guard at the Oriental."

A shadow crossed Christy's features, and her eyes darkened in pain. Nevada reached for her hand and gripped it. "Sara?"

Christy squeezed his fingers. "She disappeared last night when I ran to the doorway to help John get you out of the building."

"Townsley's men?" Nevada's voice showed he felt the strain, and he closed his eyes.

"We don't know." Christy whispered the words, but they shimmered with fear and uncertainty. "You need to rest now and quit talking."

Nevada pushed himself up with his elbow. "I'm not...lying around...any longer."

Christy pressed him back against his pillow. "You're in no shape to get up yet. Doctor Goodfellow says you need to rest for at least another day or two." She held up her hand. "It won't help to argue. John, Nellie, and I will see you stay put if we have to tie you to the bedrails."

"No need." A faint smile tipped the corner of his mouth. "Don't think I'd get far. But...I'm worried about Sara. No word...around town?"

John narrowed his eyes. "There's someone I might ask. A fellow I met the other day is keepin' his ear to the ground. I'll do some checkin' and see what I can round up." He patted Nevada's back a bit awkwardly and grinned. "And mind your pretty nurse so she don't have to tie you down."

* * * * *

Christy slipped out of the room when the doctor arrived, knowing Nevada was in good hands. Worry over Sara gnawed at her mind, and the pressing needs of her mother and brother increased her agitation.

Nellie hurried to meet her as Christy closed the door behind her. "How's the lad doing?"

"He's awake, talking and trying to get out of bed."

"Praise be!" Nellie raised her hands in the air and beamed. "I'm thankin' heaven he's all right. From what I understand the whole building collapsed not long after John pulled him out."

"Yes." A shiver passed over Christy's skin. "I hope we never have to experience anything like that again."

"What are ya goin' to do now, dear?" Nellie walked with Christy toward the entrance.

"Go home and check on Ma and Joshua, and start packing the things worth taking out of that hovel."

"Yer movin'? Where to?" Nellie planted her hands on slender hips.

Christy shrugged. "I'm not quite sure. Ma lost the house." Warmth rose to her cheeks at her own blunt words.

"Well then, I'll tell ya." Nellie grasped Christy's hand and squeezed. "You'll move 'em both right here. You and yer ma can share a room. You said yer brother is an invalid. We can keep an eye on both of 'em at the same time that way." Her bright eyes met Christy's.

Christy wagged her head. "There's no way I can allow you to do that. It's very generous of you, but we can't afford to pay for two rooms, even if we share."

"Remember, missy, I need more help around here. You can work off yer room, and there'll be no charge for yer brother as long as he's ill. When Joshua is better, he can do odd jobs still cryin' to be done. I keep a room open for people in need, and it's not bein' used at the moment. Sure now, that'll be just the thing."

Christy's throat closed on a lump, and she swallowed hard. "Thank you," she whispered and pulled Nellie into a hug.

"There, there, don't go on about it." Nellie patted her back and stepped away. "Go fetch yer family as soon as ya can. I'll send someone over with a wagon later to pick up their things. No need to bring them now." She pushed a lock of hair from her face. "How far away do ya live? Should I send a wagon for yer mother? I seem to remember ya sayin' she's not doin' well."

"We're only a block down Toughnut Street. The fresh air and short walk'll do her good. Can you keep an eye on Nevada while I'm gone?" Christy shot a look down the hall toward the room where the doctor still lingered.

"Of course. Now shoo away with ya and quit yer worrying. God is big enough to take care of all yer troubles, don't ya know."

Christy smiled. "I'm starting to figure that out, but yes, He is. If only we can find Sara, things will be put right." She hurried out the door, her heart lighter than it had been in days. They had a place to live, Nevada would get better, and with God's help, Sara would be safe.

Once home, Ma's excited voice came through the open window, but Christy couldn't make out the words. She walked through the front room and into the kitchen.

A whiskered man with a scar on his cheek sat slouched in a

chair at the table. He swiveled toward her, and his gaze traveled from the top of her head to the hem of her skirt. "Now who'd this be, Ivy?"

Ivy Malone beamed at her daughter and held out her hand, drawing Christy to her side. "This is my middle child, Christy. She come all the way from California to stay with me while I been sick. Ain't she a pretty girl?"

"Yes, ma'am, she's right purty." The big man smacked his lips like he planned on sitting down for a full meal.

Christy crossed her arms over her middle and stared. She'd heard that voice somewhere in the past but couldn't quite place it. A saloon she'd worked in, maybe? But his face stirred nothing in her memory.

Ma tugged at Christy's arm and frowned. "Cat got your tongue, Daughter? Can't you speak to your pa's cousin Jake? He's family. We want to treat him decent."

Christy moved away from her mother. "Logan wasn't my pa, or Joshua's. Did you send the telegram about Logan's death?" Something about this man didn't sit right.

"Yes, ma'am, that would be me." He leaned back in his chair and bared his teeth, then used his grubby finger to remove a wad of tobacco from his cheek. "Where's your spittoon?"

"We don't have one." Christy jerked her head at the back door. "Step outside if you need to spit. I just scrubbed the floors."

He rose slowly from his seat and stepped to the door, pulling it open and letting a stream of tobacco shoot from his lips.

Christy turned to her mother and lowered her voice. "What's he doing here?"

Jake turned back around and grinned. "Why, Cousin, I've come to find the man who shot Logan and kill him. I don't aim to leave town until I do."

* * * * *

Sara awoke, shivering in the heat of a tent. She lay on a hard, narrow cot, a foul odor assaulting her senses. Turning bleary eyes to the side, she noticed a chamber pot too close to the bed, and unwashed clothing draped across a nearby wooden chair. Her stomach recoiled, and she willed the little she'd eaten to stay down.

Or had she eaten at all? What day was this, and why was she here? She pushed up on one elbow and groaned. Her head felt stuffed with wool.

Somehow she managed to sit but gripped the hard rail of the cot beneath her. The last thing she remembered was...

She shook her head, trying to clear it, willing a memory of some kind to return. Fire. There'd been a fire. Her room? No. Something much worse.

Suddenly it all came rushing back. Gordon locking her in her room and posting a guard. The long night filled with tears. The day spent begging God to save her baby and to rescue her from the hellhole they called a saloon. Nevada and Christy coming as an answer to that prayer. The joy and relief of escaping the burning building.

Then what? She'd gotten out, felt the hot wind of the summer's evening, and breathed in the smoke-tainted air across the street from the Oriental.

Nevada. Now she remembered. John had gone back in after Nevada, and Christy had run to his aid. Sara had stayed where she was, unsteady on her feet and knowing they'd come.

She'd started to drop onto the edge of the boardwalk to rest when a hand clamped over her mouth. A cruel voice she didn't recognize whispered in her ear to stay quiet. Fear dug its knife into her mind. A hard wrench of her head and the man's hand slipped away. She'd tried to cry out when a damp, sweet-smelling cloth was pressed over her mouth. The last thing she remembered her legs collapsed and she sank into a dark pit.

No. There was something else. Men's voices outside the tent in the early hours of the morning. Morning? So she'd been here all night. Voices arguing over something she couldn't quite catch, then a louder one—Gordon Townsley—cursing his fellows and demanding one of them stand guard. How long had it been? An hour. Maybe two. She'd dozed and awakened again.

Sara turned toward the closed tent flap. A shadow fell across the canvas. She fell back onto the cot and closed her eyes just as the makeshift door rustled.

A man's voice she didn't recognize grunted. "She's still sleepin'."

"Sure is a purty one. Wish the boss would let us have a few minutes with her."

"He'd kill you for even sayin' that, so you'd best shut yer trap."

A low growl was the only response and the tent flap came down with a thump. "I'm gonna get a drink. It's hot out here, and I'm sick of standin' guard over a woman who ain't wakin' up anyway."

"Think it's safe to leave?"

The disgruntled second man replied, "Don't know why not. One

of the saloons what burned is servin' beer from a keg down the block a mite. We can walk down, grab a mug, and come right back."

"All right. I guess Townsley won't be back for another hour anyway. Can't hurt to wet our whistles just this once."

Sara opened her eyes and stared at the two dim figures outside the tent. Their shadows grew indistinct, and their voices disappeared in the distance. When she swung her feet to the ground again and stood, a wave of dizziness nearly knocked her back to the bed. She bent over at the waist and gulped in deep draughts of air. A few moments later she straightened, new resolve stiffening her spine. From what they'd said she might only have minutes to get out of this horrible prison.

She slipped to the tent flap and peered outside. No sign of the guards. In fact, the street was surprisingly empty. It only took a moment to push her way through and another to get her bearings. She was on the backside of Toughnut Street, not far from the Good Enough Mine. Where had Christy said Nevada was living? A boardinghouse. The Russ House, that was it. She headed away from the tent as fast as her wobbly legs would manage. If only she could get out of sight before those men returned.

Chapter Twenty

....

Christy collapsed on the edge of the bed at the Russ House, feeling like a lantern whose oil had run low. Somehow she'd managed to get rid of the odious Jake and convince her mother they had no choice but to move. John Draper had helped get Joshua to his new room, and Ma slept in the bed adjoining her own. All she wanted now was to find Sara and get a sound night's sleep. Somehow she doubted either would happen.

It wasn't often her spirits sank so low that she teetered on the edge of defeat. Somehow she must rise above the hovering dark cloud and find her way back to the sunshine. *God, please take care of Sara and Nevada.* Gratitude washed over her at God's wonderful provision over the past few days. Somehow she knew she could trust Him with her future, even when she couldn't see it clearly yet.

She closed her eyes, trying to envision what a happy future might look like. Nevada's image sprang to her mind, and her eyes flew open in surprise. From the little information Jake had shared she believed Nevada had indeed shot Logan Malone. After all, hadn't his telegram said a man named King did it? How could her heart be drawn to a killer—especially one who'd murdered her stepfather?

She wanted to end this once and for all. Nevada had been

resting for the three hours it had taken to move her family so might be awake and able to talk now. The need for answers pressed her forward as she tiptoed down the hall toward his room. The door wasn't latched so she knocked softly, unsure whether he might have carried through on his threat to get out of bed.

"Yes. It's open." His voice seemed stronger than when she'd visited him earlier.

"Is it all right if I come in?" Christy waited outside the door, sudden apprehension gripping her stomach. What would she do—walk in and demand to know if he killed Logan Malone? Maybe she was stupid to have come. She backed away from the door, turned and picked up the hem of her skirt. Let him think what he may, she didn't care to approach him after all.

The door opened behind her and Nevada's voice sounded close to her ear. "Christy? Did you want to see me?"

She jumped and whirled, her hand over her heart. Glaring at him, she noted he was fully dressed except for his boots. Her gaze traveled to his belt, and she gave a slight start. The man put on his gun before his boots? Well, maybe it wasn't foolish, if Jake were any indication of the enemies he'd made over the years.

"Why are you out of bed?" she demanded.

"Because I can't lie there and pretend I'm not needed." He leaned one hand against the doorjamb, his handsome face marred with concern.

She met his eyes fully for the first time since before the accident. Something in their depths gave her pause.

The moment moved into long seconds. A spark burned in his gaze, and he took a step toward her, reaching out a hand to touch her cheek. He tilted up her chin with one finger. "You're beautiful, Christy Grey." He breathed the words so quietly she wasn't sure she'd heard them, and then he bent his head toward her lips.

The moment lingered as he drew closer, his breath soft on her cheek. She closed her eyes, a hungry anticipation sending her pulse into a rapid gallop....

A minute later, running footsteps thudded in the hallway behind her, and Christy jerked back from Nevada's touch, her heart pounding the blood into her ears. She whirled to see John Draper sliding to a halt.

"She's here!"

"Who?" Nevada and Christy echoed the word in the same breath.

"Sara. She just walked in the front door."

* * * * *

Nevada spun toward John, relief mixed with frustration hammering at his mind. If only his friend would have delayed his arrival another few minutes he'd—what would he have done? Kissed Christy and gotten slapped for his pains? He was a fool to think she'd welcome his advances. He didn't even know if she'd heard his whispered words and had shocked himself when he'd said them. Something too big to resist had come over him as he'd gazed into those mesmerizing green eyes. He'd felt bewitched and unable to stop himself from kissing her. Maybe it was a good thing John interrupted after all.

The words John had spoken leapt to life. Sara was here. Nevada bolted down the hall after John and Christy, his lungs burning and limbs shaking with the exertion. The memory of his sister, Carrie, swam before his vision. It didn't matter if he fell flat on his face in the lobby; he wanted to see for himself that Sara was safe.

He rounded the corner in time to hear a happy cry erupt from Christy. She dashed forward and wrapped Sara in a hug as both women burst into tears. Strange this was the first time he'd seen that kind of emotion from Christy, but he felt moisture touch the corners of his eyes too. The girl appeared unharmed, but he'd know more once she removed herself from Christy's embrace.

John stood back, his face wreathed in a smile, while Nellie hurried forward, her coos of delight filling the air. "This must be little Sara, who we've been prayin' for all night." She reached out to stroke the girl's disheveled blond curls.

Sara loosened her hold on Christy and stepped back, swiping at the tears still coating her cheeks. "You've been prayin' for me?"

Nevada experienced a jolt of surprise at the realization that he too had spent much of the time between wakefulness and sleep petitioning heaven on her behalf. And here Sara stood, safe and alive, when he'd doubted God would hear. Sorrow at how far he'd fallen warred with a tremendous surge of joy that, in spite of his lack of faith, God had seen fit to answer. Something akin to trust stirred deep in his spirit, and his soul sent out the first tentative shoots towards his heavenly Father in years.

Nellie took a handkerchief from her dress pocket, pressing it into Sara's hand. "Yes, dearie. I knew the good Lord would bring ya home safe. And glory to His name, He did!"

"Home?" Sara looked around with a puzzled expression.

"Aye, that it is. I own this place. I've a room waitin' upstairs for ya, with a comfortable bed all turned back and ready to tumble in. Unless ya'd care for a bath first and a bite to eat?"

Sara's eyes widened, then she broke into renewed sobs. This time Nellie wrapped her arms around the girl and smiled at the others. "I'll take the wee one upstairs, get her cleaned up, and put her to bed. Come along, sweetness." She urged Sara forward, and together they disappeared down the hall.

Silence fell on the three standing in the foyer, and then John cleared his throat. "Guess now that Sara is back, I'll get over to my shop. Got a brace of work waitin' for me."

Nevada rubbed his hand over his jaw, feeling the stubble and wishing for a bath. His hair smelled like smoke, and his skin itched. "I'll be there tomorrow to help you get caught up. Just need one night to rest, and I'll be right as rain."

John rounded on Nevada and scowled. "Not on your life. You come over any time sooner than a week, and I'll toss you out on your ear. And I don't mean maybe, either." He turned and stomped out the door without looking back.

Christy covered her mouth with her hand, but a giggle broke through. "My, he can be fierce when he wants to, can't he?"

"John's a good man to have on your side, but I guess I'd best not rile him by traipsing over there tomorrow." Feeling himself sag, Nevada gripped the edge of the counter.

"You need to get back in bed." Christy reached for his arm.

The door swung open again, and Nevada turned with a retort, ready to level a jest at John, but the words died before they were born.

Tom Parks, the man who'd agreed to help him hunt Jake, stepped into the room. He removed his hat, nodded at Christy, and held out his hand to Nevada. "Good to see you again."

"Same to you. What brings you here? You looking for a place to bunk?" Nevada gripped the other man's hand.

"No, I've got it covered. I'm looking for a woman by the name of Christy Grey."

Nevada heard a sharp intake of breath beside him and felt Christy move forward. "I'm Miss Grey. How can I help you?"

He gave a small bow and smiled. "Tom Parks, ma'am." He shot a look at Nevada before returning his attention to her. "I work for the Wells Fargo Company, and I have some questions about the stage robbery."

* * * * *

Christy fumed at the interruption. A stranger stood in the foyer, demanding to know about the holdup, when all she wanted to think about was Nevada. If she didn't know better, she'd imagine the cowboy had been about to kiss her. Had she dreamed his breathless "you're beautiful, Christy Grey," or had the words come from his mouth? She praised God for bringing Sara back safely but couldn't deny the fact she wished John's announcement had come a bit later. What might have happened if they hadn't been interrupted? Her insides quivered with the memory of Nevada leaning over her, his eyes half closed. If only…

Then a man cleared his throat, and Christy was startled back to the present.

She stared at the nice-looking individual who could've passed for a rancher. He worked for Wells Fargo but didn't say if he was employed as a detective or was a clerk sent to ask questions. Either way, she knew what he'd come about and didn't care to respond.

"This isn't a good time," she said stiffly. "I need to check on my mother." She made a half turn.

"I'll only require a couple of minutes, and then I won't bother you again, Miss Grey." Disapproval tugged at his lips.

Nevada took a step back, glancing from one to the other. "I think I'll go lie down for a while."

Concern shot through Christy's heart. "Of course. You need to rest."

Tom Parks peered at Nevada. "Anything wrong?"

"Nothing a good night's sleep won't cure." He nodded to Christy. "Maybe I'll see you tomorrow?"

"I'm sure." She watched him move slowly back up the hallway before turning to the stranger still waiting inside the door. "Would you care to sit down?" She motioned to two stuffed chairs tucked into the corner of the lobby.

"No, thank you, ma'am. Like I said, this shouldn't take long."

She eyed the man, certain she knew what was coming. The marshal had been unsuccessful in getting information, so Wells Fargo must have sent this agent instead. It didn't matter. She had no intention of telling what she knew if President Garfield himself appeared at the door.

"If you're here to ask me to describe the men who held up the stage, I already told the marshal I can't do that."

"That's not my intent."

"Oh?"

"I need to know if you can remember anything distinctive about the leader. His voice, how tall he is, anything at all."

"Only the leader?" She rocked on her heels.

"Yes."

Christy felt her guard slipping and grabbed it with both hands, pulling it back up like a shield. "I don't remember anything about him."

"Would you say he was a tall man, or short and stout?" Parks turned his hat in his hands.

"Hmm." She slanted her head to the side and thought. "Rather on the large side, I think. Broad, powerful shoulders and longish brown hair that fell past his collar under the mask."

Parks grinned. "Now that wasn't so hard, was it, Miss? Do you remember anything else?"

She shook her head, then stopped as something niggled at her memory. "His laugh. It sounded like something was wrong with his throat. Rough and tight. I can't really explain it."

"Ah-huh. That's a big help, thank you." He took a step towards the door and reached for the knob.

Christy stared, not daring to hope she'd get off so easily. "That's it? You didn't ask me about the man who bandaged my arm." As soon as she said the words, her heart sank in dismay. She couldn't believe she'd been so stupid. Parks was ready to walk out the door and she as much as asked him to stay and question her further. She turned to leave. "Good night then, Mr. Parks."

"Miss Grey?" The tone of his voice halted Christy in her tracks.

"Yes?" Her breath caught in her throat.

"You seem to be protecting someone, and I'd like to understand why."

Warmth stole to her cheeks. "I won't pretend I don't know what you mean."

He nodded but didn't reply.

"One of the men bandaged my wound when I thought I might bleed to death. He took me aside and spoke to me as he worked, explaining he wasn't part of the gang."

"And you believed him?" His brows rose, but the rest of his face remained impassive.

"Not at first, as I assumed he must be with them. Then I realized he came several minutes after the others attacked. He assured me he'd only stumbled across their camp the night before and stopped for a meal. He didn't know what they intended until after I'd been shot."

"So you think he came to help you, rather than take part in the robbery?"

"I do."

"Right now I can assure you I'm only interested in the leader of the gang. All right?"

She swiveled and eyed him through narrowed lids. "I don't understand."

"You don't need to at this point. You can trust I know what I'm doing."

"How? I've just met you."

"That you have, Miss Grey, that you have. Let's suffice it to say I have a reason for not disclosing everything I know." He placed his hat back on and touched the brim. "I bid you good day."

* * * * *

Nevada paced the confines of his room, his insides twisting in knots. Tom Parks an agent for Wells Fargo? Somehow he'd known the man wasn't merely another cowpoke or ranchman whiling away time in Tombstone. Why hadn't Parks admitted his occupation when they'd talked that evening in the Golden Eagle? It was possible the man suspected his involvement in the stagecoach holdup and hoped to uncover the truth from Christy. But he'd expressed an interest in Jake, the leader of the outlaw band, so that might be all there was to his visit.

Whatever the reason, Nevada had better be prepared with a plan if things started unraveling, or there'd be a neatly knotted rope around his neck. He stuffed his hands in his pockets and encountered something soft. He withdrew a square of cloth and allowed the corners to fall open on the palm of his hand, exposing the delicate cameo brooch he'd demanded from Jake after the robbery. How could he have forgotten to return this to Christy? He'd meant to do it long ago.

Time to set things right. He headed for the door and then paused, his hand touching the knob. If Tom Parks still waited in the lobby, it wouldn't look good to appear holding an item taken from one of the passengers. Stepping over to the bureau, he plucked the brooch from the cloth and set it carefully on the smooth surface next to the water pitcher. Tomorrow would be soon enough to return it, when he knew there'd be no chance of involvement from the investigating agent. Hopefully Christy would be pleased to have her grandmother's brooch again and wouldn't think too poorly of him for waiting so long.

Chapter Twenty-one

....

Christy leaned over Sara's bed and smoothed the hair from the sleeping girl's forehead, hating to wake her but knowing she must be hungry after her ordeal.

Sara stirred, her head moving from one side of the pillow to the other. "No, don't touch me. Leave me alone!" Her voice rose in a near shriek, and her hands struck at Christy.

"Shh. It's me, Christy. No one is going to hurt you." She kept talking in a soothing tone until Sara quieted.

The young woman's eyes opened. "I'm sorry. I guess I must have been dreamin' one of the customers—" Silent tears coursed down her pale cheeks.

"It's all right. No need to explain. I understand." Christy pulled up a chair and sat, then cradled Sara's hand in both of her own. "You're safe now. No one will ever touch you again in that way."

Large, sad eyes, still misty with tears, focused on Christy. "How long have I been here?"

"A couple of hours. We let you sleep, but it's almost suppertime, and I thought you might like me to bring you a tray. Are you able to eat?"

"I don't know." Sara hitched herself a little higher against the headboard, and Christy placed another pillow under her head. "Maybe a little."

251

"Nellie has some wonderful soup and fresh bread, along with real milk. Does that sound good?"

Sara brightened. "Yes. But I can come down." She tried to sit up.

"You mustn't get up tonight," Christy said gently. "We want you to rest. Doctor Goodfellow will be by to see you in the morning and check on your baby."

Sara's hand flew to her middle. "Is everything all right? I haven't lost it, have I?"

"No, honey, and I'm sorry I worried you." Christy leaned over and placed a tender kiss on Sara's forehead. "Nellie and I thought it would be a good idea for the doctor to see you and make sure everything is fine."

"Okay." She turned a puzzled gaze on Christy. "Who's Nellie?"

"She's the lady who owns this place. Do you remember her bringing you upstairs and putting you to bed?"

"Not very well. I was so tired and frightened—and thankful to get out of that tent—I wasn't thinkin' clearly."

"Who took you, Sara? Was it Gordon Townsley?" Christy had never trusted the saloon manager, and right now she'd like to impose some bodily harm on him.

"Yes, but he sent some of his flunkies to do his dirty work. One of them mentioned 'the boss' and the other said Townsley wants me for himself. I tried to ignore the rest of what they said about me, although it wasn't much compared to things I've heard men say in the past." Sara turned her head away and faced the brocade-covered wall on the far side of her bed. "That's all I'm good for, you know. Pleasing men."

Christy placed her finger under Sara's chin, drawing her around.

"Don't ever say, or think, that again. You are precious in God's sight, and He loves you so much. It's not your fault you ended up in a horrible place where men did despicable things to you. And even if you'd made that decision for yourself, God will still forgive you if you ask Him to."

Sara gave a small shake of her head, dislodging Christy's hand. "I didn't choose to go there, but I didn't have much say in it, neither. After my folks died, I was near to starvin' and gettin' sickly. That's when Gordon found me. He promised me a place to live, food to eat, and made it sound like a home. I went 'cause I believed him. It was true the first couple of weeks, till I got stronger and gained a little weight. Then he told me I needed to earn my keep."

"He brought you to the Oriental?" Christy gritted her teeth to keep back the flow of words she'd like to heap on the man's head. No sense in frightening Sara further. The poor girl had been through so much.

"Yes. At first he only asked me to serve drinks and didn't let anyone touch me. But after a while, things changed. Men started offerin' him good money to 'spend time' with me. I could tell he didn't like it at first, but that didn't last long. He started by sendin' Joshua to my room. I think he figured Joshua wouldn't repulse me, and I wouldn't fight him." She blushed, then the color drained from her cheeks. "But after two or three weeks he sent horrible men to my room...." Sara rubbed her upper arms, her chin quivering.

"It's behind you now," Christy murmured. "We're going to make sure you have a new life."

"But I can't afford to stay here. I need to make my own way."

"Nellie wants you to stay. She's given me a job, and when you're strong enough, you can help with light work in exchange for your room and board."

"Why would she do that? I'm a stranger and a fallen woman. No one who's decent—except you—wants anything to do with me."

"That's not true. There are other Christian people who won't look down their nose at you. Granted, some will, but those kind aren't worth bothering with. Nellie loves the Lord and is committed to doing His work here in Tombstone. She's helped many people, and some of the men are already calling her 'The Angel of Mercy,' and I agree." She brushed a strand of golden hair from Sara's cheek. "Rest for a while, and I'll bring you supper. And no more thinking poorly of yourself. You need to get strong for the wee one you're carrying."

"Thank you, Christy. I don't know how I'd have survived without you." Sara squeezed Christy's hand. "I believe in God's love because you've shown it to me."

Christy drew the door shut behind her and stood in the hall, her shaking hands swiping at the tears rolling down her cheeks. Love like she'd never felt swelled her heart until she thought it would burst. Peace and joy threatened to swamp her, and gratitude to God Almighty brought on more tears. She pressed her back against the wall and bowed her face into her hands, suddenly overwhelmed with the impact of Sara's words.

She'd made a difference in someone's life and shown them God's love. It was real. All of it. Everything Alexia had tried to tell her these past four years. God accepted and loved her, just for who she was. She didn't need to prove anything to Him, other than returning His love. But now she knew she could. Freely. Without reservation. From this day on, she belonged to Him.

* * * * *

Early the next morning Christy checked on her mother sleeping peacefully in the adjoining bed and slipped out of her room. It was the first night in many that her mother's coughing hadn't kept Christy awake through the night. And now Ma's skin looked cool and dry. Joshua needed exercise as well, beyond sitting in the chair in his room, and Doctor Goodfellow agreed it was time for him to be up and around. The wounds had healed in his stomach, but the doc didn't want her brother taking chances by doing too much. Keeping him corralled might be a problem. At least the fact that his favorite gambling haunt burned down would keep him from traipsing back to the poker table anytime soon. Besides, she'd hogtie him if he even hinted at gambling again.

She headed for the lobby, hoping to find Nellie. Sitting around without doing her part didn't sit well on Christy's conscience. Rounding the corner in the front of the building, she heard Nellie singing an old familiar hymn. She paused to listen. Not once since arriving in Tombstone had she considered attending Sunday services, but the lovely melody coming from her new friend ignited a longing to do so.

Nellie looked up from polishing the surface of a low table in the lobby. "Good mornin', dear. Yer up awfully early. Couldn't ya sleep?"

"I think I had my first restful night since arriving in town. I hoped to find you before the day got busy to see what you'd like me to do."

"Why, take care of yer family and Sara. Nothin' else."

"No, ma'am, that won't do at all. Sara will more than likely be up and around today, and Ma's sleeping peacefully. Josh needs very little care anymore, and you hired me to work." She rocked on her heels. "So give me a job."

A tinkling laugh broke from Nellie. "All right. How about takin' over the dustin' and sweepin' the foyer before any more dirty feet come this way? After breakfast ya can fill the water pitchers in the occupied rooms. Tap on the door and see if anyone's at home. If not, slip inside, get the pitcher, and bring it to the kitchen for fresh water. My boarders are used to havin' that done of a mornin'."

"All right, thank you. How about meals? May I help with those?"

"No. My cook and servin' staff are well trained to care for the boarders and any payin' customers who stop in, but thank ya for offering. Now go along with ya and check on your mama and Sara before breakfast is served." She shooed Christy out of the room with her rag, her rich contralto laugh echoing down the hall.

* * * * *

Nevada stopped inside the dining room door, willing his nerves to remain steady. This was the first morning he'd be sitting down to the table with Christy. Being in her presence sent the blood pulsing through his body and made him feel more alive than he had in years. He'd not spent any time near her since Tom Parks' departure last night—and, right before, the incident in the hall. Nevada still found it hard to believe he'd come so close to kissing her. He wasn't sure what had possessed him to try, but he didn't remember seeing a desire to flee shining in her beautiful eyes.

The dining room wasn't set up with the typical long table most boardinghouses boasted, but rather smaller-sized tables seating two to six patrons. The number of customers eating each morning varied, but right now there were at least six people staying here besides Christy's family. Of course, anyone off the street was welcome to pay to eat at this restaurant, and there always seemed to be a number of extra guests. He stepped away from the door and into the shadows. Let the others arrive first and see what happened.

Chattering voices came from the hall to his left. Two men with their wives on their arms advanced into the room. The gentlemen withdrew chairs from a table and seated the ladies, then took the remaining two chairs. A couple of minutes later, two bearded men entered and chose a table a stone's throw from the group already seated. A handful of strangers trickled in, but still Nevada waited.

A familiar voice pulled his attention away from the dining area. Christy and Sara walked down the hall with Joshua moving cautiously between them. Nevada peered at Christy's brother as he drew closer, wondering how he'd fared these past weeks since his injury. The young man seemed a little pale and walked with a halting gait, seeming to favor the leg where he'd been shot.

Nevada glanced at Sara and experienced a slight shock. The animated girl was a far cry from the fear-filled visage of the night before. Was it only relief at being in a safe place?

Nevada stepped forward as the trio stopped at the open archway to the dining room. He bowed to the ladies. "How are you all this morning?"

Sara gave a cry of joy. Standing on her tiptoes, she planted a kiss on his cheek. "Thank you, Nevada. I never had a chance to tell you how grateful I am you got me out of that horrid room before it burned down around me." She dropped her arms to her sides. "I'll never forget what you did for me. Never."

Joshua stepped forward and thrust out his hand. "Me too, mister. I don't know who you are, but Sara tells me you and the blacksmith toted me home the day I got shot." He bobbed his head toward Sara. "Besides, you saved Sara. Not sure how I'll ever repay you."

Nevada shot a look from Joshua to the beaming girl, whose eyes were turned on the young man in happy adoration. "Glad I was there for you both, but any decent man would've done the same."

Joshua shook his head. "Not everyone in this town is decent. Just the same, I'm beholden."

Christy held out her hand. "Would you care to join us, Nevada?"

"How about your mother?" He scanned the hall behind the group but saw no sign of anyone else exiting a door. "Isn't she coming?"

"Not this morning. I told her to stay in bed and rest. I'm taking a tray to her when we finish." Christy touched his arm with the tips of her fingers. "You'll come, won't you? Please?"

Nevada didn't want to move. He prayed she'd keep her hand there a moment longer, but she stepped away and motioned inside. He cleared his throat. "I'd like that. Thanks."

They made their way to a table and the men held the chairs for the ladies, waiting for them to be seated before taking their places. Nevada had faced numerous guns pointed his direction over the years and dodged more bullets than he could count, but he'd never experienced the panic hitting him now as he sat next to Christy Grey.

Sara spoke in a low voice to Joshua, and he leaned closer to hear. As their heads bent over their conversation, they seemed to shut out the world around them.

Christy's eyes twinkled as she gazed into Nevada's. She leaned close and lowered her voice. "I think Joshua may be smitten."

Nevada's tension eased, and he grinned. "Somehow I don't think he's the only one."

"It might be what they both need." Straightening, she plucked the linen napkin off the table and spread it over her lap.

Nellie approached their table. Her fine-boned face lit as she came to a stop. "How is everyone this mornin'? Sara, honey, did ya sleep well?"

Sara nodded, shyness settling over her features. "Yes, ma'am, right fine. Thank you again for lettin' me stay. I'll pull my weight, I promise."

Nellie patted the girl's back. "There now, I'll not have ya worryin' about it anytime soon. Eat hearty, then get some rest." She gestured to the small placards stacked in the center of the table. "Those are breakfast menus for the guests. You can choose anything you care to eat. It's smaller than the one we offer on weekends, but the food is wonderful. There's coffee or tea, as well."

They spent a few minutes reviewing the menu, then placed their order for oatmeal, fresh apples, pudding, ham, bread, and coffee.

Nevada turned to Christy. "Nellie's amazing. I've never met someone as kind and generous."

"I know. It was enough she offered me a job, but to invite my entire family and Sara to live here…it's almost more than I can take in." The final words came out in a whisper.

Nevada bent a little closer to Christy. The fragrance of lavender tickled his nose. He closed his eyes briefly to savor the delicate scent that made him acutely aware of this feminine woman. The old longing for a home and wife of his own rose within him. He wanted to reach for her hand and not let go.

But he had no right, and she'd not shown any indication she might care. Each time he was in her presence his awareness of her grew, but not just due to her physical body or lovely looks. Christy's inner beauty, her sweetness, her generous spirit and kindness to those around her, drew him at a deeper level than he'd been drawn to any woman in the past—even Marie.

The knowledge surprised him. He'd never believed he'd care for anyone else in the way he'd loved Marie, but they'd been barely out of their teens when they'd fallen in love. He was a man now, with a man's awareness, appreciation, and needs, and something inside convinced him Christy would meet those needs like no one he'd ever known.

The touch of her fingers on his jerked him back to the present, and he started. She dropped her hand, soft color suffusing her cheeks. "I'm sorry. I spoke to you, and you didn't appear to hear me."

A warmth rushed to Nevada's heart. He cared for this woman more than he had a right to, but he couldn't help it—nor did he want to let go of the feeling. "Forgive me. I was gathering wool for a moment."

"Is something bothering you?" Her rich green eyes drew him into their depths.

Nevada settled back into his chair, trying to break the spell. If an old enemy walked through the door hunting him at this moment, he'd be doomed. "No, I'm fine." He smiled at the waitress as she poured coffee into his mug, then took a sip of the hot brew before continuing. "I *have* been wondering about Tom Parks' visit, though."

"Ah, yes. Mr. Parks." A dimple showed. "You've nothing to worry about on his account." She glanced at Sara and Joshua and dropped her voice. "He's hunting the leader of the outlaws who robbed the stage, and he didn't pressure me to describe the man who bandaged my arm. He asked me a couple of questions regarding the leader and then departed."

"That's it? Nothing else?" Nevada asked.

"I did inquire as to why he didn't press me for more answers. He acted like he might believe me when I told him your story about coming upon the outlaws the night before. Said he had his own reason for not explaining." She shook her head. "I'm not sure what he meant, but I was satisfied when he didn't pursue the matter."

Nevada's heart rate increased. "His own reasons, huh? Wonder what he meant." He picked up his cup and took another drink. "Let's not worry about it now, shall we? How about you? What are your plans?"

"I'm not sure I know what you mean. Just to care for my mother until she's well, and work for Nellie. Nothing more."

"How about beyond that? Do you want to live in Tombstone after your mother regains her health?" He leaned back farther as the server placed a bowl of porridge near his cup. Steam rose off the top, emitting a mouthwatering fragrance.

The waitress took a small pitcher from the serving tray she carried and put it in the middle of the table. "There's sugar in the bowl for your porridge and more milk in the pitcher." She continued to place bowls in front of the other three. "Someone will be along shortly with the rest of your meal."

Christy waited until the woman left, then reached for the milk and poured a portion into her bowl.

A giggle broke from Sara, and Joshua chuckled. They didn't seem aware of the food in front of them.

Christy gently cleared her throat. "Joshua, you might want to eat before it gets cold."

"Huh?" He raised a bemused face. "Oh. Yeah. Sure." He fumbled for his spoon and dipped it into the porridge, not seeming to notice the milk.

Christy rolled her eyes at Nevada. "To be young again."

Nevada smiled. "You can't be much older than Joshua."

"I'm afraid I am. He's nineteen, and I'm twenty-five, but at times, I feel much older."

"I have four years on you. I don't think I'd care to—be that age again, I mean."

She raised her brows but didn't reply.

"I went through more at that age than I care to remember." He ducked his head and raised the spoon.

"Someday I'd like to hear about it, if you'd care to tell me." Her voice was quiet, soothing.

Only the clink of spoons against the edge of the bowls and the buzz of conversation at neighboring tables could be heard as the four bent to their task. Plates of food were put before them, and the bowls whisked away as the last bite was scraped from the bottom. Nellie walked past again but didn't pause this time, just glanced at their coffee cups and beckoned to a server, who hurried over to refill them.

"You didn't answer my question." Nevada put down his fork and lifted his napkin to his lips. At her quizzical look he continued. "About what you hope to do after your mother is well."

"I guess I haven't thought that far."

"How about marriage?" The instant he said the words, he clamped his teeth shut in horror. What a stupid blunder. Would she think him bold or coarse to ask such a thing?

She tilted her head to the side and seemed to carefully consider the question. "I think I've about given up on marriage and am resigned to live alone. At one time I thought it would happen. In fact, I was engaged to a very kind man."

Jealousy reared its head in Nevada so quickly it threatened to choke him. She'd loved someone else, but the man hadn't married her? What a fool. Nevada had to ask. "What happened?"

"He died." The simple words were spoken without much emotion, as if they were simply a statement of fact. No deep grief or anger burned in her eyes. "Kicked in the head by a horse."

"I'm sorry." It sounded so inadequate, but what should he say? "I'm happy he's dead"? Shame washed over him at the pleasure bubbling inside. He had no right to be gratified at someone else's misfortune.

"Yes. He was a good man and loved me." She toyed with her fork, then laid it beside her plate and raised wistful green eyes. "But I'm afraid I didn't deserve him. I cared about him but would never have been able to give him the love he desired."

Nevada controlled his next words, making sure he kept his emotions in check. "But you planned to marry him."

"Yes. He…accepted me. In spite of everything. I honored him for that and wanted to make him happy. I don't think there's another man who could ignore my past, and I've made my peace with that fact." She folded her napkin, laying it beside her plate. "If you'll excuse me, I must get some chores done for Nellie."

Nevada leapt from his place and grasped the top of her chair, sliding it back so she could rise. "Christy?"

She turned and faced him, but her features that had been so open and vulnerable only seconds before were shuttered. "Yes?"

"Don't be so sure."

"About what?" She gathered the fabric of her skirt and swept it aside, stepping around the chair.

"I know at least one man who doesn't care a fig about your past…only about making you happy."

A flash of wonder and the briefest glimmer of hope darkened Christy's eyes as she stared up at him. Then the light dimmed, and she shook her head. "No. I'm sure you mean well, but I can't accept that after knowing you shot Logan."

Nevada's senses went on alert, and his muscles stiffened. "Logan Malone? How do you know him?"

Christy took a step back. "He was my stepfather. It's true then? You're Nevada King, the man Logan's cousin Jake telegraphed us about." She twisted her fingers together in front of her waist. "I didn't want to believe it before, but you're the one who killed Ma's husband."

Nevada's tongue stuck to the roof of his mouth. Words wouldn't come. How could he have lived in this town all these weeks, taken water to Christy's home, and not known her mother was married to Logan Malone? A deep, wrenching groan broke from his throat, and he extended his hand toward her. "Christy. Please at least let me explain."

Christy only stared at him. "I've got to go." She walked away without looking back.

Joshua and Sara's voices behind him barely registered on his senses. The look in Christy's eyes before she lowered them had pierced Nevada's heart. Now he knew how the men he'd shot had felt when they realized they were dying. As far as he was concerned, his hope of happiness had just walked out the door.

Chapter Twenty-two
....

Christy prayed she wouldn't bump into Nevada while refilling water pitchers. She intentionally left the handsome cowboy's room for last. She knocked at his door once, then again, with no response. Gripping the knob, she turned it gently and waited, then pushed the door a few inches and stopped. "Nevada? Are you here?"

No masculine voice answered, and she swung the door the rest of the way, walking across the threshold. Her mouth dropped open as she surveyed the room. The bed was neatly made, with the sheet tucked under the mattress, and the single blanket pulled up to the pillow. Clothing hung on pegs behind the door, and no dust showed on the flat surfaces in the room. Nothing seemed out of place.

She trembled, just thinking about the man who lived here. Her emotions had swung like a metronome since meeting him, and she still didn't know how she felt. The truth of her accusation against Nevada cut deep. He'd asked for a chance to explain, but what could he say? She'd been repulsed in years past by Logan's reputation as a troublemaker and gunfighter, and the thought that Nevada might be cut out of the same cloth rankled.

From all appearance, he wasn't someone to trifle with—handy with both his fists and a gun. She'd been convinced of his status as an outlaw and then observed the tender, kind side that gave to others with no thought for himself. He'd helped her family, saved Sara, and procured this job for her with Nellie. Those weren't marks of an outlaw or someone intent on doing evil, but he hadn't denied his involvement in her stepfather's death.

Maybe allowing him to explain was the right thing to do, if she could be certain he'd tell the truth. She hated this indecisive seesawing. The best thing would be to simply stay away from Nevada as often as possible.

Then why the rush of longing as she remembered those whispered words at the table? Could it be possible he'd overlook her past and accept her as a wife and companion? No. He hadn't said he was that man, and she wouldn't read anything more into his words. Besides, the last thing she needed was someone fast with a gun who'd probably end up dying young.

Enough daydreaming about a future that wouldn't happen. This was her last room, and she needed to check on her mother. She hurried across to the bureau and reached for the pitcher, lifting it off the surface. A small object slid over the edge and landed on the braided rug between the bureau and the end of the bed. She set the pitcher back down and bent over. Hopefully whatever it was hadn't broken.

Christy hiked up her skirt and knelt, then leaned over and peered under the edge of the bureau. Light glistened off of ivory. She reached underneath and grasped the small object, pulling it out in her closed hand. Pushing to her feet, she steadied herself by gripping the front edge of the dresser. Nevada needed to be more careful and not leave things where they could get lost. Christy uncurled her fingers to set the object back where it belonged—and gasped. Her grandmother's cameo brooch lay on the palm of her hand.

* * * * *

Nevada had wandered the streets for the past hour with little memory of where he'd gone or who he'd spoken to. Logan Malone had been married to Christy's mother. The horrible truth flayed his emotions until they felt raw. Never had he hated what he'd become as much as in that moment. He wanted to crawl into a hole and never come out. How had his life come to this place? So much hurt, anger, and unforgiveness. He slowed his aimless walk on the outskirts of town, his mind examining that word. Whom hadn't he forgiven? Sure, there were men who'd wronged him in years past, but he'd never held a grudge. So where did the idea of forgiving spring from?

A bitter taste sat on his tongue, making him want to spit. The old anger surged as his thoughts flew back to his fiancée, Marie. It was God's fault he trod this path today. In the past he'd always nurtured that thought, stroked and welcomed it, but today it didn't hold the same attraction. Christy's expression as she accused him of her stepfather's death nearly buckled his knees. God hadn't forced him to shoot that man, or any other who came against him. Sure, he could justify them as self-defense, but it didn't ease his conscience any.

Sara's humility as she thanked him rang in his ears. He'd saved her from a horrible life, but then he'd collapsed and nearly died in the process. John claimed he wouldn't have found him if God hadn't shown him the way through the smoke. Memories from the past bubbled to the surface—times when he should have died but hadn't. Was God protecting him all those times, in spite of his anger and unforgiving spirit?

Shame coursed through his mind. He leaned against a building and hung his head as waves of conviction lapped at his soul. God loved him and hadn't forgotten him. God had never abandoned Marie when she died, or Carrie when she'd run away from home. He'd been there all along, bringing comfort to the grieving and peace to those who sought it. But Nevada had neglected to see those things—had chosen instead to turn his back and walk away. "Forgive me, Father, for I have sinned. Please, if You can forgive me, take me back."

Nevada stood with his head bowed in his hands. Recapturing the peace he'd once known from his heavenly Father was all that mattered. "God, I give it all to You. Everything. Christy, my past, my future."

The last trace of guilt and shame melted under the overwhelming peace filling his body. Grace, bigger than anything he'd understood before, poured like a waterfall over his bruised and battered emotions. His spine stiffened, and his chin lifted. New strength ran through his veins. Forgiveness. He'd given and he'd received. From now on, he'd walk it out. He'd find a way to never pull the trigger on another man as long as he lived.

He pushed from the wall and headed for the Russ House. Maybe God would provide an opening to talk to Christy and ask her forgiveness, and a chance to explain. So many things in his life needed to be dealt with, but this one pained him like a sore tooth.

The parlor appeared deserted, and no one stood behind the desk. Nevada took a step toward the back hall when a rattling cough halted his progress. He pivoted midstride, certain of who he'd see. Christy's mother sat in a high-backed chair, gasping for air. Nevada

crossed the room and knelt beside the ailing woman. "Can I help you, Mrs. Malone?" He winced as the name tumbled off his lips.

She raised watery eyes, a handkerchief covering her mouth. "Water, if you please?" The cloth muffled the words.

He pushed to his feet and hurried behind the counter. Pouring a glass almost to the top, he returned to the woman and pressed it into her hand.

She sipped at the liquid and leaned back in her chair, fixing him with a narrowed gaze. "And who are you, young man?"

"The name's Nevada, ma'am." He drew in a short breath. "But my Christian name is James King. I'm the one who brought your son home. I've been delivering barrels of water."

She studied his face. "You're Christy's friend?" A frown furrowed her brow, then disappeared. "Pleased to meet you, and thank you for the water."

"Would you like me to help you back to your room?"

"I hoped to find my daughter, but she doesn't appear to be around." She placed the glass on a table and put her hands on the arm of the chair. "That would be a kindness, if you don't mind helping a sick old woman."

"Surely." Nevada helped her up, then tucked her hand into the crook of his elbow. "Lean on me if you need to." He walked slowly down the hall to the room she'd been assigned, his heart beating a rapid staccato against his chest. He'd seen the impact his name had on Mrs. Malone and dreaded the moment she figured out his identity.

They'd almost arrived at her door when hurrying footsteps approached from the opposite direction, and Christy rounded the corner. "Ma! What are you doing out of bed?" She rushed forward, her attention fixed on her mother.

Nevada's stomach clenched. "I'll bid you good evening, ma'am."

Christy's mother turned with a smile and patted his arm. "Thank you, young man. You're a godsend to our family."

Despair hammered at Nevada's mind, but he pushed it aside. He'd given his life back to God and wouldn't pick up his burden of self-loathing again. He'd started down the hall and was almost to the corner when he heard Mrs. Malone's piercing voice.

"Christy, I remember now. I've been tryin' to figure out where I heard that man's name before. He said it's King. That's what the telegram from Jake told us. A gunfighter named King killed Logan." A loud moan issued from her lips right before her body thumped to the floor.

Chapter Twenty-three
....

Christy stared in horror, then dropped to her mother's side. "Ma!" She stared up at Nevada. "I need to get her in bed."

Why hadn't she told her mother about Nevada before now? Probably because it had never occurred to her that Ma would learn his last name or recognize him as the man who might have shot Logan. Christy only had herself to blame if this worsened her ma's condition.

Nevada touched Christy's shoulder, concern etching his rugged features. "Let me help." He didn't wait for a response but scooped the woman into his arms with one easy motion. "If you could get her door?" Christy held it open, and he laid the unconscious woman gently onto the bed. "Should I call the doctor?"

"I think that might be best, thank you. See if Nellie could come as well?"

Christy poured water into the washbowl and dipped in a clean cloth, then wrung it out. She wiped her mother's face as Nevada hurried away, his boots thudding on the wood floor and disappearing into the distance.

The silence that had settled over the room was suddenly broken. Ma rolled onto her side. A cough came from deep inside. She gasped, moaned, and the coughing spasm began again.

Christy rushed to rinse out the cloth. She bent over her mother and drew in a harsh breath. Blood tinged the spittle forming around Ivy's lips, and the pillow cover was spotted with drops of deep red.

* * * * *

Christy and Nellie took turns sitting beside Ivy Malone as the woman drifted in and out of consciousness over the next forty-eight hours. She rallied for a couple of hours at a time, then sank back even deeper.

Joshua hovered outside the door but appeared afraid to stay more than a few minutes at a time, although at one point Christy heard him whisper his love as he bent to kiss his mother's forehead. However, when he offered to tote water and bring trays of food, Christy's heart soared at the evidence of her brother's growing maturity since his own personal brush with death. He'd not once suggested returning to the gambling halls and had even hinted at finding a job to help with the family expenses.

A tap drew Christy to her feet, and she opened the door several inches. She'd started her shift and sent Sara to dinner with Joshua. Nevada stood in the hallway, his hat in his hands, his eyes sorrowful.

She glanced back at the quiet form in the bed, then slipped out into the hall. "I'm surprised you came." She regretted her words as soon as they left her. He'd helped them tremendously, but she still struggled to get past the bitterness.

Nevada's eyes reflected his hurt, but he bowed his head in acknowledgment. "How is she?"

"Sleeping peacefully. The doctor gave her laudanum. He's coming back to check on her later this evening."

He shuffled his hat brim around in a circle. "Do you think we could talk for a moment?" Longing suffused his face.

Christy's heart lurched in spite of her desire to remain angry. "I don't see how. I need to stay with her."

Footsteps padded on the floor, and a cheery whistle preceded Nellie's appearance from around the corner. "Christy, my love, ya haven't eaten a bite all day. I insist ya go to the dinin' room. I know it's not my shift to sit with yer mama, but I'm free right now." She waved her hands at them. "Shoo. Yer lookin' downright peaked, both of ya."

Nevada offered his arm. "I'd love to."

Christy hesitated, then gave in. No sense in claiming she wasn't hungry or didn't desire to sit near this man; she wanted the latter with a vengeance, regardless of the consequences. "Thank you, Nellie. For everything." Tears welled in her eyes and she blinked rapidly. "I don't know what our family would do without you."

"Oh, go along with ya. Just doin' my Christian duty is all." She clicked her tongue and pushed through the door into Ivy Malone's room, shutting it gently behind her.

* * * * *

Nevada settled into the chair across the small table from Christy, not certain he'd be able to swallow a morsel of food, no matter how appetizing. "Are you feeling better about your mother's condition now that Doc's seen her?"

She sighed. "For now, but I'm afraid he doesn't hold out a lot of hope for the future. He thinks she's in the final stages of consumption and might not have long to live." He couldn't miss the pain that flickered across her face.

"I'm sorry."

Her hand was resting on the tablecloth, and he gave it a gentle squeeze. She didn't withdraw it, but decorum demanded he not allow his hand to linger. So he sat back but kept his gaze steady on her. "If there's anything I can do…"

His words fell in the space between them like bricks hitting a rock road. He'd already done too much—damaged this family in a way that could never be repaired.

Christy shifted in her seat. "You've been a help since you arrived in town, even though it's hard—" She raised agonized eyes and stared at him. "Why?"

The whispered word was so low Nevada wasn't sure she'd spoken.

She leaned forward, afire with intensity. "Why did you shoot him, Nevada? Couldn't you have walked away?"

Nevada flopped against the wooden chair. This was the conversation he'd always dreaded and never had—explaining his actions to a grieving family member.

She clasped her hands on the surface of the table. Her knuckles showed white.

He tried to gather his thoughts but failed miserably. "I don't know if there's ever true justification for a shooting, but there's always a reason. Logan Malone called me out. I avoided him for days. He boasted around town that he planned to kill me. More than one man told me about Logan and his cousin Jake. Face Malone, or expect them to hunt you down." He paused, suddenly aware of the relationship between Christy and the man. "Never mind. Let's leave it at that."

"No. I need to understand. It's important."

He blew a hard breath and slowly nodded. "Word was if I didn't meet Malone in the street, he'd ambush me like he'd done with others, and then claim to have killed me after I drew my gun. When Logan called me out that final day, I told him to walk away. Told him he'd die. But he laughed. They all do." Sorrow rose up and threatened to overwhelm him. The old feelings of hopelessness that swamped him after a shooting struggled to surface.

Nevada shrugged. "He wouldn't back down. If I'd only wounded him, I'd probably be dead. Most men will keep shooting until they empty their gun. If I'd walked away, every gunfighter in the territory trying to make a name would hunt me down. They'd think I turned yellow. I'd be an easy target. Or worse, Logan and his cousin Jake would've camped on my trail till I faced them, or I'd have died with a bullet in my gut from some hidden location." He clamped his lips shut. More than likely she'd hate him now after revealing the truth about her stepfather.

"I'm not surprised." Again, the words came out in a near whisper and then gained in strength. "That sounds like Logan. I don't know Jake. I'd never met him before he came to Tombstone a few days ago and stopped by our house to see Ma."

A jolt shot through Nevada's body. "You talked to him?"

She scrunched her brows. "Yes. Why?"

"What does he look like?"

"Large, dark hair, unkempt, with a scar on his cheek."

A sickening knowledge surged through Nevada's mind. "I've been afraid of this. I wasn't sure until now, but—"

Christy's eyes widened. "What is it? What's wrong?"

"You didn't recognize his voice?"

"No…wait. There was something familiar about him, but I couldn't place it."

"I'm positive Jake is the man who held up the stagecoach the day you arrived. He's the leader of the outlaw gang."

Her skin turned chalky white, and her hand flew to her heart. "His men were responsible for shooting me? My stepfather's cousin?"

Nevada nodded. "But in all fairness, he couldn't have known you were onboard. I didn't realize who he was the night before in the camp. He wasn't in town the day Logan died. If you've never met him before, he wouldn't have recognized you even without your veil."

Her teeth worried her bottom lip. "I don't care. He's despicable. Why is he in Tombstone? I'd think he'd have run as far as he could after the robbery."

"Tom Parks thinks he's planning another job. I know he is. I overheard him talking in the Oriental. The fire may have kept him from pulling it off. But there's another reason he's here." Nevada placed his forearms on the table and leaned forward, his voice low. "To kill me."

* * * * *

Christy gaped at Nevada, not sure she'd heard him correctly. "I've lost my appetite. I think I'll go check on Ma."

"Wait. Please?" Nevada's hand once again covered her own.

His warm touch sent a quiver of pleasure up Christy's arm, but she gently removed it and clasped her hands in her lap. "What is it?"

He sat back, his expression clouded with worry. "I can't hope you'll understand or forgive me, but I'm praying you don't hate me."

"I'm not sure what I feel at the moment." She studied him, and the icy lump sitting in her throat started to dissolve. "But it's not hatred."

Nevada slumped against his chair. "Thank you."

She waited a moment, trying to sort out her thoughts. "Would you care to walk with me? I can't eat right now."

"I'd enjoy that." He came around to her chair and assisted her in rising.

They walked from the room in silence until they reached a small parlor back of the dining area reserved for guests and their friends. The empty room beckoned to Christy, and she motioned toward two chairs situated a couple of feet apart with a round table between. "It's probably too hot outside to walk."

"I agree." He waited for her to be seated, then sank into the adjoining overstuffed chair.

Christy studied the brocade walls then allowed her gaze to roam the beautifully appointed area. High-backed, comfortable chairs, a flowered settee with a crocheted throw, and tightly woven colorful rugs all exuded a soothing sense of home. Strong awareness of the man beside her caused her to swivel and stare at him. "I think I owe you an apology."

Nevada tensed. "You have nothing to be sorry for."

"Since the first time I met you, I've judged you." A smile trembled at her lips. "I suppose I can be forgiven for thinking what I did after our…um…unusual start. But since then, you've shown nothing but kindness and consideration to my family and me."

He started to answer, and she held up her hand. "Wait. Let me finish, please?" She needed to get the words out before she lost her courage. There'd been so much misunderstanding the past few weeks between herself and Nevada, but she knew the time had come to set things right.

Nodding, he sat back in his chair and waited.

Christy drew in a deep breath and let it out through her nostrils. "I believe you about Logan. I never liked him and never trusted him. He was a terrible influence on Joshua. He gambled, fought, and drank much of the time. I had no idea he'd stoop so low as to ambush someone, but I can't say I'm terribly surprised." She stopped. So much hung on this next question. "Why did you have my grandmother's cameo brooch in your room?"

The warm tone of his tanned skin paled, and a muscle twitched in his cheek. "You found it on the bureau?"

"Yes." She noticed he didn't ask why she'd entered his room. "When I went in to change the water in your pitcher."

He met her gaze squarely. "I'm glad."

Surprise pulsed in her mind. This was not the answer she'd expected. Hot denial or some kind of excuse, but not the evident relief she saw. "Why?"

"I didn't know how to return it to you without you assuming I'd taken it for payment."

"Didn't you?" The words had simply spilled out, and it was too late to take them back. Besides, he needed to explain, and she didn't care to help him.

"No. I told Jake I wanted it for payment so he'd give it to me after I saw how much it hurt you to lose it. Even before I knew who you were I..." He hesitated and didn't continue.

"Please. I'd like to hear the rest."

"All right." He placed his hands on his knees, his expression earnest. "I couldn't stand it that they'd shot a woman, and you thought I had something to do with it. Then they took your brooch, and even though I couldn't really see you, I heard the pain in your voice. I've done some things I'm not proud of, but I've never been party to harming a woman. I decided I'd do what it took to get the brooch back and hopefully prove I wasn't in on the holdup. Every day for the first two or three weeks I expected the marshal to come calling."

"I still don't understand why you didn't just give it to me." Christy kept her attention fixed on him, not wanting to miss even the flicker of an eyelash.

"You'd already believed the worst of me, and I figured giving it to you would convince you I'd been part of the robbery." He gave a rueful laugh. "Guess I should've done the right thing and not tried to figure it all out."

"But I don't understand why you've even stayed in town if you were worried about the law. And why did it matter so much what I thought?" The words dragged themselves out of her innermost being. She'd longed to know the answer to these questions and had finally mustered the courage to ask.

He sat still and stared at her without speaking. His eyes warmed to dark pools, and a glow transformed his rugged features into something beyond handsome. It was...breathtaking.

"Because I care for you, Christy Grey," he said simply. "I think

I've cared ever since I heard you demanding that someone fix your arm before you bled to death. And after getting to know you, well…" His lips curved. "I'm afraid the caring has grown to something beyond that."

She opened her mouth, not sure how she planned to respond.

Pattering feet drew her attention away from Nevada.

Sara rushed into the room. "Christy, your ma's callin' for you. I think you need to hurry. It's not good."

Chapter Twenty-four

Christy raced ahead of Sara down the hall, rounding the corner to the room where her mother lay. Sara's expression sent fear pumping through Christy's body. As her hand touched the knob, she called back, "Have you sent for the doctor?"

Sara swiped at her damp cheek. "Joshua insisted on goin' to fetch him. I told him he wasn't strong enough yet, but Joshua said he hasn't been there for his ma in the past. And he wasn't goin' to let her down this time."

"Thank you, Sara." Christy pushed open the door and slipped inside the darkened room, hearing the harsh breathing even before she neared the bed. "Ma? It's Christy." She bent over her mother's tiny form and grasped her hand. It was clammy and almost limp. "Ma, can you hear me?"

Ivy opened her eyes, but her deep cough shook the mattress. Christy reached for the damp cloth on the table and wiped the bloody froth from her ma's mouth.

"Water." The word rasped like a file run over a stone.

Christy grabbed a glass sitting next to the bed and lifted Ivy's head. "Here. Drink slowly now. Joshua went to get Doctor Goodfellow. He'll be here soon."

"Wait. Important…I tell you." Ma struggled to rise, but another coughing spasm pressed her back into the bed.

"No. Don't talk, Ma." Christy dipped the rag into the basin of water nearby and rinsed it, then gently dabbed at her mother's face. "Rest now so you can get better."

"Not this time, Daughter. Must talk…before I…die. Please."

Panic swept through Christy's heart. Ma couldn't leave them. They'd not made peace on so many accounts. "Shh. You're not going to die."

"Listen." Ivy fumbled for Christy's hand and gripped it with a strength surprising to her. "Need to tell you." Distress wrinkled her forehead.

"All right, Ma. I'm listening." She reached back with her free hand and inched a chair close to the bed, then sank into it.

"I'm sorry for treatin' you bad…all these years. So afraid…" Ivy lifted her other hand and covered her mouth as she coughed again. "After Molly died…scared I'd lose another child. Wanted to make… you strong."

Christy's throat closed, and tears welled. "It's okay, Ma. Please don't worry yourself."

"Need…to finish." Ivy barely raised her head off the pillow. "I… love you, Christy. So proud of you. Tell your brother"—her breath came in short gasps—"I love him. He's been…a good boy. Took care of me…when Logan left. Tell him, Christy…." Falling back against the pillow, she closed her eyes for several long moments, then opened them again. "Not to grieve me…like he did Logan. I'm ready to go. Tell him"—she paused and closed her eyes—"to go straight…be a man from now on."

"I will, Ma. I'll tell him, don't you worry. I love you too—so very much."

Silence settled over the room for a couple of minutes, then Ivy stirred and her lids fluttered open. "Forgive me?"

"There's nothing to forgive, Mama. Nothing at all." She kissed the damp forehead.

"Yes. Did somethin' bad." Ivy panted, sucking in several shallow breaths. "Shouldn't have."

"Shh. It doesn't matter now."

"Ne...va...da." The single word carried a world of sorrow in the three syllables.

Christy's heart rate quickened, and she leaned forward. "What about Nevada, Ma?"

"Sent word to Jake...Nevada killed Logan." Her eyes closed for a moment, then opened. "Sorry I did." She struggled to force the words out between trembling lips. "Sara told me...he saved you both... from the fire. Logan was...no good. Knew it...didn't want...to admit. Wanted someone...to love me." She sank back. A tear slipped out of the corner of her eye and trickled down into her hair. "I asked... God...to forgive me. Hope you...will too."

Christy let out a low cry and laid her cheek against her mother's. "I love you so much, Ma. Of course I forgive you." She draped her arm around Ivy, pulling her close and rocking her gently.

Dimly she heard the door open. Footsteps approached the bed. A man's firm but gentle hands drew her upright. He leaned over the bed for several long seconds, then spoke in a low but decisive voice. "I'm sorry, Miss Grey. I think your mother is gone."

Chapter Twenty-five
....

Nevada hovered outside the open door with Sara, waiting for the doctor to finish examining Mrs. Malone before they entered. Joshua stood on the far side of the bed, his tortured eyes fixed on his mother.

Christy's cry brought Sara racing into the room. She clutched Christy's hand and drew her away from the bed, encircling her shaking body in a fierce hug.

Nevada stood on the other side of the threshold. Christy's sobs pierced the wall he'd erected around his heart and brought out a protectiveness he hadn't realized he possessed. He wanted to watch over this woman and care for her in any way possible. She'd been through so much lately, and now she'd lost her mother. He didn't know if his love would make a difference, but if she'd have him, he'd do everything in his power to restore joy to her life.

Joshua stood beside the bed, hollow eyes staring at his mother. He raised them to the doctor, and his voice croaked, "She'll be all right, won't she, Doc?"

Nevada stepped into the room and walked over to stand beside the young man, his hand resting on Joshua's shoulder. Guilt and shame assailed him at the pain he heard in Joshua's voice. Because of Nevada, the only man Joshua had known as a father was dead, and now he'd lost his mother. Nevada bowed his head and whispered a silent prayer for strength and comfort for the grieving sister and brother.

Doctor Goodfellow turned toward him. "I'm sorry, son, but she's gone. Her lungs couldn't hold out any longer."

Joshua's body began to tremble, but he didn't bolt or cry out. He reached down and plucked his mother's hand from the sheet where it lay and carried it up to his cheek. "Ma? Forgive me for wastin' all your money and makin' you lose the house." A sob tore from his throat. "Please don't hate me, Ma."

Christy pulled out of Sara's embrace and stepped behind her brother. "Joshua?" She turned him toward her and placed her palms on the sides of his cheeks. "Look at me, little brother."

Nevada walked to where Sara stood, his heart aching at the scene playing out in front of him. He was dimly aware of the doctor pulling the sheet up over Ivy Malone and grateful Christy had turned Joshua's back to the bed.

Christy continued to cradle his face in her hands. Love shone from her eyes. "She gave me a message for you before she died. She loved you, Joshua, so much."

He shook his head, almost dislodging her hands. She moved one to his forehead and brushed his dark auburn hair away from his face. "Ma made her peace with God before she passed, and we'll see her in heaven someday. But she asked you to go straight and not grieve her so deep like you did with Logan. She wanted you to know how proud she was to call you her son, but she wanted you to be the man she knew you could be."

The slumped shoulders straightened. Joshua looked up with a

stunned expression. His desperate eyes begged to believe Christy's words. "She said that? She was proud of me?"

"Yes. You stuck with her and cared for her after Logan left. Joshua, you need to know she didn't blame the man who killed Logan." Christy shot a glance toward Nevada before returning her attention to Joshua. "She understood why he had to do it. She loved us both and wanted us to make a good life for ourselves."

He gave a shuddering sigh and drew her close. "All right, big sister. I'll try. No more gambling or drinking. I'll make you both proud."

Sara moved silently over to stand beside the two and touched Joshua. "I'm proud of you too."

Joshua patted Christy's back, then turned to Sara. She held out her arms, and he walked into them, pulling her close.

Nevada took two steps toward the door. He'd imposed on this family's privacy long enough. Time to head back to his room.

"Nevada?" Christy's tone slowed his pace as he crossed the threshold.

"Yes?"

She fell into step beside him until they reached the middle of the hall. "You heard what I told Joshua about Ma?"

"I did. She said that about me?"

"Mama knew Logan was no good, but she didn't want to admit it. She asked me to forgive her for doing something she realized was wrong." Christy placed her hand on his arm and her damp lashes rose to reveal deep green depths of pain. "I'm afraid she sent word to Jake that you're in Tombstone. He'll be hunting you now in earnest."

Nevada placed his hand over her fingers and squeezed. "I'll not shoot another man, I promise you. I've been the cause of too much grief for your family already."

Christy didn't remove her hand but instead placed her other one on top of his, encasing it with a warm embrace. "You told me something in the dining room earlier. Did you mean the words you said?"

His thoughts raced until they landed on the declaration he'd made. His heart gave a sharp lurch. When Sara had interrupted them, he'd assumed Christy hadn't heard the words he'd blurted about how much he cared. "Every one and more."

Her gaze didn't waver. "I care about you, Nevada, and I can't lose you. Give me your word you won't allow Jake to shoot you down in the street."

Gratefulness again threatened to overwhelm him, but he couldn't permit himself the luxury of considering her words right now. "I can't promise, Christy, but I'll do my best to stay alive. All I can promise is I won't shoot another man. And especially not another member of your family."

* * * * *

Frustration narrowed Christy's eyes and tugged at her nerves. All she could think about was keeping Nevada alive. Why did he have to choose this time to lay down his guns? She hadn't understood before how a man could get into a shooting scrape, but the knowledge that Jake planned on killing Nevada had shaken her deeply.

She tightened her grip on his hand. "He's not family. Logan was

my mother's third husband, and Jake is his cousin. He's a killer who ambushes men, as well as a thief. If you don't face him, he'll shoot you in the back the first chance he gets—now that he knows who you are."

Nevada smiled, the skin at the edges of his eyes crinkling. "I'm not easy to kill, darlin'."

"Then what?" She wanted to stomp her foot and demand an answer, but the quiet strength pouring from this tall, rugged cowboy stopped her.

"Something is different." She peered up at him and tried to find the answer, but he kept on smiling. "What is it, Nevada? What's changed?"

"Me." The simple word came out with a bold assurance. "I've given up trying to run my own life. That's God's job now. If He wants me alive, He'll show me a way to take Jake without killing him."

Relief washed over Christy. She basked in the peace created by Nevada's words. "All right. I'll trust Him, as well."

Nevada bent his head and touched his lips to hers in a brief but sweet kiss. "When this is over, I have a few more of those tucked away and maybe a question or two I might want to ask."

Joy exploded in Christy's chest and she stood on tiptoe, placing her palms against his cheeks. She met his lips, allowing hers to linger for several seconds. Nevada stood as though bolted to the floor, then his arms slipped around her waist and drew her close. His kiss deepened, and his hands stroked the small of her back.

Christy wanted to lose herself in his embrace forever. Cradled in his arms, she felt complete. No fear, self-doubt, or anxiety about the future could touch her. Finally she drew a short distance away and smiled up into his eyes. "I'll be waiting for that question, Cowboy, and don't you forget it."

He laughed, his joy echoing hers. "Not much chance of that."

* * * * *

Christy was grateful the undertaker was able to provide a casket quickly so they could bury her mother the following morning. The intense heat of late June didn't allow for a long period of mourning, and the small procession followed the horse-drawn black hearse to the outskirts of town. They stopped beside a newly dug grave in Boot Hill and spent a few moments in silent meditation before the pastor spoke a prayer. Ma hadn't wanted any big production, and Christy decided to honor her desire.

She wished Nevada had felt comfortable attending but understood his need to stay away until Joshua could come to terms with who Nevada was and the part he'd played in Logan's death. She'd told Joshua about Jake, as well as Logan's plan to bushwhack Nevada. She'd stressed the cowboy's need to defend himself, but Joshua didn't want to hear. Even sharing Jake's plan to hunt Nevada down hadn't penetrated Joshua's fog of grief. Hopefully, once her brother got past his first couple days of shock he'd understand. After all, it was Nevada who saved Sara from the gambling den and rescued them both during the fire.

Nellie Cashman, Sara, Joshua, Christy, and the pastor made their way back to town, each caught in their own hushed reflections. Nevada promised to have dinner with her at the Russ House after the service, and she prayed their lives would return to normal. Maybe

Jake would drift away and nothing would come of his threats, or she could convince Joshua, Sara, and Nevada to leave town with her now that her mother no longer required care.

Joshua mumbled something and slipped into the boardinghouse without looking back.

Sara stopped beside Christy and gave her a tight squeeze. "Thank you for standin' by me and bein' my friend. I'm sorry you're hurtin' so much right now."

Christy placed her arm around Sara's waist. "I'm all right. It's Joshua I'm worried about."

Sara shrugged. "Joshua needs to sort out what you told him about Nevada, that's all. He'll come around. He wants to do what's right."

"I know."

"I'm goin' to my room to lie down. This baby's been kickin' me somethin' fierce lately." She patted her belly and laughed. "Joshua says that means it's a boy for shore." She pushed through the front door and disappeared inside.

Christy gazed after her. In all the distress of the recent days, she'd almost forgotten Sara believed she carried Joshua's child. Of course there was no certainty of that, but she'd been with Joshua a number of times before Townsley sent others along. Whatever the case, the two young people seemed at peace with the circumstances. What a miracle—that something as terrible as what the girl had gone through could produce something that would bring joy to her heart for years to come. And to Joshua's, if she read the signs correctly.

She sank onto a bench beside the door. How wonderful to rest and not have anything important or ugly pressing in on her mind. A new chapter of her life would open somehow, and God would show her what to do and where to go. The promise she'd seen in Nevada's face offered hope for her future she'd never thought possible.

Footsteps thumped on the boardwalk, and Christy looked up. Nevada walked toward her, his countenance alight with excitement. "I talked to Tom Parks, and he's planning on arresting Jake today. He's gathered enough evidence to put him and his cronies behind bars for the stage holdup, among other crimes. Maybe our worries about having to shoot him were unfounded, and I'll get to ask you that question sooner than I expected."

She sat up straight and beamed. "That's wonderful—"

"Nevada King!" came a shout from up the street. "Turn around and draw your gun."

Chapter Twenty-six
....

Nevada's hands froze where they were. If Jake thought he was going for his gun, he wouldn't hesitate to shoot, and Christy was in the line of fire. He didn't turn his head but spoke loud enough for her to hear. "Get inside, Christy."

She gave a low cry and pushed to her feet. "I'm not leaving."

Frustration lodged like a rock in his throat. "I can't worry about you and stay alive. You've got to do as I say and get out of sight. Now."

He heard Christy's footsteps on the boardwalk and the opening of the front door, but he still felt her presence. No doubt she'd moved to the nearest window and peered outside. No help for that, and he couldn't spend time worrying about it now. In the next few minutes he'd need all his concentration to keep from dying.

Four long strides took him past the Russ House and into the street. The sun shone brightly on the dusty town. Hammering could be heard as workers put the finishing touches on structures being rebuilt after the fire. Shopkeepers peered out their doors at the two men advancing toward the street, then quickly slammed them shut. A woman grabbed the hand of her young child and dragged him down the boardwalk before disappearing into a nearby store.

Jake stood on the far side of the road, his hands spread wide at his sides. "Today's the day you die, King. I been waitin' a long time to put a bullet into your gizzard."

Nevada stopped and faced the man, holding his hands away from his guns. "I'm not going to fight you, Jake."

"Ha. I knew you was a yellow dog the day you stayed at the camp 'stead of helpin' us rob the stage. All you done was care for that blamed woman's arm. Worthless, that's what you are." He leaned over and spat on the ground. "And a plumb yeller coward."

"That blamed woman, as you put it, was Logan Malone's step-daughter." Nevada watched Jake and didn't miss the jerk of surprise as his words hit their mark. "Didn't know one of your men shot your own kin, did you?"

Jake spat again and wiped his mouth with the back of his hand. "Don't matter now. She wasn't bad hurt. It's you that has a score to settle. Logan was the closest kin I had left, and you shot him. Now I'm gonna kill you."

"I'm not going to draw, Jake. You plan to shoot a man in cold blood?" Nevada took a step forward and watched for a reaction, but the gunman didn't appear to notice his advance. Another short step and another. A flash of light caught him in the eyes, and he shifted his gaze without moving his head. If he wasn't mistaken, the glint had come from the sun reflecting off the barrel of a rifle.

"It won't be murder. You'll draw. They all do." Jake shrugged. "Guess if you don't, it's your funeral." He emitted a coarse laugh. "And that's one I'll be more'n happy to attend."

Nevada walked another two paces toward his opponent, closing the gap to half the width of the street.

The man seemed to suddenly awaken to the movement. "Hey there, stay put." His fingers curved into a claw-like position and hovered above his gun. "I'm gonna give you the chance to draw first."

"I told you, I'm not fighting you." Nevada took another three long strides as Jake's eyes bugged. "At least, not in the way you're wanting." As the final words left his mouth, Nevada leaped forward and dove for Jake's legs just as the man's gun cleared the holster.

* * * * *

Christy couldn't stand it. The man she loved was walking toward a gunman determined to kill him, and Nevada had sworn he'd not draw his gun. Why was he getting so close to Jake? Didn't he realize at this distance there was little to no chance Jake would miss? Her palms broke out in a sweat, and her mouth went dry. She didn't want Nevada to kill another man, but more than anything she wanted him to live. "Please, God, take care of him," she whispered.

Her stomach tensed as Nevada lunged for Jake as the gun came free. A shot rang out and Christy closed her eyes, dreading what she'd see. Would Nevada be lying in the street with blood streaming from his body? She couldn't stand not knowing what was happening so she peered back out the window.

Another louder report rent the air. Tom Parks stood under the overhang of the Palace Lodging House across the street, his rifle aimed upwards towards the roofline of the doctor's office. Nevada and Jake were tangled on the ground, fists flying and dust churning. Relief nearly knocked her knees from under her, and she sagged against the wall. The next moment she raced for the door and jerked it open.

Christy took three steps their direction and halted. A man lay sprawled on the street where he'd apparently tumbled from the roof, a rifle not far from his outstretched arm and blood oozing from his side.

The two combatants rolled in the street, exchanging blows so swiftly Christy could barely tell one from the other. It appeared Nevada had the upper hand as he landed a hard punch to the outlaw's belly, sending the man rolling backwards. A movement off to the side turned Christy's attention away from the battle.

Parks strode across the street and her brother, Joshua, emerged from the shadows of the building next door, his gun drawn and aimed at the two men continuing to struggle.

Tom walked over, plucked the rifle from the ground next to the man facedown in the dirt, and turned him over. The Wells Fargo agent grunted. "This is one of the men who held up the stage you were on, ma'am. Probably the one who shot you, as he seems a mite trigger happy to me."

"Is he…?"

"Yep. Dead as they come. Good thing he missed when Nevada jumped Jake. One less hombre the courts will have to convict." He turned his attention to Joshua. "Son, why don't you saunter on over to that fracas and keep your gun trained on Jake."

Joshua pulled his gaze away from Nevada and Jake, staring at the agent. "How'd you know I didn't come out here to shoot Nevada?"

Tom reached up and fingered his mustache. "You had plenty of chance and didn't do it, so I figured you must be here, same as me… to make sure this remains a fair fight."

Joshua seemed to grow two inches before Christy's eyes, and a wide grin transformed his face. "Yes, sir. That's exactly what I planned."

TOMBSTONE
1881
AZ

"Good man. I might have to see about gettin' you a job with Wells Fargo. Now get on over there." He motioned with his rifle to the two men still exchanging punches.

Nevada grabbed the front of Jake's shirt and jerked him to his feet. He drew back his arm and let loose with a hard right, knocking the outlaw to the ground. Jake clawed to his hands and knees, then stood, swaying on his feet. Blood trickled from a cut lip, and his right eye had swollen almost closed. He bellowed and lunged, his blows going wild.

Nevada stepped back, allowing the crazed outlaw to stagger past him.

Jake swerved and turned around, seeming to remember the gun still in his holster. He planted his feet square, his chest heaving, and swept his hand down.

With one quick movement, Nevada stood toe to toe with the man. He delivered a lightning fast jab to Jake's cheekbone and followed it with a second to his chin. The big man staggered backwards, then fell hard in the dirt, rolling over onto his belly.

Panting, Nevada stood over the prostrate man as sweat streaked the dust coating his grim face. "Stay down unless you want me to plant you in the dirt again."

Jake groaned and did as he was told. Nevada cast him one more glance, then half turned as Joshua crossed the street. "Glad you're on my side, Joshua."

The young man grinned, then the blood drained from his skin. "Look out!" He lifted his gun and pointed it at the man still lying on the ground.

Christy stared in horror as Jake raised a gun in his clenched fist and aimed at Nevada. Her heart sank as his finger tightened on the trigger. Joshua stood like a carved statue, his eyes riveted on Logan's cousin. Nevada whipped his pistol from his holster just as a shot rang out from across the street.

The bullet struck Jake in the shoulder, and the gun dropped from his hand. He shrieked, then lay silent in the dust. Tom Parks dropped the muzzle of his rifle and walked forward.

Nevada shot him a glance. "Thanks, Parks. I owe you."

Tom kept his eyes on the prone figure. "Maybe I'll have occasion to collect someday. But for now we'd best gather up these guns before anyone else tries to take another shot at you, King." He bent over and plucked the pistol from the unconscious man's hand, then rolled him over and removed the second one from his belt.

Christy let out a sob of relief and rushed across the road, meeting Nevada as he holstered his gun.

He opened his arms and caught her to him, then drew her away from the grisly scene and onto the boardwalk. "I'm all right, honey, but I'm too dirty to hug."

She tightened her grip around his waist. "I don't care. You're alive, and that's all that matters."

He pulled her close and laid his cheek against her hair. "And I aim to stay that way till I'm old and gray, God willing."

Raising wet eyes to meet his, she smiled. "You still have a question you promised to ask me. I'm not letting you out of my sight until that matter is taken care of."

Nevada touched a strand of her hair, then stroked her cheek. "Darlin', you don't have to ever let me out of your sight again, if you don't want to." He bent his head and kissed her gently. "I'm right here, and I'm not going anywhere."

Christy tightened her arms around Nevada's neck, giving herself completely to the kiss as it lingered and slowly deepened. Nothing mattered right now—not the people staring from the nearby buildings or the dirt coating Nevada's clothing. He was alive, and he loved her.

After several long seconds Nevada raised his head but kept his fingers laced across the middle of Christy's back. "I love you, Christy, and I want to make you happy. You're everything I've ever wanted in a woman, and more. Would you do me the honor of becoming my wife?"

Christy drew in a deep breath and let it out in a gentle sigh. "I thought you'd never ask, Cowboy. There's nothing I'd like better than to become Mrs. Nevada King."

"I'm afraid that's going to be Mrs. James King. Nevada is a thing of the past and doesn't plan on returning."

She stood on tiptoe and gazed into his eyes. "No sir. I fell in love with Nevada and have no intention of marrying anyone else. You can call our first son James if you want to, but you'll always be my Nevada."

His face blazed with joy, and he hugged her closer. "You win. I'll be whatever you want me to be, Christy Grey, and for as long as you'll have me."

Epilogue

....

Christy nearly danced with excitement as the stage rolled into town. How different from the day she'd arrived. She still suffered pangs of loss that her mother hadn't lived to share her happiness, but she continually thanked the Lord Ma had made peace with God and her children before she passed on to heaven. She couldn't believe three weeks had gone by since Jake was arrested.

Nevada wrapped his arm around her and laughed. "A mite anxious, are we?"

She nudged him in the side with her elbow. "There's no 'we' about it. You don't look a bit anxious. Besides, it's not every day my best friends come to Tombstone."

His twinkling gaze rested on her. "It's not every day you get married, either. I hope that's not too far down your list of things you're happy about."

Christy grinned and gave him a peck on the cheek. "Wouldn't you like to know?"

The driver halted his team with a flourish in front of the Grand Hotel. "Welcome to Tombstone, folks. Wait till I climb down and get the door open, and watch your step. Park your guns with the new marshal, Virgil Earp. He don't allow no shootin' in his town."

Nevada winced and gave a half shrug. "Hopefully things will

tone down in Tombstone. I heard that Townsley couldn't get hired as the manager at the rebuilt Oriental and left town for new diggings."

Christy hugged him and grinned. "Joshua told me the news." She shaded her eyes and watched the stage approaching up the street. "I think Sara's sleeping better now that he's gone."

"I'm glad."

The driver gripped the door and swung it open. Christy shrieked. Alexia, her husband, Justin Phillips, their son, Toby, and little daughter, Grace, stepped from the stage. Alex opened her arms and Christy launched herself at her friend, enveloping her in a fierce hug. Laughter and tears mingled with snippets of words as the two clung to one another. A finger tapped Christy on the shoulder, and she loosened her hold on Alex just enough to look around.

Nevada stood close by, wearing a broad grin. "You going to introduce us?"

Justin chuckled and Toby left his father's side to tug on Christy's skirt. "Aunt Christy, I want my hug too."

Christy scooped the young boy into her embrace and swung him around in a circle. Bystanders laughed and moved out of her way as a man handed down bags from the top of the coach. "You've grown up since I saw you last. I think you've gained ten pounds at least!" She set him on the ground and tickled him, loving the giggles filling the air.

Christy stepped toward Nevada and held out her hand. "Everyone, this is my soon-to-be husband, Nevada King."

He cleared his throat. "Well, it's actually James King, but I've gotten kind of used to my other handle."

Justin slapped his back. "Works for me, and pleased to meet

you. Let's get the ladies and children somewhere more comfortable, and then we can talk." He leaned down and hoisted one of the bags. "How far to where we'll be staying?"

"Two blocks. We'll hire a couple of men to tote your stuff over." He turned to look over the crowd and brightened. "John. Where you been, old-timer?"

John Draper stood with folded arms and narrowed eyes. "Old-timer, huh? I only got ten years on you, fella, and can work circles around you any day of the week."

Nevada threw back his head and laughed. "Finally got you stirred up, huh? Work keeping you busy these days?"

"Yeah, since my best help went and got himself engaged and don't have time for me anymore." He shot a sly look at Christy. "Now who's all these folks? Friends of yours?"

"Yes." Christy tucked her hand through Alex's arm and made the introductions. "John, why don't you come to the house with us? Nellie's serving dinner after everyone has a chance to clean up."

He motioned to the bags littering the boardwalk. "Need help totin' these?"

Nevada nodded. "I was going to hire someone."

"Nah. The three of us can make it without a problem."

"Make that four." Joshua sauntered up with Sara on his arm. "I've got an announcement to make, and I can't wait any longer." His chest puffed out. "I'm pleased to tell you Sara has agreed to be my wife."

A cheer went up from the small crowd, and even Justin and Alex beamed at the young couple, their happiness contagious. Shouts of congratulations rent the air, and both received numerous hugs and slaps on the back. The men loaded their arms with luggage, and the happy group made the short trek to the boardinghouse.

Alex fell in beside Christy. "Nevada is charming, and you look utterly lovely. I don't think I've ever seen you so happy."

Christy's heart lifted at the genuine praise. "I guess it's because I'm in love, and I've finally found peace." She shot a glance at her friend. "You always tried to tell me what it would be like if I got my heart right with God, but I never realized…." She stopped and choked over the last word. "I also made peace with Mama before she passed, and Joshua has quit gambling and drinking."

Alex tucked her hand through Christy's arm. "I'm so happy for you. And Sara is a very pretty girl. Does her family live here?"

Christy wondered how much to reveal, then remembered who she was talking to. Alex had been the first person in Last Chance to accept her when she came to town and her background as a dancehall girl became known. They spent the next few minutes walking slowly behind the men and getting caught up, with Christy filling Alex in on Sara's past and the changes they'd seen in the young woman.

"I think Sara has accepted the Lord. She hasn't come right out and said so yet, but I can tell she's different, and it's not just due to my brother." She grinned at Joshua's back. "As much as she's smitten with him, I believe it goes deeper than that."

Alex hugged Christy's hand against her side. "I'm glad. It sounds like she's overdue for joy in her life. How about you? Are you ready to become Mrs. King?"

"More ready than you can imagine."

Alex giggled. "I'm not too old to remember my own wedding day. I know exactly how you're feeling."

Their two heads slanted towards each other and touched in silent agreement. Once again Christy sent up a prayer of gratitude for another gift God had given her. This woman had become her closest friend. Christy hugged the secret to her heart that she longed to share with Alex, but it wouldn't be fair to Nevada. She'd wait until they could talk to Alex and Justin together to deliver the news of their decision to establish a ranch in the Auburn area. No, it wasn't Last Chance, but it was only a day's ride away and so much closer to friends and family than Tombstone. Her one prayer was that Sara and Joshua would choose to follow, and somehow she knew in her heart they would.

* * * * *

Twenty-four hours could make such a difference in a man's life. Yesterday at this time they'd all stood on Allen Street waiting for the stage to arrive, and today he stood at the front of the new chapel at the corner of Safford Street waiting for his bride to appear. Pastor Peabody Endicott stood to one side with his friend John close by on Nevada's right. A small group of beaming people sat in the front pews of the auditorium as light streamed through the new stained-glass windows on each side of the recently finished Episcopal Church.

Years ago he'd thought it would be Marie coming to meet him, but now he couldn't envision what she'd looked like. All he could see in his mind was Christy's shining eyes, and all he wanted was to feel her presence by his side. He'd been an immature young man who'd fancied he'd lost the love of his life, but now he'd found the treasure he'd been searching for. He felt complete, whole, and at peace. Not only in Christy's love, but in his newfound life with his Savior. So much had changed these past months since he'd fled from Albuquerque, and he gave thanks to God daily for the gifts he'd been given.

The organ that had been carted by wagon over the trail played off to the side. Christy had suggested a simple ceremony in Nellie's parlor, but he'd insisted on the church. His strongest desire was they start their lives together united in their faith, as well as their love.

The side door at the edge of the platform opened, and Sara walked out. Christy had asked Alex to stand up with her, but she'd urged Christy to give the honor to Sara. The young woman had been through so much, and Alex believed it would bolster her confidence.

Sara's beaming countenance lit up the area at the front of the church. Nevada didn't miss Joshua's jaw dropping to his chest. He stifled a chuckle as the pretty girl dressed in a pale shade of blue walked over and stood at John Draper's side.

All internal mirth died as the door opened again and Christy stepped over the threshold. Her long auburn hair was piled on the top of her head in a cascade of tresses, and loose curls teased the back of her slender neck. He had no idea what kind of fabric she'd found for her gown, but the ivory color set off her skin, making his hands break out in a cold sweat. The sleeves flared just below her elbows revealing delicate wrists and slender arms, and the fitted waist and lace-covered bodice turned his muscles to jelly. If he'd thought her lovely before, he'd been wrong. She was nothing short of amazing.

Pastor Endicott positioned them both in front, and Nevada captured Christy's warm hand in his own, pressing it to his side. His heart soared at the love he saw reflected in her eyes. So much to be thankful for—so much to live for, encompassed in this woman who stood next to him.

The service floated by, and Nevada prayed he'd given the correct responses, but he couldn't have sworn to it. Christy's presence and the fact she'd soon be his wife had him more addled than he'd thought possible.

"Mr. King?" The pastor reached out and touched his arm. "Sir?"

Heat rushed up Nevada's neck as he realized he'd missed whatever he'd been asked. "Yes. What am I supposed to say next?"

"Nothing. Just kiss your bride." A chuckle rippled through the dozen people sitting in the sanctuary, and then a hush fell over the building as Nevada bent to Christy's upraised face. Their lips met and the kiss lengthened. He placed his hands on her waist and drew her closer, wanting this moment to go on forever.

An elbow caught him in the ribs, and the familiar voice of his best man brought him out of his trance. "You got the rest of your life to do that, son. Let the lady come up for air."

Laughter broke the solemn moment, and a smattering of applause erupted as the pastor faced the crowd. "Ladies and gentleman, I give you Mr. and Mrs. James King."

Nevada let out an exultant whoop. He turned to sweep Christy off her feet and into his arms, swinging her around before planting her back on the floor. He kept a firm grip around her waist and grinned. "Mrs. King, I've waited my whole life to hear those words. Now let's go share our happiness with our friends, then head to the bridal suite at the Grand Hotel."

Author's Note
....

In April of 2010 my husband, Allen, and I traveled to Tombstone and spent four days completing historical and local research, along with gaining a feel for the topography of the land, plant life, and buildings. We stayed at the Sagebrush Inn—a small motel built in the 1940s and remodeled a few years ago, a popular lodging place for John Wayne and Maureen O'Hara while shooting movies in the Tombstone area. We had the privilege of staying in John Wayne's favorite room.

While Christy and Nevada's story is purely fiction, there are many elements that are true. Doctor Goodfellow, Pastor Endicott Peabody, Marshal Ben Sippy, Doc Holliday, Buckskin Frank Leslie, the Earp brothers, Nellie Cashman, and Big Nose Kate, who dated Doc Holliday, along with all of the businesses depicted, were real and shown as accurately as possible based on my research. The statement made by Doctor Goodfellow when Christy came into his office the first time—"I just finished with a surgery. Bullet wound. Had to dig so deep I felt like I was performing assessment work. Rich in lead but too punctured to hold whiskey"—was close to a direct quote he made after patching up a bullet wound.

Tombstone's post office was established December 2, 1878, and has yet to be discontinued. And, of course, the most famous gunfight in Western history occurred at the OK Corral, October 26, 1881, when the Earps shot it out with the Clantons and the McLaurys. Boot Hill cemetery is still in existence and well cared for. The vast majority of people resting there were taken by the black horse-drawn hearse mentioned in the story.

Consumption, or tuberculosis as it's known now, ran rampant in Tombstone, especially among the women in the red-light district. They often ended up contracting pneumonia, and many died young. Some of these girls were young teenagers, and many were dragged unwillingly into the life by circumstances beyond their control. Death of family members, destitution, and even being sold into prostitution were common reasons many women found themselves working the gambling hells of this era, even as they do today. A few women saw the profession as a lucrative way to make money and escape the poverty of their past, but the majority rarely had options.

As I depicted, Nellie Cashman, the owner of the Russ House, *was* called "The Angel of Tombstone" by many a miner and local resident. She did indeed minister to the downtrodden, the poor, the ladies in the red-light district, and even criminals condemned to die by hanging. Details about her Irish ancestry, her appearance, and the description of the outside of the Russ House are accurate, although the building was being remodeled when we visited and I wasn't able to see past the lobby through the open front door.

The story about the stagecoach holdup where Christy gets shot in the arm is based on a real event. A young woman shot during a Wells Fargo coach robbery was bleeding badly and insisted one of the outlaws assist her. He took her aside but couldn't see as his mask kept slipping. When she agreed to keep his identity a secret, he removed the mask, bound up her arm, and the stage eventually went on its way. The outlaws got away with a shipment of Wells Fargo gold meant for the payroll at the mines. During repeated questioning by the town marshal, the young lady continued to refuse to reveal the outlaw's identity.

A Wells Fargo agent was dispatched by the company and pretended to fall in love with the woman, going so far as to propose marriage in hopes of obtaining the identity of the outlaw. He suggested there should be no secrets between a man and his intended, and insisted she divulge what the outlaw looked like who'd helped her. She firmly refused and broke her engagement. It was later disclosed he'd played a role in hopes of obtaining the information. From the historical account I read, she kept her secret the rest of her life.

Other episodes, such as the one with the city slicker whose hat was kicked down the street and returned to him with more than enough money to purchase another, were common occurrences in Tombstone during this time period. Also, the menu choices shown at the Russ House were from an actual menu used during 1881.

The fire in the latter part of the book occurred on June 22, 1881, and burned a large section of the business district, including the Oriental Saloon, as depicted. Water was scarce during that time period, as no underground lines had yet been run from the mountains. Barrels of water were transported into town by wagon at a high price per gallon, but not in quantities large enough to fight a fire of this magnitude.

The fire resulted from a mishap with a barrel of bad whiskey. At the Arcade Saloon (in the same block as the Oriental Saloon) the owner wanted to measure the amount left in a barrel so he could return it to the vendor. Upon doing so, he accidently dropped the measuring gauge into the barrel. He made the mistake of holding a lit cigar while trying to remove the gauge from the barrel. The cigar ignited the gas, creating an explosion, and spread burning alcohol everywhere. The Golden Eagle, later renamed the Crystal Palace, right across the side street survived, as did a few of the other landmarks in town. The Crystal Palace is still in business today and looks much the same as when it was rebuilt.

It took about two weeks for the townspeople to rebuild most of the business district, bringing lumber from a mill at the base of the nearby mountains. Then, in May of the following year, Tombstone got hit by another devastating fire, and much of the town once again burned (including the Grand Hotel), but was soon rebuilt. Until a water line was brought in from the mountains a couple of years later, the people were helpless to fight fires.

We visited one of the original mines and discovered many of the old tunnels still honeycomb the ground beneath the town. A fire in 1886 destroyed the pumps removing the water from deep in the mines and operation ceased. Mining reopened in 1901, but boiler problems and serious flooding once again closed them. Silver prices dropped substantially when the gold standard was set in place, and the remaining silver in the shafts was abandoned.

The Bird Cage Theater began construction shortly after the first fire and is still standing to this day with many of its original furnishings. One of the mining tunnels can be accessed from a room in that building.

In 1929 the county seat moved to Bisbee. Tombstone's future was uncertain, but a group of determined citizens coined the phrase

"the town too tough to die" and invited the public to come help them celebrate the town's past. Tombstone has continued to hold onto life over the decades, catering to tourists with an insatiable appetite for a glimpse into the old West.

Walking the preserved streets of old Tombstone and riding in one of the stagecoaches provided for tourists gave me a small idea of what it must have been like in the wild mining heyday of the early 1880s. I hope this book has brought you pleasure and provided you with a glimpse into a colorful part of our nation's past.

I'd love to hear from you, if you'd care to drop me a line. Or visit my website to see pictures from our Tombstone visit at **www.MiraleeFerrell.com.**

About the Author

....

 MIRALEE FERRELL grew up in a small town and married Allen, her high school sweetheart. They raised two children who both serve the Lord. After they left home, she prayed about filling her time. In 2005 she received the answer. While at church the pastor prayed with her, stating he believed God was calling her to write and be published. After praying, she embarked on a new adventure. Two years later her debut novel, *The Other Daughter,* released, and since then four more novels have followed.

Miralee serves as president of the Portland, Oregon, chapter of ACFW. She speaks at women's groups, libraries, and churches.

Miralee and her husband have been married for thirty-eight years. They live on eleven acres in Washington State, where they love to garden, play with their dogs, and go sailing. Miralee also rides her horse on the trails near their home with her daughter who lives nearby.

www.MiraleeFerrell.com

POST CARD
CARTE POSTALE
Love Finds You

Want a peek into local American life—past and present?
The *Love Finds You*™ series published by Summerside Press
features real towns and combines travel, romance,
and faith in one irresistible package!

The novels in the series—uniquely titled after American towns with romantic or intriguing names—inspire romance and fun. Each fictional story draws on the compelling history or the unique character of a real place. Stories center on romances kindled in small towns, old loves lost and found again on the high plains, and new loves discovered at exciting vacation getaways. Summerside Press plans to publish at least one novel set in each of the fifty states. Be sure to catch them all!

Now Available

Love Finds You in Miracle, Kentucky
by Andrea Boeshaar
ISBN: 978-1-934770-37-5

Love Finds You in Snowball, Arkansas
by Sandra D. Bricker
ISBN: 978-1-934770-45-0

Love Finds You in Romeo, Colorado
by Gwen Ford Faulkenberry
ISBN: 978-1-934770-46-7

Love Finds You in Valentine, Nebraska
by Irene Brand
ISBN: 978-1-934770-38-2

Love Finds You in Humble, Texas
by Anita Higman
ISBN: 978-1-934770-61-0

Love Finds You in Last Chance, California
by Miralee Ferrell
ISBN: 978-1-934770-39-9

Love Finds You in Maiden, North Carolina
by Tamela Hancock Murray
ISBN: 978-1-934770-65-8

Love Finds You in Paradise, Pennsylvania
by Loree Lough
ISBN: 978-1-934770-66-5

Love Finds You in Treasure Island, Florida
by Debby Mayne
ISBN: 978-1-934770-80-1

Love Finds You in Liberty, Indiana
by Melanie Dobson
ISBN: 978-1-934770-74-0

Love Finds You in Revenge, Ohio
by Lisa Harris
ISBN: 978-1-934770-81-8

Love Finds You in Poetry, Texas
by Janice Hanna
ISBN: 978-1-935416-16-6

Love Finds You in Sisters, Oregon
by Melody Carlson
ISBN: 978-1-935416-18-0

Love Finds You in Charm, Ohio
by Annalisa Daughety
ISBN: 978-1-935416-17-3

Love Finds You in
Bethlehem, New Hampshire
by Lauralee Bliss
ISBN: 978-1-935416-20-3

Love Finds You in North Pole, Alaska
by Loree Lough
ISBN: 978-1-935416-19-7

Love Finds You in Holiday, Florida
by Sandra D. Bricker
ISBN: 978-1-935416-25-8

Love Finds You in
Lonesome Prairie, Montana
by Tricia Goyer and Ocieanna Fleiss
ISBN: 978-1-935416-29-6

Love Finds You in Bridal Veil, Oregon
by Miralee Ferrell
ISBN: 978-1-935416-63-0

Love Finds You in Hershey,
Pennsylvania
by Cerella D. Sechrist
ISBN: 978-1-935416-64-7

Love Finds You in Homestead, Iowa
by Melanie Dobson
ISBN: 978-1-935416-66-1

Love Finds You in Pendleton, Oregon
by Melody Carlson
ISBN: 978-1-935416-84-5

Love Finds You in Golden, New
Mexico
by Lena Nelson Dooley
ISBN: 978-1-935416-74-6

Love Finds You in Lahaina, Hawaii
by Bodie Thoene
ISBN: 978-1-935416-78-4

Love Finds You in
Victory Heights, Washington
by Tricia Goyer and Ocieanna Fleiss
ISBN: 978-1-60936-000-9

Love Finds You in Calico, California
by Elizabeth Ludwig
ISBN: 978-1-60936-001-6

Love Finds You in Sugarcreek, Ohio
by Serena B. Miller
ISBN: 978-1-60936-002-3

Love Finds You in
Deadwood, South Dakota
by Tracey Cross
ISBN: 978-1-60936-003-0

Love Finds You in Silver City, Idaho
by Janelle Mowery
ISBN: 978-1-60936-005-4

Love Finds You in
Carmel-by-the-Sea, California
by Sandra D. Bricker
ISBN: 978-1-60936-027-6

Love Finds You Under the Mistletoe
by Irene Brand and Anita Higman
ISBN: 978-1-60936-004-7

Love Finds You in Hope, Kansas
by Pamela Griffin
ISBN: 978-1-60936-007-8

Love Finds You in Sun Valley, Idaho
by Angela Ruth
ISBN: 978-1-60936-008-5

Love Finds You in
Camelot, Tennessee
by Janice Hanna
ISBN: 978-1-935416-65-4

COMING SOON

Love Finds You in
Martha's Vineyard, Massachusetts
by Melody Carlson
ISBN: 978-1-60936-110-5

Love Finds You in
Prince Edward Island, Canada
by Susan Page Davis
ISBN: 978-1-60936-109-9

Love Finds You in Groom, Texas
by Janice Hanna
ISBN: 978-1-60936-006-1

Love Finds You in Amana, Iowa
by Melanie Dobson
ISBN: 978-1-60936-135-8

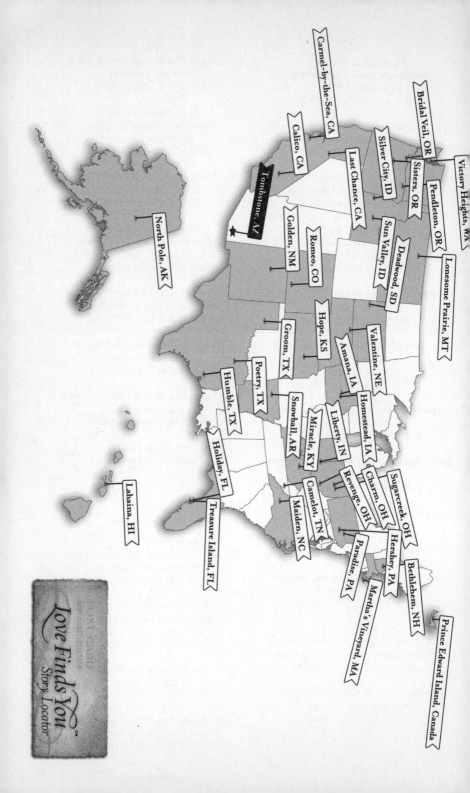